BLOOD LINE

A DETECTIVE MARCY KENDRICK THRILLER

THEO BAXTER

INKUBATOR
BOOKS

Published by Inkubator Books
www.inkubatorbooks.com

Copyright © 2024 by Theo Baxter

Theo Baxter has asserted his right to be identified as the author of this work.

ISBN (eBook): 978-1-83756-339-5
ISBN (Paperback): 978-1-83756-340-1
ISBN (Hardback): 978-1-83756-341-8

BLOOD LINE is a work of fiction. People, places, events, and situations are the product of the author's imagination. Any resemblance to actual persons, living or dead is entirely coincidental.

No part of this book may be reproduced, stored in any retrieval system, or transmitted by any means without the prior written permission of the publisher.

1
ONLY BACK THREE DAYS
MARCY

I hadn't slept well at all. My mind was still a mess because I was struggling to let go of Henry, or the idea of Henry. I wasn't sure which.

Angel Reyes, my partner, was back now too, after being in the hospital and physical therapy, but he was on desk duty for the next month. I knew from what he'd said that his leg was going to take three to six months to fully heal, and that was only if he followed exactly what the doctors told him to do. Either way, it meant it would be a while before he could be let loose on the city again. I supposed it was good that Captain Jack Robinson allowed him to come back and ride the desk after being out for so long.

I walked into the station and headed for the detective pool, hoping that Jordan, who was not only my ex-husband, but was now a lieutenant and my immediate supervisor, would be away in meetings or locked in his office. I really didn't want to see him. I saw Angel seated at his desk, which was right next to mine, and smiled. I had missed him, not that I hadn't seen him over the last month, I had, but not here at work.

He grinned and waved to me. "Hey, I saved your seat," he said with a laugh.

I rolled my eyes and grinned at him. "Cheezy, glad you're here. Sucks you can't go out on calls with me though."

"Yeah, I'm not looking forward to riding the desk, but this leg won't heal if I try to do too much too fast."

"I know, I'm just glad you're here."

"Me too, I was so sick of my own company, I was ready to check myself into the mental ward."

I smiled and put my purse away as I sat down. "I went by your place, thinking you might need a ride. How'd you get here?"

"Uber," he replied with a grin. "If I'd known you would pick me up, I wouldn't have bothered."

"I can take you home; no need for an Uber." I grinned and glanced to the break room, then frowned. I wanted a coffee, but not the muck that was back there. "Want a coffee? I saw the mobile Coffee Guys truck down the street. Gotta be better than what's in the break room."

"Sure. I'm shocked you didn't stop at the coffee shop on your way in."

"I was running late after stopping at your place; not that I'm blaming you, I was already a bit late. Didn't get much sleep," I replied as I stood up.

Ten minutes later I was back with our coffees and two pastries. I handed a coffee and one of the tasty treats to Angel and sat down at my desk with my own. Just as I was about to take a bite, Jordan strode out of his office and into the room. His eyes landed on me and narrowed.

"Kendrick, you're up. Take Hummel and head over to

Glassell Park. Some sort of robbery going on; patrol is there and needs backup," he said, handing me a slip of paper with the address.

I took the paper and was about to protest taking Hummel, but the moment I opened my mouth, Jordan stuck his finger in my face.

"I don't want to hear one word about you not wanting to work with anyone but Angel. He's on desk duty, and you're just going to have to suck it up. Go!"

I gritted my teeth and grabbed my purse and keys. "I'm driving," I said as Hummel joined me. "Where's Vance? Why are you being partnered with me?" I muttered as we walked out of the station.

"Vance is on vaycay. He's on a cruise to Aruba, lucky bastard." Hummel chuckled.

"Must be nice," I replied, climbing into my car. "Siren's under the seat."

Hummel took his time putting his seat belt on and grabbing the siren. That was the problem with Hummel, he did everything slowly. It drove me up the wall. As soon as he got the siren on the dash and hit the button to turn it on, I threw the car into reverse and backed out of the parking spot, then slammed it into drive and took off.

"Slow down!" Hummel cried as I swung the car out of the lot onto the street.

I glanced at him out of the corner of my eye. Working with Hummel was going to try my patience, and I was already short on patience for the day. Ignoring him, I swerved in and out of traffic to get to Glassell Park. We hadn't been given much information on the situation, which was just like Jordan to send us out without knowing what we were walking in on.

Hummel continued to whine at me to slow down, or watch out for various elements on the trip, which I chose to ignore. It was the only way to deal with him.

I pulled my car up behind one of the patrol cars on Verdugo Road, just behind the back of the Glassell Recreation Center, not in the parking lot where cars were fleeing from, and parked. I couldn't tell you the last time I saw Hummel move so fast. He pulled his seat belt off and opened the door, jumping out.

"You're crazy," he said, huffing.

I glared at him and headed for the patrol officer standing on the walkway, motioning vehicles to get out of the lot. I wasn't sure why Porter was letting them all go, and I wanted to know the situation we were walking into. I could see off to the right, near the ball fields, a carnival of some kind had been set up, and wondered if someone had tried to hold up the ticket people or maybe the concession booths.

"What do we have?"

"We're not sure," Porter replied, "but witnesses are saying the perps are calling themselves the Cursed Diablos."

"So why call us out? Why not gang and narco division?" I questioned, wondering why I was there if this was gang activity.

"Because there is no gang called the Cursed Diablos. If they are a gang, it's too new, so they aren't on gang and narco division's radar yet, and this is basically robbery and homicide, so I guess that's why they sent you."

I shook my head. Bureaucratic nonsense was what it was. "How many perps are we dealing with?"

"Wilson's got one of them in the car, and he's not talking, but we know there's at least a handful more running around

Glassell Park. We've got patrol searching, but there's a lot of ground to cover and a lot of people to weed through."

"Have you had the attractions shut down and the tourists and fairgoers cleared out?"

"We're working on it, pool and tennis courts are shut down, fairgoers are being directed out now, and the rides and games are being shut down," Porter answered. "Been trying to get a bus for the dead guy by the Ferris wheel, but they haven't shown up yet. You got here faster than they did, and you came from farther away."

"Kendrick drives like the devil is chasing her, so that's not surprising," Hummel muttered as he joined us.

Porter's eyes flashed to me, but I ignored it.

"So the dead guy, tourist, resident, or perp?"

"Tourist from Wyoming. Wouldn't cooperate with the shooter and got shot for his trouble, according to witnesses."

"Where are you keeping the witnesses?" I asked, looking around.

"They're in the rec center. We've got officers doing interviews in the community room and people waiting in the gym to be interviewed." Porter pointed behind us at the building. "Once we've got their information, we're getting them out of the area as quickly as possible. Hence me standing out here directing traffic."

"Gre—" I started to say as the area around us was lit up with gunfire. "Get down!" I yanked Porter back and to the ground, then pulled my gun.

Hummel dropped down next to us, his back to the patrol car as a series of bullets sprayed the front and side of the car. "What the hell?" he shouted as he pulled his own weapon.

I popped up, bracing my arms on the hood of the car, and returned fire.

The tattoo-covered assailant fell to the ground as my bullet hit his chest.

I glanced at Porter. "Glocks with a switch? They've got fully automatic Glocks, and you didn't think to tell us that?"

He shrugged. "I didn't know. The witnesses didn't say any specific weapon was used; they just said guns. And the guy in Wilson's car wasn't carrying."

I felt my eye twitch. "How many of them had guns? Did they say?"

He shook his head.

"Hummel, with me," I muttered, keeping my weapon out as I headed for the downed assailant.

We cautiously headed into the parking lot, my head on a swivel as I looked for other potential threats. I kicked the Glock away from the dying man's hand and nodded for Hummel to grab it. He picked it up by the slide as I kept my weapon trained on the perp, who was too busy bleeding out onto the cement to notice me.

"Go call this in; we need more backup," I demanded. "And we need medical support as well."

Hummel took the weapon with him and rushed to my car to use the radio. As he reached it, more gunfire sounded from farther away, along with screams from people who had started running in our direction.

"Porter!" I called.

"Yes, ma'am?" he said, reaching my side.

"Cover him, I don't think he's going anywhere, but I can't stay here. I need to go see if I can find the other shooters."

"Yes, ma'am."

I kept my weapon pointed at the ground as I ran through the throng of people running toward me. "Police! Where are the shooters?" I called out, hoping one of the people sprinting for their life would answer.

"Carousel," someone replied.

I didn't bother to find out who had responded, I just used it as a direction finder. I was like a salmon swimming against the current as I tried to get through the fleeing people. As I moved, I shouted, "Police, move out of the way!"

Finally, the crowd seemed to lessen the closer I got to the merry-go-round. I saw a man, dark hair, tattoo-covered face, holding a woman by her ponytail, his weapon pointed at her very pregnant stomach. She was screaming and crying, a man lay on the ground at her feet, and three children, two girls approximately four and eight and a boy around nine, stood to the side, holding each other and crying for their mother.

My mind flashed back to the night St. Martin murdered my mom and I couldn't do anything. I had felt helpless. I wasn't now though.

I didn't even pause. The guy didn't see me coming as he was saying something about points, but I didn't care. I only saw what he was going to do to that woman in front of her kids. I pulled the trigger, and the guy fell back away from the woman, his grip loosening on her hair enough for her to run to her kids.

My shot hadn't been a kill shot, regretfully, because he raised his arm and started to pull the trigger, his gaze still on the woman.

I didn't think about those kids watching. I was livid and now had tunnel vision as I continued to pull the trigger, emptying my clip into the man's chest as I continued to run toward him.

"Kendrick!" Hummel's voice finally broke through to me.

Instead of focusing on him, I kicked the gun away from the perp, then turned to the woman and her children a few feet away. The man had gotten a shot off, and I needed to make sure none of them had been hit. "Ma'am, are you all alright?"

She was on her knees, holding all three of her kids to her chest, sobbing. She looked up, her tearstained cheeks streaked with dirt and debris. Her chest was heaving. She swallowed hard. "Y-yes, yes, we are but... but my... my husband," she stuttered, her eyes sliding to the man on the ground.

I followed her gaze and nodded, then headed over to him and felt his neck. "He's got a pulse," I said, surprised. I flipped him over to find the gunshot wound to the upper chest on the right side, and put pressure on it. "Hummel, get medical here asap! We've got a live victim!"

Hummel spoke into his phone, and within moments a pair of EMTs were running toward us. Hummel then moved to the perp I'd emptied my gun into and checked for a pulse. "Bit of overkill, don't you think, Kendrick?" He stared at the massive mess in the guy's chest.

"Nope." The guy was a sick bastard who deserved every bullet I put into him. I knew I was going to catch some flak for shooting the guy like that, but at this point I didn't care. The man had a gun to a pregnant woman's stomach and was threatening to shoot her in front of her kids after already shooting their dad. He was vile. He deserved to be sent to hell. Just like St. Martin.

I watched as a group of patrol officers escorted seven handcuffed assailants by us. "Is that all of them?" I asked, checking the area. Everything seemed to have calmed a little, and as I kept my head on a swivel, looking for more assailants, I noticed Hummel on his phone, his gaze darting to me and away. I sighed. He was probably reporting what I'd done to Jordan.

"Yes, ma'am. We've got eight more vics, two men and a woman, deceased, others with varying injuries, two life threatening. Medics are with them now."

"Okay, I'm glad they're getting medical attention. Do we have officers doing a sweep to make sure we got all the perps?"

"Yes, ma'am. We've set up a perimeter search as well. And we've got officers checking IDs as people leave or are directed to the rec center as witnesses."

I nodded. "Good man. I'll wait for crime scene here; send them over when they get here."

"Yes, ma'am." The officer hurried to catch up with the others headed toward the parking lot.

Hummel moved from the carousel where he'd been on the phone next to the dead guy and over to me. He held out his hand. "Give me your weapon."

"No. I'll turn it in at the station." I glared at him. "You aren't my superior, Hummel."

"Captain wants you back at the station, asap."

"We aren't done with the scene—"

"You are."

"But—" I huffed.

Hummel handed me his phone. "Take it up with the captain."

I took the phone and said, "Kendrick here, sir—we've got—"

"Hummel can handle it from here. I want you in my office within half an hour."

Sighing, I gave the woman and her children a last look.

"Yes, sir." I tossed Hummel his phone and strode over to her. "Detective Hummel will get your information so you can go to the hospital with your husband. Someone will interview you all there. I'm so sorry you had to go through that."

The woman sniffled. "Thank you so much for saving me. For saving us. That man... he said he'd get fifty points for shooting me... I don't understand how anyone could be so depraved... It was like a game to them." She sobbed.

I gave her a hug. "Go, take care of your family."

She nodded and turned back to the EMTs, who were loading her husband up on a stretcher.

I really hoped he'd pull through. She didn't need to lose him with three kids and one on the way. Dealing with the aftermath was going to be hard enough for her.

I headed back toward the rec center and then over to my car. I turned on the siren and drove toward the precinct without Hummel. Mulling over everything that had happened, I didn't think there was anything I would have done differently.

As I walked into the station, everyone stopped and stared at me. I just stared right back. I was pissed off that Hummel had interfered and called the captain to tattle on me.

Before I reached the detective pool, I could see Jordan in the doorway, waiting on me. I sighed. He was the last person I wanted to deal with. I stopped about three feet away since he was blocking the entrance to the room.

"Three days, Kendrick! You were back less than a week, and you couldn't keep from shooting people!"

I stared at him. I wasn't going to explain. Not to him. Captain Robinson had already said I needed to get to his office, and I had three more minutes to do that and not be late. "Move."

Jordan was seething, his eyes were narrowed, and his jaw ticked as he berated me. "You're reckless and dangerous!" he shouted as I brushed past him.

My eyes met Angel's as I made my way past him toward the captain's office. His gaze was full of empathy and something else I wasn't sure of. Compassion? Regret? Both maybe. I gave him a tight smile.

"He said to send you right in," Jason said, tilting his head toward Captain Robinson's office door.

I nodded and headed for the closed door. I knocked and waited for the captain to acknowledge me, then opened the door. I went in and closed the door behind me, right in Jordan's face. That made me smile, but I quickly dropped it before turning back to Robinson.

"Sit."

I did as he asked.

"I need your weapon and your badge."

"Are you firing me?" I said, taken aback.

"No. You're on suspension. IA has already been in touch. They want psych evals on you, and I can't say I blame them, from what Hummel relayed over the phone."

"What did Hummel tell you happened, sir? If you don't mind me asking what I'm being accused of?"

"He said that after taking out one perp, you ran toward the gunfire, then emptied your clip into the other perp without identifying yourself."

"Did he also say that the man had a pregnant woman hostage and was getting ready to shoot her in the stomach?" I demanded, seething. "Did he tell you that the man said it was a game and he'd get fifty points for shooting her? Did he tell you that the man had already shot her husband? And that their three children were right there watching and listening?" I demanded, seething.

"No, he didn't, still... you downed the man and kept shooting, Kendrick. I can't help but think there is something going on with you."

I gritted my teeth. "I don't like women, mothers particularly, being threatened and murdered in front of their kids."

"Look, I know you've been through some horrible things, Kendrick, that's why I'm not firing you. I want you to get some more therapy. I want you to pass those psych evals. Do what you have to do, okay?" he said, his eyes full of compassion. "You're a good cop, one of our best, and I don't want to lose you over this."

I sighed. "I'll talk to Doc Adams. I'll do what she recommends."

"Today. She's expecting you in ten minutes."

"Yeah, I'll go up to her office now." I stood up and turned for the door.

"Kendrick?"

"Yeah?"

"Still need your weapon and badge."

I paused, then nodded. I unholstered my Glock and checked it, then laid it on his desk before pulling my badge from my belt, setting it down next to it. I glanced at them with frustration. I wasn't happy about giving up my badge. Even if it was temporary. I hoped it was temporary at any rate.

"It's just until you get your mind in the right headspace; you'll be back," he said, keeping his voice gentle.

I nodded, then opened the door and headed out. I didn't even look toward the detective pool; instead I headed down the hallway to the bank of elevators and hit the button for the fourth floor, where Dr. Adams had her office. She was one of a few employed by the LAPD for psych evaluations on suspects as well as officers. She also did short-term therapy with many of the officers who were involved in shootings. I'd seen her before, but usually just for one or two sessions to get cleared to go back to work. I was pretty sure that wasn't going to be the case this time.

I walked up to her front desk.

Her receptionist smiled at me. "Detective Kendrick, it's good to see you. Dr. Adams is expecting you. She told me to send you right in."

I gave her a small smile that I didn't really feel. "Thanks." Striding forward, I headed for the closed office door and knocked.

"Come in, Detective."

I opened the door and saw her behind her desk, looking as professional as ever in a fitted suit in a shade of blue that matched her eyes and her blonde hair done up in a French twist. "Hi, Doc."

"Have a seat." She gestured to the comfortable chairs that were positioned in front of the window with a coffee table in front of them.

I did as she asked and waited.

"So, how are you feeling?" she asked.

I almost laughed at that, but then sighed. "Not great." I looked down at my hands folded in my lap. "I'm on suspension again."

"Yes, and I think that might be my fault."

I glanced up at her, my brow furrowed. "How on earth would it be your fault? I'm the one who shot the suspect."

"Yes, but I think I may have cleared you for duty too soon. I missed something."

I expelled a breath and then shook my head. "No, I'm okay."

She arched her brow at me. "Are you? Really?" She pursed her lips and then said, "I got a phone call from Captain Robinson as you were headed up here."

That surprised me. "Oh?"

"He mentioned you filled him in on today's events, but I picked up something that I'm not sure he did."

I bit my lip as I stared at her. "What?"

"Despite the fact this killer was using a gun and not a knife, you were most likely reliving your mother's murder. You saw a mother, her life in danger in front of her children, and reacted as you would have if Lemuel St. Martin had been the killer."

Her words made my spine stiffen. She wasn't wrong. If I'd had a gun that night, I would have done exactly what I'd done to that suspect. "I am not going to deny that my mind might have flashed to that night, but I knew what I was doing. The first shot I took allowed the woman to get free of him, but he took a shot at her anyway, even though he'd been shot himself. And thank goodness he missed because he wasn't giving up. I continued to shoot to stop him."

She nodded. "I can understand you reacting that way. It's natural to want to protect someone who can't protect themselves. The issue is the excessive amount of force you used. I think that goes back to the anger you feel toward St. Martin, and probably to Nicholas Pound as well. I think that while you have dealt with Mr. Pound making you relive your mother's death repeatedly, you haven't dealt with the anger you felt at being subjected to watching your mother's murder as a child."

I felt the muscle in my jaw twitch. I had a feeling I wasn't going to like what she was going to suggest.

"I'm going to recommend some one-on-one therapy as well as group therapy so that you can work through these issues." She pulled a business card from her notebook and handed it to me. "This is the number for Dr. Fellows. He is expecting your call."

I took the card and looked at it. "How long do I have to go through therapy this time?" I asked, feeling resigned to it now.

"That depends on you and the work you put into it, Marcy."

2

LOST DREAMS
MARCY

"Are y-you all right?" Henry asked as I lay in his arms after we'd finished making love.

I turned my head on the pillow and gave him a smile. "I'm great. You?"

The concerned look on his face turned to a happy smile, and a twinkle lit his eye. "I'm great too. That was... amazing," he murmured, kissing my temple.

I snuggled into his side and lifted my face to his. "It was. We'll have to do it again sometime." I giggled.

It had been a long time since I'd felt so cared for, so well loved. Jordan and I had been married for ten years, but the last few years had been contentious, and then we'd gotten divorced just a few months ago, so being with Henry like this was refreshing. I had missed it.

I missed him. I ran my hand over his face, cupping his cheek as I leaned in to kiss him. "I miss you," I murmured against his lips.

"I'm right here," he said, giving me a loving look.

"Don't go," I cried as I pulled him to me, but as I did, he faded away, disappearing from the bed.

I woke when my alarm went off at six a.m., lying on my side, holding the extra pillow as if it had been Henry. I sighed as I stared at the empty bed and clicked the alarm off. It didn't matter that I'd never shared this particular bed with Henry. We'd only been together that short time at his house since he'd feared leaving his home because of his stutter. It had never bothered me, and when we were together, his stutter wasn't a problem, it had almost gone away toward the end.

My heart ached at the loss of him. He hadn't deserved what happened to him. To be killed by that psycho because of me. Tears filled my eyes and spilled down my cheeks at the anguish I felt. I'd been falling in love with Henry, and then he was stolen from me. And in such a brutal way. I was broken, but after seeing Dr. Fellows twice a week for one-on-one therapy and doing group therapy three days a week, I was starting to heal. Not just from his loss, but also the anger I had held from when my mom died, which was the reason I was in such intense therapy in the first place.

Speaking of the group, I needed to check in. I wiped my face, headed to the bathroom, cleaned up, then got dressed. Once I was decent, I sat down at the table and opened my laptop. I logged in to my therapy group at six fifteen for our six-thirty meeting and clicked the Zoom link. Dr. Fellows had accommodated those of us who had odd working hours or needed to be at work by eight by having such an early meeting time.

Once the screen came on, adding me to the group, I raised a hand in greeting. "Hey," I murmured to everyone.

"Marcy, glad you could make it this morning," Dr. Fellows said. He was always cordial when he greeted each of us.

"Hey, Marcy, how's work going?" Katrina, one of the other participants, asked. She was actually my mentor of sorts. We'd bonded over our losses and even spoken outside of our group therapy sessions.

"You passed your evals, and Dr. Adams approved you going back to work?" Dr. Fellows asked before I could answer Katrina.

I'd been gone a little more than two months if you didn't count the few days I had been back before being suspended for a month, but now, after passing Dr. Adam's psych evals and being cleared by IA, I was easing my way back into work.

I smiled at both Katrina and Dr. Fellows. "Yes, I…" My throat tightened as I thought about how much of a breakdown I'd had in that first session with Dr. Fellows. "I started back this week. Half days. It's been… difficult."

"Do you want to talk about it? What's making it difficult for you?" Dr. Fellows asked.

I thought about it for a minute. "It's not the work, exactly. It's the people. My co-workers." I looked up at the ceiling and tried to keep myself from crying. I had never been one to burst into tears at the drop of a hat. A cross word to me and I gave as good as I got, at least I used to, but now, it was like I'd grown sensitive. "I feel like they are looking at me differently, like I'm fragile."

"Not Jordan," Katrina asked, sounding surprised.

I gave a humorless laugh. "No, not Jordan. He's as much of an ass to me as he's always been." I rolled my eyes.

"Angel's been great though, solid. I think he gets it, but everyone else..." I shook my head.

"So even though you saved his life, he's still treating you like he was before?" Dr. Fellows asked.

"Pretty much. I think he's blocked out the fact that I was the one to get him out of that predicament. He's now focusing on what happened when I came back to work before. Basically, he's back to trying to control everything I do. Captain Robinson has told him to lay off me more than once this week. He does his best to keep Jordan off my case, but he's the lieutenant, so I can't just ignore him."

"Have you been sent out on any cases, or are you on desk duty?" Dr. Fellows interjected. "You know I mentioned to Dr. Adams and you that you should ease back into work..."

I nodded. "I've been sent out a few times, just run-of-the-mill things, no major cases. No serial killers, nothing that reminds me of Mom or Henry. As far as I'm aware, we don't have any active serials in the city right now. Mostly it's been a couple of robbery-related shootings and some domestics. And Angel's been with me on all of them."

Angel had kept me sane and up to date on what was going on in the department while I'd been out.

"Glad to hear we are serial killer free," Mitchel, another participant, murmured. "I don't know how you deal with that." He shivered.

I glanced at Mitchel. He was young, no more than twenty. I recalled that he'd lost his girlfriend to a drug overdose. "I'm trained for it," I answered him.

I didn't tell him that I'd basically trained myself to go after those types of killers. I'd wanted to make a difference after what the Face Flayer had done to my mom. I had been there when he attacked and killed her. I had been hiding under the bed with my brother. Stephen had probably saved my life that night, keeping me quiet and still under that bed, because I'd wanted to slide out and save Mom from Face Flayer. It wouldn't have worked; I was just a kid at the time. After that, I decided I was going to be a cop so I could stop psychos like him. There were people out there who thought I was a vigilante cop, but I wasn't, not really. When I said I wanted to stop them, I meant legally. I never went out looking to kill them, just to arrest them and make sure they paid for their crimes.

There were some killers, though, who would rather die than be taken in. I hated being the one to pull the trigger, but if it came down to me, their victim, or them, I sure as hell would pull the trigger and put them down. I wouldn't allow them to continue their killing spree. That just wasn't how I rolled. I would always act. I would always protect. It was who I was.

"How's your brother?" Blake asked.

I glanced at her corner of the screen and winced. Blake was a real sweetheart who actually knew Stephen. He'd done some work for her company a year or so ago. I knew she'd hooked up with him, but I hadn't known that at the time I'd shared details of Stephen's mental breakdown.

"He's doing better. Getting some good help," I answered.

After visiting his therapist with him when he'd explained about the abuse he'd suffered from our mother, he'd been doing good, but then backslid and started drinking heavily along with taking an overdose of pills. It had been dumb luck that I'd found him, because normally I'd have been at work. I had gotten him to the hospital in time, and was grateful I'd been thinking about him after my own intense therapy session and decided to drive by to see him. I'd found him on the living room floor with a bottle of Jim Beam and an empty bottle of sleeping pills. He'd barely been breathing when the ambulance arrived. The hospital had pumped his stomach and gotten him stable, and then his psychiatrist had admitted him for a seventy-two-hour hold.

When the seventy-two hours were up, Dr. Faulkner, his psychiatrist, had convinced him he needed more intense therapy, and to check in to a clinic. He seemed to be doing better the last time I spoke to him. With him convalescing, I'd been taking care of his apartment and feeding his fish since my own therapy allowed me to at least stay at home.

"I'm glad to hear it," Blake replied.

"Is he still at Shine View?" Dr. Fellows asked.

I nodded. "Yes, for a little longer, I think."

"I will check in on him, if you'd like?" Dr. Fellows offered. "I can't give you any diagnostic information, not without his permission, but I can do a general wellness check for you."

"Oh, you don't have to do that, his psychiatrist, Dr. Faulkner, makes sure I am in the loop, and Stephen calls me regularly."

"All right. I just don't want you to be stressed with worry about your brother."

That was a nice thought, but even with the wellness checks, I'd still worry. I was his sister, we were the only family we had left, so of course I was going to worry. "Thank you," I said, despite that.

"How have the nightmares been?" Dr. Fellows asked.

I shrugged. "I wouldn't really call them nightmares. More disturbing dreams that mix with memories."

"That's natural. Our subconscious minds tend to take

certain traumatic memories and play out different scenarios. It's a way of dealing with the trauma of what happened, and helps you do things differently in the future if that sort of event takes place again."

I nodded, but I wasn't sure I agreed with that wholeheartedly. Not with the particular dreams I'd been having about Henry, but I didn't say anything. I really didn't want to go into details about the dreams I'd been having in group. It was too depressing, and there wasn't anything anyone could do. They couldn't bring Henry back. Nothing could. He was gone, his life stolen by a serial killer who had been and still was obsessed with me. And I had the letters from the mental institution to prove it.

"Have you received any other letters?" Dr. Fellows asked.

Funny, seemed like he'd read my mind. "No. Not since I got the restraining order a couple of weeks ago. They don't allow him to mail me anything anymore."

"I'm glad to hear that." Dr. Fellows nodded and then turned to Matt. "How has your week been?"

The conversation moved on to some of the others, and I made appropriate comments of encouragement to each of them. Then our hour was up, and we were setting up a time for our next session.

Before signing off, Katrina said, "Hey, Marce, how about we meet up for coffee or lunch later?"

"That'd be great. I'll text you if I have a time open up. You know with my job it's hard to know exactly when I'll be able to take a break." I laughed a little.

Katrina nodded. "Girl, I get it. I couldn't do your job. I'll check in with you later if I don't hear from you first."

"Sounds good; see ya later." I waved and then shut down the program before closing up my computer.

I spent the rest of my morning cleaning my apartment and grocery shopping. I didn't go into work until three that day, so I made lunch and watched a movie. It was lonely to say the least. I honestly hated time off because I spent too much of it thinking about things I couldn't control or change. Like Henry's death. If only I had stayed, then he would still be alive.

My head said that probably wasn't true. Henry might not have died right then, but that psycho was going to murder him no matter what just because we were together. He would have done it the moment I left, no matter when that was. I couldn't have saved him.

If only I had realized who he was sooner, then maybe... but it was useless to play the what-if game. I couldn't change things. I could only move forward. Those thoughts weren't productive. The problem was they continuously crept into my head when I was on my own, secluded in my apartment. I thought about contacting Dr. Fellows and asking for a one-on-one therapy session, but I didn't. It was bad enough doing the group therapy thing. It helped me, but I hated being so vulnerable.

I knew I shouldn't bottle things up, but sharing was hard for me. I'd learned to stop sharing after what happened to Mom right in front of me and then spending the rest of my childhood in the foster system. I couldn't be placed with a family and had to live in a group home and do one-on-one therapy with a state-ordered therapist. Sharing got you put on pills and told your trauma would never go away without them. That wasn't true. The trauma didn't go away with pills. It was always there. It was all in how you dealt with it. The pills didn't deal with it, merely masked it, and made you numb to it. At least that was my experience.

I dealt with my trauma by focusing on becoming the best damn cop I could be. I worked my way up in the ranks and was now an LAPD Police Detective Third Class in the Homicide Special Section Unit (HSS). I had been up for lieutenant, but the job had gone to Jordan. I supposed I could try again, but I wasn't sure I wanted that role now. I liked being able to just do my job. I liked catching killers and not having to be in charge of a bunch of officers.

The things people did to each other would turn anyone's stomach, if they had to see it. It was a wonder more cops weren't in therapy, though a lot of the ones I knew self-medicated with alcohol. Going to therapy was thought of as a weakness.

Hence the way my co-workers were treating me. As though I was fragile and unable to do the job. They compared me to Jordan, who had been kidnapped and tortured a bit, and said if he could deal with that without therapy, then I should suck it up and be fine. I wasn't kidnapped and tortured, was I? No. I just had to deal with a psychopath who'd decided to emulate the man who'd murdered my mother, then deal with him killing someone else I really cared about. Not traumatic in the least.

Sighing, I clicked the TV off and went to get ready for work. I headed into my bedroom and changed from my loungewear into a pair of black dress slacks, a light-blue, button-down shirt, then pulled my blazer from the hanger in the closet. I set it on the bed as I put on a pair of socks and my trainers. I threaded a belt through the loops, added my badge to it so it wouldn't fall off, and buckled it. I put my hair up into a low bun, added mascara and lipstick to my face—I didn't bother with much makeup—and decided I was presentable.

Grabbing my blazer and my purse, I picked up my keys and headed out the door, locking it behind me. I'd kept the added deadbolts on my door after Nick had broken in, and always made sure to lock up tight. I made my way to my car and drove to the precinct.

3

THE BURNED BEAUTY
MARCY

Pulling into the parking lot, I turned the engine off. I sat there for a couple of minutes, trying to psych myself up to go in because I hated seeing my co-workers' faces. Most of them were just waiting for me to have a mental breakdown. To flip out and go crazy. I wouldn't give them the satisfaction.

The only people I had in my corner were Angel and Captain Jack Robinson. Neither of them treated me differently.

The problem was Angel was still operating at half-capacity due to the car accident he'd been in, which had broken his leg pretty badly. He still had to go to physical therapy, so like me, he was on half days too.

Captain Robinson wasn't always available to intervene because he had to spend most of his day with the top brass. Another thankless job I really didn't aspire to. He had to deal with not only Jordan, but also the mayor and the chief of police and sometimes even the governor. There were always meetings to go over budgets and statistics and crime rates. I knew he was often unappreciated for everything he did.

Taking a deep breath and letting it out slowly, I climbed from the car and schooled my expression into the mask of a hardened detective. I was calm. I was centered. Nothing was going to bother me. At least that was what I told myself as I entered the building.

I managed to make it all the way to my desk and put my purse down before Jordan shouted at me.

"Where the hell have you been, Kendrick?" He stormed toward me, his hulking frame hovering over me seconds later.

I gritted my teeth. He knew damn well that I was on half days, and I wasn't about to allow him to try to intimidate me. "Do you really want an itinerary of what I've done today? Because I'm more than happy to share, Lieutenant. I woke up, used the bathroom, spoke with my therapy group, cleaned my apartment, and went grocery shopping. After that I ate lunch and watched a movie, and now, I'm here at the time I was *scheduled* to be here." My heart was pounding hard in my chest. Jordan pushed my buttons nearly every time we spoke, and I always ended up angry and seething.

"You know that wasn't what I was asking. You're late. What, did you stop by the cemetery and have a little heart-to-heart with your cross-dressing dead boyfriend?" His voice was loud and drew the attention of half the department.

I could see Hummel smirking and his partner, Vance, making snide remarks—which was his MO—from out of the corner of my eye, but I couldn't hear them, thankfully. I kept my focus on Jordan, ready to lay into him. "You—" I started.

"Kendrick, my office," Captain Robinson called, interrupting me. "Now!"

I shut my mouth, but didn't move as I glared at Jordan, clenching my fists. I wanted so badly to punch him. Henry wasn't a cross-dresser, and Jordan knew it. The way he'd said it almost sounded like he was jealous, but that was ridiculous. He was the one who'd cheated on me, not the other way around. The ink was barely dry on our divorce papers when he'd married the Barbie doll more than a decade younger than me.

Jordan smirked. He turned and walked away, presumably heading to his own office, thinking Robinson was going to yell at me in his place. I doubted that was the case, but either way, I'd rather deal with an angry Jack Robinson than my asshole ex-husband.

"Reyes, you too," Robinson called from his office door.

I turned to see Angel hobbling toward me on crutches. I smiled. "Hey. Looks like the captain wants to see us."

He nodded, but his expression was troubled. "You okay?" he asked.

I shrugged. "I'm fine."

"Marcy, what Jordan said—"

I shook my head. "Drop it. It's fine. I'm fine. Everything is fine. Let's go before Robinson has to call for us again."

He sighed. "It's not fine, but I'll drop it for now."

As we entered the captain's office, Robinson gestured for us to have a seat.

I took the farthest one, leaving the more accessible one for Angel. "What's up, sir?"

"Just got a call, suspicious death." Captain Robinson looked shaken. "An extremely wealthy heiress has died, and I don't want it bandied about. I'd like to keep the death out of the media for as long as possible. It doesn't look good."

"Who is it?" I asked. We were in LA, and there were any

number of wealthy heiresses here, along with celebrities, sports figures, and politicians. There was no way I could possibly guess who had died.

"Audrina Dixon."

"Seriously?" Angel said; his jaw dropped open. "What happened?"

"I'm not sure. The fire department was called, but so was LAPD. It's a jurisdictional mess. Crime scene is there, and after their initial assessment, they've asked for you." He looked at me.

"Me specifically?" I frowned.

"Stone said the death looks suspicious, and asked if you were back on the job. Are you up for it? If not, I can get Hummel and Vance—"

"No, yeah, I'm good. We'll go." I wasn't about to turn this down. I wanted to go back to doing real detective work. Besides, Hummel sucked. I would swear the man couldn't detect his way out of a paper bag.

He stared at me as if he could see into my head. "You're sure you're up for this? It could get ugly."

Nothing could be as ugly as the last major case was, but I didn't say that. That would be jinxing things. "I promise I'm fine, sir."

He nodded and looked at Angel. "You up for this? PT going okay?"

"Yes, sir. Just another week or so on the crutches, but I can go without them if I have to."

Robinson shook his head. "No, follow the doctor's orders. We want you back at one hundred percent. That won't happen if you don't."

"Yes, sir." Angel nodded. "Anything else we need to know?"

The captain handed me the paper with a Beverly Crest address on it. "No, just get over there, and no lights. I don't want attention drawn to the scene. Bad enough that half of the fire department is there. I'm serious about keeping the media from getting a hold of this before we even know what's happened."

"Yes, sir." I wasn't sure we could stop the media from finding anything out, but I'd do my best to keep any leaks to a minimum. "We'll head over there now."

"I want your report as soon as you get back. If I'm in a meeting, write it up and leave it on my desk personally. I don't want any other eyes on this. If the door is locked, tell Jason what I just told you, and he'll let you in."

It was unusual, Captain Robinson wasn't normally so paranoid, but considering Jordan had a way of being demanding and interfering with my reports, I figured he was saying this so I'd have an out if Jordan asked for the report. "Of course, sir." I stood and waited for Angel to get through the door before I followed him out of the office. "I'll go bring the car around and meet you in front of the precinct."

"Sounds good." Angel maneuvered around a desk to get to his own, where he'd left his jacket.

I grabbed my purse from my desk and pulled out my keys. I hadn't had time to take my blazer off earlier before Jordan started in on me, so I just headed straight to the car. I pulled the car to the front and got out, then moved around the vehicle to open the door for Angel. I took the crutches and slid them into the back seat, then jumped back in the driver's seat.

I pulled my seat belt over my shoulder. "Ready?" I looked over to be sure he was buckled.

"Yeah, I'm good." He shifted in the seat, getting comfortable. "I wonder what happened. Audrina Dixon was a gorgeous woman."

I frowned. "I hadn't ever heard of her, but then I didn't really follow celebrities. "Who is she?"

Angel pulled his phone out and began typing as I headed for the 101. "She's pretty famous on Insta, both for her beauty and the jewelry she designs. Though her family is where a lot of her money came from. She's a billionaire. Or was, I guess." He held his phone up to show me a photo of the woman.

I glanced over, not wanting to take my eyes off the road. From what I could tell, Audrina had been a beautiful redhead, probably in her late thirties to early forties. It was hard to tell from the picture. Her blue eyes were bright, and her smile was perfect. "Was she married?"

"Divorced. It was pretty antagonistic, from what I've heard."

That raised my eyebrows. "Was it? Kids involved?"

"A couple of boys, I think." He scrolled on his phone and a moment later held it up again for me to see. "Yeah, two boys."

"Okay, good to know." I signaled to switch lanes. "Wonder what we're walking into," I murmured.

"Guess we're gonna find out." He nodded toward the building we were headed to.

Out front of the four-story, luxury apartment building, there were two fire trucks, the fire chief's truck, an ambulance, LAPD patrol cars, the crime scene vehicles, and the coroner's car. The road was full of emergency personnel. I pulled in behind the coroner, Damien Black's car, and parked. Climbing out, I went around the front of my car and opened the back door to grab Angel's crutches, then opened his door.

Once he was on his feet, we had to push through the gaping crowd that had gathered on the sidewalk, probably wanting to know who had been hurt or killed. When we reached the crime scene tape, I motioned for one of the patrol officers to let us in. I swept my blazer aside and showed my badge to the female officer.

"Everyone's around back, ma'am," Officer Liz Allen said.

I glanced at her and realized she was the officer who had been at the Hollywood Hills house where Kelly Norton had been murdered. "Is there a gate, or do we have to go through the building?"

"Through the building, ma'am."

I glanced at Angel. "You okay?" This was a lot of movement for him, and I knew he wasn't supposed to be vertical for long periods of time.

"I'm good, barely a twinge. Don't worry about me, Marcy. I know you're just concerned for my health, but I promise I'll say something if I need to sit." He grinned.

I took him at his word. Angel wasn't one to complain, but I knew if he needed to take a break, he'd say so. "Okay, let's head in."

4

MYSTERIOUS MURDERER
ANGEL

Marcy and I headed into the luxury apartment building; it was all marble floors and glass tables, with several large plants and leather sofas and chairs in the lobby. There was a reception counter, where a woman sat behind a computer. I wished I weren't on these damn crutches so I could just nudge Marcy and get her attention as I normally would, but trying to do that now would throw off my balance and send me crashing to the floor.

"Marce, we should check with reception, don't you think?" I paused my forward movement.

Marcy stopped, and her lips twisted as she thought it over. "Lindsey did say it was a suspicious death when she spoke to Robinson, so yeah, we'll probably need to do that." She glanced at the blonde woman on the phone behind the counter. "Let's go see what we're dealing with; we can grab surveillance video and talk to the receptionist after. They aren't going anywhere."

She wasn't wrong; we didn't know anything yet. I gave

her a nod and followed her down the hall and out through the sliding glass doors that led to a flagstone patio and deck surrounding a huge swimming pool. I could see the victim lying about two feet shy of the shallow end of the pool. It was hard to tell if it was actually Audrina Dixon.

"Kim," Marcy said as we approached, "what's going on?"

There were about twenty people standing around the body; Officer Min-Ji Kim was one of them, along with Fire Chief Sorenson; Lindsey Stone, who was head of crime scene investigations; Damien Black, the coroner; and Michael Portsmith, a crime scene photographer. There were various other firefighters and patrol officers, including Officer Julie Desmond, Kim's partner.

"Hey, Kim," I said, swinging my body up near them. These crutches made it difficult to get around, but at least I was mobile.

"Detectives, glad you could join us. We're having a little jurisdictional dispute." He nodded toward Sorenson and Lindsey Stone.

I frowned. "Why? The fire department doesn't normally try to take over crime scenes unless it's all about the fire, yeah?"

Kim shrugged. "I'm sure they're going to want to have access to the crime scene because of that, but the dispute is over the vic's body."

"I'll go talk to Lindsey." Marcy started toward the attractive brunette with the chocolate brown eyes. She paused and looked over her shoulder at me. "Coming?"

I gave her a nod and moved my crutches forward, swinging my body with them. It took me a minute to reach them.

"She is a fire victim; the crime scene is ours," Sorenson argued.

"She didn't die from the fire. She clearly fell from the balcony, which makes it HSS' crime scene," Lindsey bit out, a look of frustration on her face.

"She wouldn't have fallen if she wasn't on fire; the room shows that—" Sorenson continued.

"Look, I get it, it's a slow week for you, but this death"—she pointed at the victim—"was probably murder, and you have no jurisdiction for investigating that. You can have access to the room to figure out how the fire started, but HSS will be taking over her death investigation."

Sorenson rocked back on his heels and, after a moment's hesitation, gave her a nod. "Fine. I want to be kept in the loop." He gave both Marcy and me a look that told us not to argue.

I didn't see a problem with it, but it wasn't my call. Marcy was actually the senior officer. I was only a second grade, while she was third. If Jordan hadn't hounded IA to investigate her shooting a suspect, she probably would have been promoted to lieutenant instead of him. They'd cleared her because it was a justified shoot, but it had screwed up her chance at the promotion.

I was kind of glad about it, not because I didn't think she deserved it, she really did, but it would mean losing her as a partner. And she wouldn't be out here doing what she does best, which is catching the actual bad guys. She was good at it. It was almost like she could get into their heads and figure them out. She did it like it was a jigsaw puzzle, and as soon as she has all the pieces, she can put it together. Working with her these past couple of years has made me a better officer. Either way, I didn't want to give up being close to her.

"We'll make sure you have a copy of our report, as long as Captain Robinson agrees," Marcy said. "Now, unless you have anything else, please take your personnel and go. We've got enough people around here fucking up the crime scene, and we don't need any more."

I smiled. I loved it when Marcy told people off. She gave no fucks at all about pissing people off. "Hey, Lindsey, what can you tell us?" I asked as the fire chief moved away without another word.

Lindsey smiled. "Glad to see you're back, Reyes. You too, Kendrick. Been a while. Okay, come on over here," she directed.

We moved with her to stand about a foot from the vic.

Lindsey pointed up to a balcony. "So, we are pretty sure she was up there when she went over the rail. The question is, did she choose to jump, or was she pushed? My first theory is that she went over on her own, not intending to kill herself, but hoping to land in the pool to put out the flames."

"With that balcony being so close to the pool, that's a good theory. Do her injuries seem consistent with that?"

"They do, but it's also possible that she was pushed." Lindsey huffed and turned to the coroner, who was squatted over the body. "Damien, have you found anything?"

"She was definitely on fire prior to the fall. You can tell by the burns to the body and clothing. Also, it's consistent with what we found upstairs. Have you two been up there yet?"

I shook my head. "We came right here first."

"You'll need to check out the room, but you'll see the pattern of movement that took her out the glass doors and over the balcony railing. Now, whether there was someone who followed her out remains to be seen, and our witnesses aren't speaking," Lindsey shared.

"Wait, there's witnesses?" Marcy's eyes widened.

"Yeah, her two fourteen-year-old sons." Lindsey opened her notebook and said, "Gottlieb Dixon-Pfeiffer, who I've been told goes by Gary, and Milgram Dixon-Pfeiffer, who goes by Mike. Can't say I blame them; those names are a mouthful."

Marcy took notes as well, writing down their names. "You said they were both fourteen, so they're twins? Identical or fraternal?"

"Identical, but they have dyed the tips of their hair. Mike's are frosted blond, and Gary's are blue."

"Okay, has anyone gotten statements from them?" Marcy asked.

"We've got medics looking them over, but neither are speaking. Probably just the shock of it. Apparently, they witnessed the whole thing, as both were home and in the same room, and they're showing signs of smoke inhalation."

I waited a moment and then asked, "So we're not looking at them as suspects?"

"I never said that," Lindsey answered, "but their traumatized nature would lead me to say no."

"So it was an accident, and her fall was deliberate with her trying to reach the pool, suicide, or some outsider came in, lit the room and her on fire, then forced her over the rail and left the boys alone. Is that what you're telling me?" Marcy asked.

"Are you thinking the ex might have been the intruder?" I questioned her.

"I don't know, maybe. I need to see the room." Marcy

glanced at the victim. "I want the autopsy report and anything you can tell me asap."

"I'll have it by tomorrow morning," Damien answered.

"Come on, Michael needs to get pictures of the upstairs crime scene," Lindsey said, waving her arm at Michael to get his attention. "You can come up with us. And you're in luck, Reyes, there's an elevator."

"You're always thinking of me, Linds," I said with a chuckle.

We returned to the lobby, and Lindsey led us over to a bank of elevators. Once we were inside the car, she tapped in a code on the keypad. We rode up to the fourth floor, and the doors opened straight into the apartment.

"Who else has that code?" Marcy asked as we stepped out of the elevator into a small foyer.

"I got it from reception. I'd suppose the boys would have it, the victim, and any of their friends who visit often, but without the boys talking, it's hard to know. Reception might have a list of anyone who does, or maybe video of them coming and going."

Marcy gave me a look, and I knew she wanted me to remember to ask when we questioned the woman at the desk. I gave her a nod. "Noted."

"Where to?" Marcy asked.

"Back here." Lindsey led us toward the back of the apartment, down a hall.

On the left was a gaming room with a big, plush sofa, a coffee table, and a large flat-screen TV on the wall with a game paused on the screen. There were two controllers on the table. On the right was a room that was still smokey, but I could see that it had probably been really light and airy and got a lot of sunlight. Inside, there was a wall of floor-to-ceiling windows with a sliding glass door, and several skylights in the ceiling. The room was trashed though, glass everywhere, with a distinct smokey odor in the air.

"That's the oil you're smelling. Which is what was used to start the fire. From the debris, we can see there were several oil lamps in this room." Lindsey pointed at the partial remains of several oil lamps. "Now, it's too early to know exactly what happened, but we think the fire started in this general area. You can see the discoloration on the stone is a bit more concentrated here?"

"Yeah," I answered.

"Go on," Marcy said with a nod.

"Right, so it looks like she was here, maybe lighting the oil lamp that was on this table over here, against the wall, before it was burnt in the fire, leaving just the metal frame." She started to move. "We think she took this path, bumping into this table next to the chair and then this one behind the sofa before stumbling to the balcony doors."

"Damn, she had to have been in so much pain. I can see her thinking that would be the fastest way to get relief, going outside and maybe aim for the pool. It was a risky move if that's what happened." Marcy frowned as she moved toward the glass doors.

"Isn't it?" Lindsey said with a nod.

"Okay, well, get pictures of everything, and put it together with the autopsy report."

"Sure thing," Lindsey replied.

"Let's go talk to reception, see who came and went to this apartment."

Once we were downstairs, we headed for the reception desk.

I smiled at the pretty blonde and noticed her drag her

blue-eyed gaze over my frame before giving me a blinding smile back. It was sad that it did nothing for me. She was a gorgeous woman, but my heart was engaged elsewhere in a place it shouldn't be, honestly. "I'm Detective Reyes, and this is my partner, Detective Kendrick. We'd like to have the surveillance video for the pool area, the lobby, and elevators for today, say starting from midnight to when emergency personnel arrived."

"Of course. I suspected you might, so I already called the owner to get permission. Here you are." She handed Marcy a disk, realizing my hands were occupied with the crutches and I couldn't carry shit. Her cheeks turned a little pink, and she seemed a bit embarrassed.

"How long have you been working the reception counter?" Marcy asked.

The woman's eyes widened. "For a couple of years—"

"Sorry, no, I meant today, how long have you been on duty?"

"Oh, I came in at six a.m. Normally I'm off by three, but then this all happened, and I figured you'd need me to stay, so I just told my replacement I'd work a double." She shrugged. "Might as well get paid if I have to be here for all of this, you know?"

"Pragmatic of you." I gave her a smile. "So did you notice anyone enter and go up to the Dixons' apartment?"

"No, nobody went up to their floor that I saw. We had a few who visited residents on level three and two, but nobody went to the Dixons' place."

"Could we have a list of names of the people who have the Dixons' elevator code?" I said, giving her a charming smile.

"Sure, we have a record of it on the computer." She

nodded toward the machine. "Just a sec." She began typing and within a minute clicked print, and a page shot out of the printer. She grabbed it, looked it over and then held it out toward Marcy. "There you go."

"Thanks. Have you seen any of these people today?" I asked.

"Sorry, I haven't, but I'm not always paying attention to people who come in, especially if they know where they're going, and sometimes my back it to them, you know?" she offered as she gestured to the filing cabinets behind her.

"Alright, thanks, we'll check with them to see if they've been here. Be sure to give your information to Officer Kim in case we need to speak to you again."

"My pleasure," she added.

We started toward the front of the building, and I murmured, "What are you thinking?"

"I doubt it's suicide, there was too much chaos in that room, and no sane, loving mother would do it in front of her children." Marcy paused.

"What if she wasn't a sane person or a loving mother?" I suggested, playing devil's advocate.

She tilted her head and then shook it. "It doesn't feel right. We're missing something. Maybe we've got a mysterious murderer who knew the code and snuck in past the Barbie at reception and made it to the elevator. With the boys not talking, it's hard to know exactly what happened." She sighed.

"So, back to the precinct?" I asked.

She nodded. "Wanna grab a burger and fries on the way?"

I grinned. "You know it."

With that, we headed back to the car, swung through my

favorite fast-food joint to get doubles with cheese and the works, large fries, and soft drinks, and ate on our way back to the station. I loved the fact Marcy was never self-conscious about eating like a lot of women I knew. She ate what she wanted and didn't apologize for it. I admired that.

"What?" Marcy asked, with a quick glance at me as she drove.

I had to grin. She'd caught me watching her. "You've got ketchup on your chin." She didn't.

She shrugged, grabbed a napkin, and wiped her face. "Gone?"

"Yep." I turned back to look out the windshield as I finished off my burger.

Marcy was an attractive woman, but she was my partner and Jordan's ex-wife. I shouldn't be crushing on her. I shoved my trash back in the bag a little more forcefully than needed, which was similar to how I'd shoved my feelings toward her into the little box I kept in my head. Being around her on the daily was hard, but it was worth it.

5

FORCING THE INTERVIEW
MARCY

I was glad to have Angel back. Working the last big case without him at my side while he recuperated had been hard, and I was concerned about him moving around so much. I didn't want him to reinjure his leg and be out again. Still, he said he'd tell me if he needed a rest. I trusted him to do that. Smiling over at him, I stopped the car in front of the precinct doors.

"You've arrived at your destination, sir; that will be twenty dollars," I deadpanned as I put the car in park and opened my door to help him out.

He laughed. "I'll give you five stars on Yelp; that's the best I can do." He winked as I handed him his crutches, then looked back in the car at the bag of trash. "Oh, crap, let me grab—"

"Reyes, get your ass in the building. I'll take care of the garbage."

He stared at me for a minute before cracking a grin. "Yes, ma'am," he said, laughing.

I waited for him to get to the doors before pulling away from the curb and finding a parking space. Entering the precinct, I saw him waiting for me in the hall. It was thoughtful, but he didn't have to. "You know, you could have gone on to your desk."

He shrugged. "Figured we could go see Robinson together, and if we ran into Jordan, I could run interference."

I saw the wisdom in his words and nodded. "Yeah, good plan."

We headed into the detective pool, where all our desks were in the HSS, and went straight toward the captain's office. Jason was seated at his desk right outside the closed door.

"Is he in?" I asked.

"He's in, one sec." Jason pushed a button and spoke to the captain and then said, "Go on in."

I opened the door and moved out of the way so Angel could enter too. "Sir?" I said, looking at Robinson.

"So, what do we have?"

"We're not exactly sure yet, sir," Angel said. "Could go either way, terrible accident or murder. We've got underage, catatonic witnesses who are under medical care, so we haven't been able to speak to them yet. Stone and Black said they'd have the crime scene report and the autopsy report for us tomorrow. And Chief Sorenson said he wants to be kept in the loop with a copy of the report."

"Yes, I've spoken to the chief at length. He'll have a copy after I have a copy. Any media leaks?"

"Not yet, sir," I answered. "There were a couple of news trucks outside the building when we left, so they may see the body being taken from the building, but Black knows to keep it covered. If they can block it, you know they will." I glanced at Angel to see if he had anything to add, but he didn't.

Robinson nodded. "All right, go dig into their lives and see if you can find any enemies, any reason for her to have been murdered and by who, just in case. And I want your initial report on my desk by end of day."

"Yes, sir," we both said.

We hadn't bothered to sit, so I opened the door and let Angel leave before me, and we headed toward our desks. I had just sat down and pulled up my doc files to type out what we knew so far when I heard a door slam open. I looked up to see Jordan charging down the hall toward the detective pool. I cringed, hoping he wasn't coming to me, but of course he was.

"Who the hell sent you two out on a call, because I sure as hell didn't," he demanded.

I blinked at him. He'd been there when the captain had called me to his office. Angel too for that matter. Had he suddenly lost his mind? The idea made me smirk.

"You think this is funny?" Jordan's eyes blazed.

"You were there when Robinson called us into his office," I stated.

Jordan paused in his rebuttal and then frowned. "You're on half-days; you shouldn't be catching anything but minor cases; it was Hummel and Vance's turn for a major—"

"We were requested by CSI," Angel put in. "What's your problem, Lieutenant?" Angel's tone and expression were dark.

Once upon a time, he and Jordan had been good friends. That was until Angel caught wind of Jordan cheating on me and tipped me off to it. I didn't think Jordan knew that Angel was the one who'd given him away. Heck, Angel didn't even realize I knew it was him who arranged for me to find out, but ever since then, Angel had stopped hanging around him. They used to go out for beers and basketball; sometimes they'd play poker... that kind of thing. Not any more from what I'd noticed.

A tick pulsed in Jordan's cheek, his jaw rigid. "What's the case?"

I figured we couldn't not tell him. He'd make an even bigger stink since he'd asked directly. Plus, it was going to break on the news sooner rather than later, I was sure. "Body up in Beverly Crest. Possible homicide."

"What do you mean *possible*? Was it, or wasn't it?" he said with exasperation.

"We're waiting on crime scene and the autopsy," Angel hedged, giving me a wary look.

"Any witnesses? Any leads?"

"We've got a couple of kids who may have witnessed it, but they're traumatized and too much in shock to speak. They've said nothing since it happened," I shared reluctantly.

"Well, get them to talk, Kendrick! Do I have to hold your hand for everything? You can't go running for outside help on this like you did on the last case where you got them killed. You need to pull on your big-girl pants and get them talking!"

I felt heat fill my cheeks. I couldn't believe he'd just said that to me. If I wouldn't get written up for insubordination, I'd have punched him in the face.

"Back off, Jordan; that was uncalled for." Angel stood up on his good leg and stared at him, the fist of one hand clenching while the other held on to the desk for support.

"It's her fucking job!" Jordan seethed. "If she doesn't want to do it, then she should find another."

I took a couple of calming breaths, trying to get my temper in check before I let my words fly and I ended up in IA's office again, but this time for murdering my asshole ex-husband. "I will call their guardian and see if we can gain access to them."

"Then stop wasting time and do it. I shouldn't have to tell you how to do your damn job." Jordan turned and marched back to his office.

I looked at Angel and rolled my eyes. "I'm not calling right now. I'm going to do what Robinson asked first. Jordan can fucking wait."

Angel shook his head. "You're writing up the report, so I'll start digging into their lives. Do we even know who took guardianship of the boys?"

"No, I'll text Lindsey and see if she knows. I should have checked on that before we left."

"They were with medical, probably headed to the hospital, right?"

"Yeah, they were loading them into the ambulance as the news crews arrived. Hopefully, they didn't catch sight of the boys being taken in."

"It would be all over the airwaves by now if they did." Angel paused. "Someone probably noticed though, so it's only a matter of time before something leaks."

"I know, you're probably right." I sighed and pulled out my phone as Angel pulled up a search engine on his computer and began his dive into the life of Audrina Dixon. I sent Lindsey a quick text.

> Hey, who's got guardianship of the boys?

I set my phone down and started typing up the report for Robinson.

Ten minutes later, my phone buzzed on my desk.

> Audrina's younger sister, Flora Dixon, is with them at the hospital. The boys still aren't talking and seem terrified of anyone who comes near them, except for Flora. Not sure about custody though.

> Okay, thanks.

I put my phone down and made a call to the hospital on my desk phone so the call would come from the precinct. When the hospital reception answered, I told them who I was and that I wanted to be connected to the Dixon-Pfeiffer room.

The phone rang about six times, and then a hesitant voice answered, "Hello?"

"Hi, Ms. Dixon?" I asked.

"I'm not talking to reporters; I can't believe you would—"

"Ms. Dixon, I'm not a reporter. I'm Detective Marcy Kendrick."

"Oh, sorry." She sighed and then sniffled a little.

"I am so sorry for your loss. We should have come by to make sure you were aware of your sister's death." I had dropped the ball. I wasn't on my A game, and I needed to get my head straight before I fucked something major up.

"Officer Desmond called me about the boys and informed me. I met them here at the hospital. Do you know what happened to my sister?"

Breaking the news to relatives was hard, and I was glad Julie had gotten a hold of her. "All we know at this time is that there was a fire, your sister was set aflame, and then she went over the balcony railing to her death. We need to speak to the boys to learn more."

"That's not going to happen. They're completely traumatized," Flora said brittlely. "They just saw their mother brutally die. I can't believe you'd expect them to talk about something so horrible right after what they've seen!" Her voice grew shrill and angry.

"Ma'am, I understand that"—I tried to keep my voice gentle—"but—"

"But nothing! They are under medical and psychiatric care! We don't even know if they'll ever speak again! I'm not letting you come anywhere near these boys. If you want to talk to them, you'll have to get a court order!"

"Ms. Dixon, please calm down. I am fully aware—"

"Did you not hear me? I said get a court order! I'm done talking to you." She hung up.

"But—" I sighed and set the phone down.

"Problem?" Angel asked, looking over at me.

I turned to him. "No dice, she's demanding we get a court order to talk to the boys."

Angel frowned. "Did she say why?"

I explained the conversation and how it escalated. "So now I have to go tell Jordan."

"Is the report done?" he asked.

I glanced at my computer screen. "Nearly. Guess I can add in that conversation before I take it over to Robinson." I looked back at him. "Did you find anything we should add?"

"So, Audrina's the one with the money. She came into the marriage with a shit ton of it. Married a guy nine years older —" He checked his notes. "Dr. Matthew Pfeiffer. He's got degrees in psychiatry and biochemistry. That's all I've got so far."

"Okay, so, should this be a homicide, he could be a viable suspect."

Angel nodded. "Definitely. I mean, nine times out of ten, it's the spouse, or in this case, the former spouse."

I turned back to the computer, added in that information. "Keep digging. I'll let Robinson know where we're at."

"Sounds good."

I printed out the report and headed toward the captain's office. Jason waved at me, telling me to just go on in. I gave him a nod, knocked on the door and poked my head in. "Sir?"

"Come in, Kendrick; got that report?"

"Yes, sir." I handed it over.

"What was Jordan shouting about?"

I rolled my eyes; of course he'd heard him. "He wanted to know how we caught the case, and then he demanded we get the boys to talk."

"He's aware they're at the hospital under medical care?"

I nodded. "I did tell him that, but he was angry that all this didn't go through him, since Angel and I are both on half-days."

"Not anymore. You're back on fulls unless you can't handle it?" He arched a brow.

"I can totally handle it, sir. And I'm sure I can speak for Angel as well that he's good to go."

Robinson gave me a wry smile. "I don't know about good to go with that leg of his, but I'm thinking he can handle a heavier work schedule. He'll let you know if it gets to be too much?"

"He will."

"So where are we on talking to the boys?"

"Kendrick!" Jordan shouted from the outer office.

Captain Robinson stood up and went to the door. "Brasswell, get in here."

Jordan strode over to us and gave the captain a surprised look and then glared at me. "She in here complaining?"

"No, stop being an ass; not everything is about you," I answered, rolling my eyes at him.

"Fine, did you set a time to go talk to the witnesses?" he demanded.

"I was just asking about that; continue, Kendrick." Robinson took his seat again.

"Yes, sir. I called the hospital and spoke to the boys' guardian, Flora Dixon. She's Audrina's younger sister."

"And?" Jordan interjected impatiently.

I flicked my gaze at him and then back to the captain. "And she said the boys are still nonverbal and under psychiatric and medical care."

"I don't care; you need to get over there and question those boys."

"She's not going to let us talk to them, and they're underage," I raged right back at him.

"Then get a damn court order and make them," Jordan fumed.

"That is what she said would have to happen for us to be able to speak to them, but—"

"No. You get the court order and go over there."

I just blinked at him and looked at the captain, who was leaned back in his chair, clearly annoyed at the both of us. I gritted my teeth and glared at Jordan. "If you will recall, I can't be the one to get the court order; that's *your* job."

Jordan threw his hands in the air. "Fine. Just add it to the list of things I have to do around here." He stormed out of the office.

I glanced back at the captain, who sighed. I didn't know what bug had crawled up Jordan's ass this week, but I was getting tired of him yelling at me over shit I couldn't control. It was one thing for him to say shit about my personal life, but that had nothing to do with work and everything to do with being my ex. I could compartmentalize that shit most of the time. This, though, was something else. Not that it belonged at work either. All I could think was that I'd never get romantically involved with a co-worker again. "Sir, I—"

"I'll talk to him." He put a hand up to stop me saying anything. "Keep digging into Dixon's life, add in the husband and the sister. I want to know everything."

"Yes, sir." I hesitated, thinking more about the court order and how ineffective it would probably be.

"What is it, Kendrick?"

"I just wondered if the court order was the way to go. It might be better to wait until the boys calm down and regain their senses. With them being nonverbal over it, I can't see how getting a court order is going to make them talk. Nothing's going to do that except giving them time to process what happened."

"You're probably right, which is why I didn't push for it when we spoke earlier. Let Jordan get the order, and we'll use it if we need to." He glanced at the clock, then back to me. "Why don't you and Reyes call it a night. We'll pick things up again tomorrow. Those boys aren't going to be ready to talk any time soon."

"Yes, sir." I returned to my desk and glanced at Angel. "Save what you've got. Robinson said to call it a night and pick it up again tomorrow."

Angel stretched in his seat. "Sounds good. Wanna grab dinner?"

A little ping of happiness zipped through me, but I quickly squashed it and reminded my heart that Angel was off-limits. I was not going to start pining over my partner like some police drama trope. I smiled. "Sure."

6

STRANGE CONSPIRACY THEORIES
MARCY

After enjoying a sit-down meal with Angel at El Cholo, where I had the Sonora-style enchilada and an LA lemonade, I dropped Angel at home and then headed over to my brother's apartment. I used my key to get in so I could feed his fish and water his plants since he was still at Shine View getting treatment. I also ran the vacuum and dusted. Luckily, his place was small, just his bedroom, one bathroom, and the kitchen-living room combo, so it didn't take too long.

Once I finished that, I locked up and headed back home. It was about a twenty-minute drive when there was no traffic, but tonight it took me nearly double that. I was exhausted by the time I finally reached my apartment building. I pulled into the lot and parked in the closest spot I could to the entrance.

Since discovering Nick was a serial killer who happened to live in my own damn building, I'd started being extra cautious when getting in and out of my car and heading inside. I looked around the parking lot like a paranoid mental patient. I probably looked like I was the one up to no good, but the guy had really creeped me out, and I was a woman who prided herself on being fearless. He'd taken my security from me, and even though he was locked up in that institution for the criminally insane, I still walked around here like he was going to jump me at any moment.

As soon as my lease was up, I was finding a new apartment. One far away from here. Well, maybe not that far away. I still wanted to be close enough to the station to make it there within twenty minutes. Commuting was a pain in the ass with the way traffic got backed up around here.

I rode the elevator up to my floor and opened the door, unlocking the several deadbolt locks. Once I was in, I bolted them all and locked the handle, then checked it twice. Dropping my keys and purse on the table, I headed to my room to change. I took off my blazer, set my badge and gun on the dresser, then removed my holster before changing into a pair of lounge pants and T-shirt and heading to the kitchen for a bottle of water.

Now that I was comfortable, I went to my purse on the table and pulled out my phone. Sitting on the couch with my bottle of water, I pulled up the number for Shine View and dialed. I put in the connecting code for my brother's room. The phone rang four times, and I was about to give up when he answered.

"Hmmm?" He sounded groggy and half asleep.

I glanced at the clock; it was only eight thirty. "Hey, Stephen, did I wake you?"

"No, just the meds. Makes my head fuzzy and sleepy," he replied, sounding despondent.

I was suddenly more worried about him than I had been in a while. "Stephen, what's going on? I mean, I get that the meds are making you groggy and stuff, but you sound... I don't know, kind of like you're giving up—"

"I'm fine. I'll be fine. Everything's fine. Don't worry about me. I hate when everyone worries about me. I just want to go home. I don't think I need to be here anymore, but Doc thinks I need to stay longer. Says I'm in a depressive state. Of fucking course I am. I'm in the psych ward."

I shook my head and rolled my eyes. "You are not. You're in a rehab facility so you can recover from the shit that happened to you, and to learn how to manage your addictions. You checked yourself in."

"Tomatoes, potatoes. Same difference."

"Completely different." I laughed and flopped down on the couch. "Is there nothing good there? I mean, I thought you were doing okay with therapy."

He sighed. "Yeah, it's okay. I've got one-on-one therapy every day with Doc, and then there's group every other day. We do crafts every other day too. Something about it is supposed to help."

"Gotten to know anybody else there? Have you made any friends?" I asked, curious.

"Oh, I've gotten to know several of the strange ones in here with me. I wouldn't exactly call them friends. There is one guy though; he's not too bad. A little bit of a wackadoo, but, eh, who isn't?"

"What makes him a wackadoo?" I wondered how weird the guy could be, but then I'd run across a lot of weirdos in my job, and the bar for not being strange was pretty high.

"He's one of those conspiracy theories enthusiasts. Keeps saying Doc is doing MK Ultra shit on us. It's really bizarre."

"What's MK Ultra?"

"Some government, CIA black ops project in the seventies that had to do with mind control. I think they used LSD and stuff to cause hallucinations and then brainwashed people."

"So, what did they brainwash people to do? What does this guy—"

"Watson."

"What?"

"That's his name. Watson Oberman. He claims he's a former CIA operative, but Doc says he's suffering from severe PTSD, paranoia, hypervigilance, and a bunch of other shit. He's kinda funny. I mean, he swears up and down that he worked for the CIA, but in group therapy, Doc confronted Watson with the truth. Guy's, like, seriously delusional. He's never been in the government. He worked as a grocery store bagger at the Publix until he got on drugs and ended up fired and homeless."

"That's kind of sad," I replied, taking a sip of my water.

"Yeah, you'd think so, but the man doubled down. He swears he was recruited while he was homeless, and all his symptoms are the result of being experimented on. He firmly believes that homeless people in every city are being kidnapped and experimented on to perfect the CIA's program."

"Okay, that is weird. So, what does he think they're brainwashing them for?" I was kind of enthralled by this guy's delusions. It was almost as good as watching TV.

"Well, he thinks they're brainwashing people for various things, including becoming sleeper agents."

"Sleeper agents? What's that mean?"

"You know, like they brainwash them, teach them a whole bunch of spy shit, and then wipe their minds, except they're given, like, a trigger sound or word or something, and it causes them to go into agent mode and do whatever they were programed to do."

"Yeah, that's pretty out there. Wouldn't the person's own personal will stop them from doing whatever it was?" I queried. "I mean, I guess if someone was weak willed, it might work, but I don't know if you could completely control anyone, could you?"

"How the hell would I know? It's not like I believe him. It's just what he says in group therapy. One of a billion conspiracies he talks about." Stephen laughed. "When he's not being a total weirdo, he's okay. We hang out and listen to music together sometimes."

"I'd say I'm glad you've made a friend, but he does sound a bit unhinged," I murmured. "You're sounding better than when we first started talking; feeling better?"

He took a breath and then said, "Yeah... the meds must be wearing off some. It's always worse when I first take them. Still wish I could check myself out, but I know I'm not going to get better if I do."

"How much longer is your doctor suggesting you stay?"

"Few more weeks or so. I'll be fine. Really, you don't have to worry. I'm not going to try to OD again."

I drew in a sharp breath. We hadn't discussed his attempted suicide since it happened. "I'm not going to make you feel guilty for trying to check out. I'm just glad you're still here. You're my only family, and I honestly don't know what I'd do without you. You scared the shit out of me. And again, I'm not telling you that to make you feel any kind of guilt. I'm just sharing what I went through after finding you. My group therapy doctor said it would be good for both of us to share how it affected me, but only after you brought it up. I wasn't to push you. I'm not, am I?"

"No. And for what it's worth, sis, I'm sorry. I really wasn't trying to kill myself, just the pain. I wanted the mental pain to go away, so I started drinking, that didn't help, then I started taking the pills, but when one wasn't working, I added more. It was stupid."

"Maybe next time just call me, and we can work through it before you start drinking?" I suggested.

"I'm learning ways to deal with it here. One of them is talking to a mentor or family, so yeah, I'll try to remember to call." He yawned.

"Good." I took another sip of water.

"So, how did work go?"

"Okay, Jordan's still an ass—"

"Nothing new there." He chuckled.

"True. Caught a new case. You'll probably hear about it on the news soon." I told him about the case and how the twins had witnessed it but were unable to speak. "Jordan is demanding a court order to make them talk, as if that will compel their brains to let them speak."

"He's a tool. Can't believe you were married to him for so long." He snorted.

Sighing, I had to agree with him, but some part of me had loved him when we'd first gotten married. I just didn't know he was a controlling asshat when I did it. Found that out quick, but it took him cheating for me to get my butt in gear and divorce him. "Yeah."

Stephen yawned again. "So what are you going to do about those twins, then?"

"I'm hoping once they've processed what happened, they'll speak on their own, but Jordan is requesting the court order and will probably demand I try before they're ready." I glanced at the clock. It was going on nine fifteen. "It's getting late. I should let you go get some rest. I'll try to call you tomorrow, okay?"

"Okay, sis. Good luck with the case. Don't let Jordan get to you. Bye."

"Night." I hung up the phone, my mind playing over the conversation. I was still worried about him, especially with how depressed he'd sounded when we first got on the phone. I wondered if a change in meds might help, but I wasn't a doctor, and I assumed his would be watching for any odd behavior while he was on those meds.

Dismissing the thoughts, I headed to my room to get ready for bed.

7

IT WAS A BATTLE ROYALE
MARCY

I woke with a start, my hand on my weapon under my pillow. I didn't know what had woken me, but I was ready for it. It took me a minute to hear the knock again. It was coming from my apartment door.

"Coming," I called, hopefully loud enough for them to hear. I pulled on a robe, looking at the clock—6:43 a.m.—as I rushed toward the door. Peering out the peephole, I saw it was the building superintendent. I quickly undid the locks. "Good morning."

"Good morning, Detective Kendrick. I'm sorry, it looks like I woke you—"

"It's fine. I needed to get up anyway." My alarm would be going off in ten minutes anyway. "What can I do for you?"

"I just wanted to let you know that we're going to be doing some rewiring in the building starting at 7:30, and it means shutting off the electric. We only found out it was happening about twenty minutes ago, or we'd have let you know sooner."

That gave me half an hour to get ready to go to work. "It's

okay. And thanks for the warning; it gives me enough time to get ready."

"My pleasure." He nodded and moved down the hallway.

I closed and locked the door before half-running back to my room. I took the fastest shower known to humankind, blow-dried my hair and brushed it out. I did up my light makeup, then got dressed for the day. After putting on my holster, I added my weapon and grabbed my phone and blazer before going to the kitchen. I speed-dialed Angel.

"What's up?"

"I'm leaving early; you want me to pick anything up on the way?"

"Coffee?"

"Sure, do you want a sandwich, or you eating at home?"

"Already got a bowl of cereal, so I'm good."

"Okay, see you in a bit." I clicked the phone off, looked in the fridge to see if there was anything I wanted to eat, then remembered I had bought a couple of microwave breakfast bowls when I'd gone to the store yesterday morning. I fixed one while I still had power, and as I ate it, glanced at my freezer. If the power was going to be out, did I have anything in there that would go bad?

"Damn, I should have asked how long they were going to be working on it," I muttered. After a moment I shrugged. Maybe it would be okay, and nothing would spoil. I hated the thought of having to replace it all.

I tossed the bowl, hurried back to the bathroom, and brushed my teeth, then headed out the door. I hit the coffee shop on the way to pick up Angel, and then drove to his place. Pulling into his driveway, I waited for him to come outside before I got out and opened the door for him. "Your chariot awaits, sir," I said with a laugh.

"Thank you, my good woman, I do appreciate punctuality." He chuckled as he settled himself in the seat.

I shoved the crutches into the back and ran around the car to the driver's seat.

"To the precinct, Jeeves."

I laughed again. "Of course, sir. Your coffee is in the cup holder," I directed as though I were some butler or chauffeur speaking to their very rich employer.

"It's cold," he said drolly.

"Well, duh. It's supposed to be; it's an iced coffee." I grinned at him as I pulled onto the street and headed for the station.

He grinned back. "You're in a good mood this morning; what's up with that?"

"Not even sure. I was woken ten minutes before my alarm by the building superintendent informing me that they were cutting the power at 7:30, so I rushed through everything, which is why I'm early. Better enjoy the mood while it lasts, because you know the minute I see or hear Jordan run his mouth, it's gonna tank."

He chuckled. "You shouldn't let him get to you. You know he says that shit to get a rise out of you."

I snorted and rolled my eyes. "You think I don't know that? He's trying to get me to hit him so he can go to IA about me. I'm not going to give him the satisfaction."

"I'm glad to hear it, but you probably need to put a lock on that mouth of yours too, at least toward him, 'cause one of these days you're gonna say something that gets you thrown into IA's crosshairs anyway."

Sighing, I nodded. "I know. I'll work on it."

"Good coffee," he said, changing the subject as he sipped it.

"It really is." I turned into the parking lot. "Park or at the door?"

"Do you mind dropping me at the door? It's easier to maneuver if I don't have to worry about hitting anyone's car with these things."

"Sure." I pulled up to the front, put the car in park, then went to help him out, grabbing his crutches from the back. "I'll see you in there."

Once he was clear of the car, I moved deeper into the lot and found a parking space, then hurried into the building. Angel was already seated at his desk when I got there.

"So, I'm going to dive into the ex; you want to do a deeper look into their divorce?" he asked.

"Sure, that will work. I also want to look at Audrina too, see who her connections were and check out her businesses, that kind of thing. See if there were any pissed-off clients or customers."

"Sounds good."

"Oh, and call and get an alibi check on the ex, too."

"Sure." Angel nodded and picked up the phone. A few minutes later, he put the phone down and turned to me. "Kim's going to head over there and inform him of his ex's death and check to see where he was at the time."

"Great."

We both got to work, digging into their lives. I started taking notes as I dug through the divorce proceedings; it was a drama-filled mess of accusations and investigations.

I was knee-deep in it when one of the techs from CSI delivered the crime scene and fire department reports, so I paused to look through those. There wasn't anything that I didn't either know or suspect in them for the most part, so I handed the reports to Angel for him to read, and returned to the divorce proceedings.

"Hey, got a second?" Angel said sometime later, spinning his chair toward me.

"Yeah, you find something?"

"Tons." He nodded. "So this guy, Dr. Matthew Pfeiffer, he was in major debt when he married Audrina Dixon about fifteen years ago. It looks like he used her money to pay off his school loans and to set up his business shortly after they married, and then he opened a bank account in just his name and began skimming money from their joint account to his. There's some documentation from a court case where Audrina accused him of fraud and theft."

"But they were married?" I frowned.

"Right, but they had a very clear prenup, drawn up by her lawyers. It looks like she did gift him the money to pay off those loans and to start the business, but the joint account was to go to household things only. He received an allowance from her trust, but it was only a thousand a month. There's documentation that he agreed to it."

"So he broke her trust and found a way to get around the prenup?"

"Looks that way. I've also found several restraining orders against him, starting about four years into their marriage."

I nodded. "That goes along with what I'm seeing in the divorce proceedings. She accused him of mental and physical abuse and apparently attempted to leave him several times in the beginning of the marriage. And it wasn't just of her, but also the boys. It looks like they were separated eleven years ago when the boys were three, and they waited a year before filing for divorce and had to share custody for that year. However,

Audrina apparently filed mental abuse charges against him, claiming he was doing psychological experiments on the boys. He counter filed and claimed she was physically abusing them."

"So the kids were pawns in their marriage?"

I shook my head. "I don't think so. Everything I have found shows that she had documentation of her accusations, records of changes in behavior, etc.... and the courts eventually ended up agreeing with her that he was the abusive one. It took nearly a decade though. The divorce was finally settled about six months ago, and the custody battle finished up around three months ago after Audrina won custody back."

"Wow. Does it say what the visitation rights were like during that time?" Angel asked.

"He had it off and on over the years. However, every time he'd gain custody, it wouldn't last more than a few months before they were back with Audrina full-time. He just kept filing to get them back. Eventually they realized he was bribing social workers, CPS and family court officials to get his way."

"That makes sense. He's got a couple of pending court dates for various charges. None have gone to court yet because he keeps filing for extensions or asking for outright dismissals, and a couple have been dropped," Angel shared. "So, what was the final outcome of the divorce decree?"

"After almost ten years of battling it out in court, Pfeiffer was asking for alimony, but it was denied. Since he signed the prenup, he got nada. And on top of that, he had to pay her court fees going all the way back to the beginning."

Angel whistled. "So he got nothing, basically?"

I nodded. "He got to keep his business, the house in Florida, and the one in Reno. Along with his car and a few stocks and bonds that were bought in both their names."

"That's nothing to sneeze at, and the guy's business is successful. He's got a psychiatry practice and is a licensed psychopharmacologist."

"What does that mean? Is it some sort of secondary practice?"

"No, I had to look that up too. It just means he can prescribe psychotropic drugs, and he knows how the body will act with particular meds, what those meds will do to a body, and how they interact with other medications."

"I guess that's a good thing?"

He shrugged. "I'd think so."

I looked over my notes and tapped my pen on the paper. "You know, with all the allegations she's made, I could see those boys being seriously disturbed. What if we're looking at this all wrong?" I was half afraid to voice my thoughts.

"What do you mean?" Angel asked, his brow furrowed.

"What if the boys aren't nonverbal voluntarily? What if they're not in shock? What if it's an act?"

Angel seemed surprised. "So you think they might have had something to do with what happened to their mom?"

"I don't know. Maybe?" I bit my lip. "Just, from the custody suits she filed, Audrina thought her ex-husband was giving them drugs and doing experiments on them. What if they somehow snapped and killed her?"

"Do you think that's possible?"

"At this point, I think everything is back on the table, and we need to be careful how we proceed from here."

He nodded. "Good idea. So what now? Keep digging?"

I thought about it for a minute and then realized we still didn't have the autopsy report. "Let's go bug Damien. He was supposed to send the report over, but we haven't gotten it yet."

"Want me to call and tell him we're headed over there?"

"Yeah, if it's not a good time, we'll grab lunch first."

"Sounds like a plan." He picked up the phone to make the call.

I turned back to my notes, writing down my thoughts.

A minute later, Angel hung up. "He said to come on over; he's just getting ready to finish. Apparently, there were a few lab reports he was waiting on, and he got backed up."

I stood up. "Guess lunch will wait." I snatched up my purse, and after turning off my computer screen, we left the detective pool.

8

OLD INJURIES
MARCY

Angel and I caught the elevator and headed toward the coroner's lab. As the doors closed, my phone rang. "Detective Kendrick," I answered as the elevator moved.

"Ma'am, it's Kim. I just left Dr. Pfeiffer's office."

"How did that go?" I questioned, putting my phone on speaker so Angel could hear.

"I had to wait for him to finish with a patient, and then I informed him of his ex-wife's death."

"How did he react?" I asked, curious.

"He was stoic. It didn't appear to faze him or surprise him, ma'am. He just accepted it and asked if that was all."

"That's an odd reaction; did he ask how she died?"

"No, ma'am, he didn't act curious at all, but I did tell him that she was set on fire. He didn't react to that either, and he didn't ask after his sons."

I glanced at Angel, who just shook his head. "No reaction to that at all? Huh." I paused because I was trying to wrap my head around this guy's reaction. What father wouldn't be concerned about his sons after a tragedy like this? I set it aside for a moment and asked, "Did you check his alibi for the time of death?"

"Yes, ma'am. He was here at his office; his secretary assured me he was in his office the entire time on the phone, dealing with an overwhelmed patient. He never left, not even for lunch."

We stepped off the elevator. "Okay, thanks, Kim. I appreciate you doing the legwork on this."

"My pleasure, ma'am."

I tapped the button to end the call. "What do you think?" I asked, looking over at Angel, who was resting his weight on his crutches.

"I can see him not being too upset by her death, but I'd think he'd be a little surprised at least."

"Yeah, especially with how she died. It's a pretty unusual death," I agreed. "It wasn't like she was killed in a completely random car accident."

Angel nodded, but a moment later added, "And I don't get why he didn't even ask anything about the boys."

"Right? He was after custody for the past ten years, and now Audrina's dead, you'd think he'd have some sort of reaction about it. It doesn't make sense to me."

"Do you think there's been some sort of falling-out between him and the boys?"

"What do you mean?" I questioned.

"They're teens now; the courts take their opinion into account when awarding custody. Maybe they said something against him?"

I considered that. "Yeah, you could be right. That might explain him not questioning anything about them, but he didn't even ask who has custody of them now that Audrina is gone. That still strikes me as weird."

"Yeah, can't disagree with that."

"Come on, I don't want to hold Damien up for too long."

We walked down the hall, stopping at the counter outside the autopsy room. We each grabbed a set of nitrile gloves from the box and then joined Damien where he was waiting for us next to Audrina Dixon's body. I pulled on my gloves, and Angel did the same.

"There you are; wondered what happened to you."

"Got a call from Kim about the ex's alibi," I shared.

"Ah, okay then. Did he have one?"

"Seems to." I shrugged.

"Well, let's get started. I'm sorry I didn't get to this sooner. It's been a crazy morning already," Damien apologized as he snapped his glove, adjusting the fingers of it.

"It's fine. What have you got to show us?" I asked.

"Okay, well, first, let's start with the initial findings." He moved to Audrina's head. "As you can see, she was burned mainly on her upper legs, torso, face, and scalp. Her upper limbs didn't take too much of the damage, though there were some third-degree burns, here and here on her hands"—he lifted her hands to show them to us—"where it looks like she attempted to pat the flames out."

I nodded. "So, any indication of how she became covered in the oil?"

Damien blew out his breath and looked down at the body. "I would say it was thrown on her, or she managed to pour it over her head. So either someone hated her enough to want her to burn alive, or she hated herself that much." He shivered.

"But no way to tell from the body which one?"

"No, sorry. All I can say is her arms and hands didn't have much oil on them, which if she lifted her arms up like this"—he demonstrated—"and poured it so it went over her face and down her torso, it would mostly miss her arms and hands."

"And if someone threw it at her?"

He shrugged. "She could have had her arms up, like this"—again he demonstrated, as if he were a robbery victim, holding his arms and hands up—"and it still would have mostly missed her arms and hands."

"So what else can you tell us?" Angel asked, shifting on his crutches next to the autopsy table.

Damien glanced at him. "She was dead before she hit the ground."

"What? How?" I wondered what could have happened to her in the middle of that fifty-foot drop.

"The shock from extreme pain is the probable cause. It induced a massive heart attack."

"Okay, so you're saying the fall didn't kill her. Would the killer have known that, if they did indeed push her or throw her over the rail?" Angel asked.

"Probably not. I'm sure she was incapable of speech, and she was aflame when her body went over the railing. If there was a killer and they threw her, or even pushed her, they would have burn marks to show that."

I looked at Angel. "You read the CSI report, right?"

He nodded. "What about it?"

"Did you see anything about burn marks on the boys?"

Angel pursed his lips and then shook his head. "Nope."

"Me neither."

"I've got more for you." Damien interrupted my thoughts. "Tox report is back and shows no drugs in her system, and no alcohol either. Her last meal consisted of a salad with chunks of chicken, tomato, and egg, along with coffee."

"Okay." I followed along as he moved down the length of the table and lifted the sheet. "Whoa, I don't need to see—"

Damien smirked. "Relax, Detective, I'm just bringing her arms and legs out to show you a few things." He tucked the sheet around her private bits and then lifted her left arm. "You see this?" He pointed out some scarring.

"Yeah, what am I looking at?"

"Old injuries." He pointed out a couple of spots on her arm. "Breaks here and here that were open fractures." He moved to her other arm. "You can see the fractures here and in the humerus. I added the X-rays to the file so you can see the actual fracture lines where they had to perform surgery to fix them, but you can clearly see the scar tissue where the bone broke through the skin."

I studied the skin, the scarring was faded, but I could see it. I wondered if they'd all happened at the same time or different ones, so I asked Damien's opinion.

"Sorry, I should have said. They happened at different times. This one looks like the oldest." He pointed to the forearm next to the wrist. "This one had to have come next, I think, and then this one." He gestured to the humerus and then the forearm closer to the elbow and then set the arm down on the table.

"Damn, did she even have any feeling left in that arm?" Angel asked.

"The nerves did appear to have some damage to them. I'd imagine that she experienced some neuropathy pain in that arm, occasionally at least." Damien moved to the legs. "There's more though. See this? She's got a nicked bone, you can see that in the X-rays as well, I think from a stab wound, probably a serrated blade, but it's old, so hard to judge exactly what kind." He pointed to her right thigh, where I could again see scar tissue, and then moved to her left foot. "And this ankle was broken, which again, you'll see in the X-rays, but you can see where they had to rebuild it in surgery."

"So, what, she was attacked multiple times? Or in several accidents?"

"I looked into her medical records, and I'm pretty sure she was abused. They're mostly pretty old, about ten to twelve years. The oldest injury I found, which was a broken finger on her left hand, was from fifteen years ago. I've added those hospital records to the file as well for you."

I blew out a breath and nodded. "She separated from her ex-husband about eleven years ago, filed for divorce a year later, so that sounds about right. She did accuse him of abuse and presented evidence. I'm guessing it was those hospital records you're talking about."

"If he did all this to her, what are the chances he hurt those boys?" Angel murmured.

"Damn near a hundred percent, judging by the bodies I see in here from domestic violence," Damien replied softly.

"Anything else?" I asked a few moments later.

"Couple of previously broken ribs, as well as fingers, and I am pretty sure she's had her nose broken as well, but it's possible that's from a rhinoplasty since I didn't find an ER report on it in her file."

I frowned. "If it weren't for the fact that CSI didn't find any evidence that someone had entered the apartment, and that the man has a pretty solid alibi, I would think Dr. Matthew Pfeiffer was our assailant."

"CSI didn't find his prints anywhere in that apartment, from what that report said," Angel informed Damien. "It was only hers, the boys, her sister's, and the cleaning crew's. All of which have been checked out, and none were on the premises at the time of death. Well, except for the boys."

"There was some debris under her nails that we're having checked," Damien added.

"Okay, that's good. Any prints on the body?"

"The only fingerprints on the victim were her own," Damien replied.

"Great. Maybe a ghost did it." I shook my head.

"Or, like you said, it was the boys, and they're just really good actors," Angel said.

I hated to think that any child could do that to a parent, but I'd seen horrible things before, and I was sure I'd see horrible things again. It didn't make it any easier to deal with though. I knew that evil came in all sizes and shapes, and it was my job to see that the perpetrator was brought to justice, and I was going to do just that.

Once I figured out who they were.

9

NIGHTMARES AND CONFRONTATIONS
MARCY

I told Henry about the case I was working on, about the twins and their mom and how I just didn't see it being an accident. Henry was always a good listener and always had something to share. When we finished chatting about the case, we set it aside to do more pleasant things. We made some popcorn and watched a movie, one we'd both seen before. Afterwards we made dinner, and one thing led to another, and I found myself in his bed.

After we finished making love, he wrapped his arms around me and held me close. "Do you have to leave?"

I shook my head against his shoulder. "No. I can stay if you'd like me to." I tilted my head so I could look into his eyes.

"I'd very much like you to stay."

He tipped his lips down to mine, and we kissed again, but then he started to choke and spit blood. His eyes grew wide with shock. I looked down, and Henry's chest was covered in stab wounds. I glanced back up at his face and screamed. Not only was his face gone, but so was the muscle tissue and his eyeballs. All I could see was the bone and blood as it dripped down.

"What's the matter?" his lipless mouth asked.

I shrieked in horror as I scrambled away from him. Then I noticed he wasn't naked anymore. He was dressed in women's lingerie. Tears flowed down my face as I scooted across the bed and fell to the floor.

My head bounced off the carpet and woke me up. I'd somehow managed to throw myself out of my bed in my dream escape from Henry's animated corpse. I pulled my knees to my chest and sobbed as I tried to get the nightmare to fade. Why was it that those always stuck with you longer than a dream?

Regaining my composure, after an internal pep talk consisting of yelling at myself that I was a tough chick and I could face anything, I glanced at the clock and saw I had only a few more minutes before my alarm would ring, so I shut it down and got up. I headed for the shower, hoping it would help wipe out the awful image of Henry that was stuck frozen in my head. I'd only seen photographs of his body; my colleagues had been kind enough not to let me see his body in person. Turned out, though, that I didn't need to see it in person for my psyche to conjure it up in full animated form.

I stood under the blast of heated water, shuddering like I was freezing to death for a good ten minutes. Eventually, I got out and got dressed for the day. Looking in the mirror, I could see dark circles under my eyes that attested to the kind of night I'd had. I did my best to cover them with makeup, but there was only so much concealer a woman could put on without it starting to look like a pound of caked-on goop.

Holstering my weapon, I grabbed my blazer and went to the kitchen. I didn't really have time for breakfast, but I wanted to check that everything in the fridge and freezer was still good after the power had been out yesterday. Seeing it was all fine, I headed to the front door, picked up my purse and keys, and locked the door behind me. I hurried to my car and drove over to Angel's to pick him up. Because of the extra minutes I'd spent getting ready and checking on the frozen food in my fridge, I was running late and hadn't stopped for coffee.

When I saw him come out the door, I got out and went to help him in. "Morning," I croaked out. My voice was hoarse, and I was sure it was from the crying, and probably screaming, I'd done through the night.

"You okay?" Angel asked, looking at me.

I shrugged and shook my head. "Honestly don't wanna talk about it, if you don't mind?"

He stared at me for a hard minute and then gave me a nod. "Sure."

"Mind if we stop for coffee?"

His cheek lifted in a half smile. "Not in the least."

I pulled out and drove to our usual coffee shop, getting a twenty-four-ounce hazelnut coffee for me with four caramel macchiato creamers, and a twenty-ounce black with two sugars for Angel. We headed for the station, and I dropped him off out front. It took me a few extra minutes to motivate myself to get out of my car and go in after I'd parked. I could still see Henry's mutilated face in my head, and I couldn't shake it. It was just hanging out there on the backs of my eyelids, ready for me to blink or close my eyes for even a second.

"Get yourself together," I muttered as I pushed open my car door. I slammed it shut, the sound making me jump more than it should have, and locked it. I added steel to my spine and strode to the door with my coffee in hand.

At my desk, I yanked open the drawer I kept my purse in and then slammed it shut with a little more force than I should have, and Angel looked over at me. I screwed my face up into a grimace, trying to will the damn tears away, but I was struggling. Out of the corner of my eye, I saw Angel rolling his chair over next to mine.

"Spill it; what's going on with you?" he said, keeping his voice low. I assumed it was so he wouldn't draw attention to us, thankfully.

I blinked, and I could feel the tears I didn't want to spill on my lashes. If they fell, all the effort I'd gone to putting makeup on to cover the dark circles would be ruined. I'd be streaky and look horrendous. I ran a finger over my lashes, trying to wipe them away before that happened. Blowing out a breath, I admitted, "I'm having nightmares about Henry's death."

Angel sighed and put his hand on my shoulder in comfort. "You want to tell me about it?"

I licked my lips and pressed them together. I knew talking about it would help alleviate some of the horror of it, and I trusted Angel. "I keep reliving that weekend. Everything we did, and then the dream changes, and Henry... instead of him being alive and well, he's the mutilated corpse I saw in the pictures. I know we weren't together very long, I know I wasn't in love with him, not yet, but the potential was there, and now all I can see is"—my voice broke—"is his missing bloody face in front of mine."

"I'm so—" Angel started.

"You shouldn't have been fucking a suspect in the first place," Jordan said from behind us.

I whirled around and stood up, seething.

"Jordan!" Angel glared at him.

"Henry was never a suspect! He was a criminal profiler helping with the case, and he's the reason I was able to save your ass, you fucker!" I went to slap him, but Angel slid his chair forward and grabbed my arm, holding me back. "You should have more respect for the dead!" I shouted at Jordan as those tears I'd been trying so hard to hold back fell.

Jordan glared at me, his face red as a tomato, his fists clenched. "I'm writing you up for insubordination!"

There was movement to my right, and I saw the captain going back into his office, and heard his door shut. Even he didn't want to deal with this. I half wondered if he'd even talked to Jordan as he'd said he would. I was so pissed off at having to deal with Jordan's shit every day. It wasn't fair. I didn't want to quit, and I felt as though that was what Jordan was pushing me to do. I didn't want to give him the satisfaction, but damn, he was pushing my buttons.

Jordan stared at me for another moment.

"You write this up, and I'll be writing up my own statement," Angel said, staring right at him, his expression grim. "For the record."

Jordan grunted and said, "Get back to work," then stomped down the hall toward his office.

I watched after him, gritting my teeth. I wanted to punch something. No, not something. Him. I wanted to punch him. Right in his stupid face. Hard. Multiple times. Until he lost teeth. Just thinking about him with a toothless smile had me calming down with a grin on my face.

"Share with the class?" Angel said, arching a brow at me, a curious look in his eyes.

"Just picturing how Jordan would look with a couple of black eyes, a broken nose, and a bunch of missing teeth." My grin, albeit sinister, grew.

Angel chuckled. "That's a good picture, but you probably shouldn't make it happen." His own grin widened.

"I thought about it for a minute though." I sighed. "Thanks for catching my arm before I struck him. Last thing I need is IA all over me for it."

"He provoked you, and I will be writing the incident up that way and making sure IA has it."

I smiled a genuine smile. "Thanks, Angel. You've always got my back, and I appreciate that."

Angel winked. "Let's get back to work, yeah?"

I nodded, sinking into my chair. I didn't bother with cleaning my face, though it was probably streaked with tears. I was sure I looked a mess, but I just didn't care. Instead, I got busy.

An hour later, I turned to Angel and said, "Hey, did anyone interview the neighbors?"

"I can check." Angel picked up the phone and made a call to CSI. After speaking to Lindsey, he turned back to me. "So, Lindsey says that they spoke to the few neighbors who were home, and she gave me a list of the ones they hadn't been able to get to yet." He tapped his notepad. "Do you want to go interview them, or do we send Kim and Desmond?"

"Let's go do it; we can grab lunch after."

"Sounds good." Angel pulled on his jacket, folded his notepad, and put it in his inside jacket pocket, then grabbed his crutches and stood up. "You gonna go get the car or stare at my pretty face all day?" he teased.

I rolled my eyes. "Yeah, yeah." I opened the drawer and pulled out my purse, then picked up my blazer. After sliding my arms into it, I made a quick trip to the bathroom to fix my face, then hurried to get the car.

Ten minutes later we were headed over to Beverly Crest. We pulled into the parking area, and I let Angel out in front of the building before parking, then joined him. We knocked on doors and spoke to several people who hadn't been home at the time Audrina went over the balcony. One particular lady seemed to have all the building gossip.

"Ms. Winters, do you know of any enemies that Ms. Dixon might have had?" I asked.

"Well, I'm not one to gossip, but—" the blonde woman leaned forward and loudly whispered, "Edward Jakes—he's one of the security guards here—well, he's ass over tea kettle for Audrina, and she made a really big stink over his leering at her while she was using the pool." She smirked. "If you ask me, she was asking for attention in that tiny bikini she always wore, so to get upset over his attention seemed extreme, but that's just my opinion. Anyhoo, when she made that big ta-doo over him gawking at her, the apartment manager wrote him up and nearly fired him. I can tell you that Eddie was really upset about it."

"Upset enough to kill her?" Angel asked. "That seems a bit excessive, don't you think?"

"Well, that may be. However, think about this—Eddie has keys to everyone's apartment, he's got the elevator code to Audrina's place, and he's got access to the security tapes." Ms. Winters pursed her lips and tilted her head in a sassy way. "You ask me, and I say he could have snuck in there without anyone knowing, confronted her and lit her on fire, then pushed her over the balcony."

I frowned. What she said was plausible, I supposed. "Did you see him go into the elevator prior to her going off the balcony?"

Ms. Winters shrugged. "Well, I couldn't say one way or another, since I was at the salon and didn't arrive back until well after everything happened. I'm just telling you if you're looking at one of us, he's the one you should really be looking at."

"Okay, well, thank you, Ms. Winters. I appreciate your candor. You have a good day," I said and turned to Angel, raising my brows.

"You're so welcome, and if you need anything else, Detectives, feel free to ask me." She smiled, pushed her sunglasses on and followed us out of her apartment. "I'm heading over to the pool. Ta." She gave us a finger wave.

Once she was gone, I turned to Angel. "I don't think I could swim in that pool knowing a woman died horribly right next to it."

"Yeah, me neither. What do you think of this lead she gave us?"

I shrugged. "She's not wrong about it being possible, but likely is another story. Still, we can have a conversation with the man."

He nodded. "Let's see if he's on duty."

We went over to reception and asked about Eddie Jakes, but were told that he was off for the next few days. Turning from the counter, I said to Angel, "How about we grab lunch and head back to the precinct and see if anything else has come in? Then we can do some research on this guy."

"Sounds like a good plan. What are you in the mood for?"

"Burgers?"

"Yeah, that works."

After passing through the drive-thru of our favorite

burger joint, we drove back to the precinct, but sat in the car and ate before we went in. As we headed into the building a little while later, I tossed our trash in the bin, then returned to my desk only to find a report sitting in my intake box. I picked it up and saw it was from the fire department.

"Looks like the fire chief sent over the report on the bottle of lamp oil that was used as the accelerant," I murmured.

Angel settled himself in his chair, leaning his crutches against his desk within easy reach. "What's the verdict? Does it have our new suspect's prints on it?"

I shook my head. "Doesn't look like it. Only prints on it are Audrina's"—I tried not to use *the victim* because I felt it depersonalized them, and I never wanted to disrespect those who had been murdered—"and her sons'. Which could mean one of them did it, or that our murderer wore gloves."

"There was that broken glass too; any indication that it was a dropped oil lamp itself that caused the fire?"

I continued to read through the report. "It doesn't look like it. The glass oil lamp was in the debris from the shattered glass table; it looks as though she might have been holding it at the time she was lit up, dropped it as she raised her hands; it hit the table, shattering it and the lamp, and sent everything else on the table crashing to the floor."

"So she saw her attacker?"

"I think so, not that her seeing her attacker helps us any since she's dead." I sighed and put the report away. "Let's start digging into this Eddie Jakes. See what we see."

Angel nodded. "I'll take social media."

"I'll look into finances and job history," I agreed.

Before I could get started, Lindsey walked into the detective pool. "Marcy," she said with a smile. "Hey, brought you the report on the last seventy-two hours of security footage from the Dixons' apartment building."

"Great, anything interesting?"

Lindsey shrugged. "Maybe, I don't know. Her sister, Flora, was there visiting two days before the incident. The cleaners were in the day before and only come every other day, and as far as I can tell, the Dixons had no other visitors."

"So that leaves Audrina herself, the boys, and any employees who happened to be there."

"Yes, and no. I didn't see any evidence of any employee taking the elevator up to the penthouse. Nor any of the neighbors either. The only time that elevator went to their floor was when the Dixons themselves were leaving or returning home."

"Hmmm." I pursed my lips. I wondered... "It could still be this security guy. He could have somehow switched the tapes, right? Or prerecorded them or maybe even recorded over them or something?"

"If he did, he's good. I can go back and have it checked for that. We didn't look to see if the tapes were tampered with."

"Would you? That would be great." I gave her a smile.

"No problem. Hey, while I've got you here, wanna go for dinner and drinks with me tonight?" she asked.

"Sure. Is this a girls' thing, or—" I slid my gaze to Angel.

Lindsey leaned around me and said, "Angel, dinner and drinks tonight?"

Angel glanced up. "I'm in if my ride is," he tossed back over his shoulder at us.

"We'll meet you at the Bistro," I said, looking forward to

eating chicken fettuccine, salad, and bread sticks with alfredo sauce. My mouth was watering, and I could taste that creamy alfredo sauce already. "Say at six thirty?"

"Perfect. See you there." Lindsey grinned and gave a small wave as she left us to finish up our shift.

10

BROKEN LITTLE BOYS
MARCY

"How you feeling?" I asked Angel as he adjusted himself in the passenger seat the following morning.

He glanced at me, then closed his eyes. "How could you let me drink so much?"

I laughed. "You had two vodkas straight. I didn't think it was going to do you in."

"I should have eaten more," he said, "but *somebody* snaked my breadsticks." He opened his eyes and glared at me, his eyes barely slits.

"You know they're my favorite, and that alfredo sauce was amazing. Besides, you were slow." I grinned at him as I pulled into the coffee shop drive-thru, placed our orders, then waited. "Here, this should help," I said, handing him his black coffee with two sugars.

"Thanks."

Back in the precinct twenty minutes later, Jordan was waiting for us, his hands on his hips.

I steeled my spine, ready for whatever crap came out of

his mouth. I was in a decent enough mood that I felt like I could handle whatever he threw at me this morning. I set my purse down, not bothering to put it away because something told me I wasn't going to be sticking around the precinct for very long. I didn't say anything but just stood staring at him, waiting for him to speak. I wasn't about to wish him *good morning* or any other bullshit. I didn't want to talk to him or see him at all. I wasn't about to be pleasant either, especially after yesterday.

He turned away from me and looked at Angel. "Hey, Reyes, the court order came in, we've got the police psychologist speaking with those boys, but I want you to head over there and question them and the aunt."

I glared at the back of Jordan's head as he ignored me and pretended that I wasn't even there. He was such an asshole. I still couldn't believe I'd put up with him for as long as I had. I should go over to his house and thank his wife, Katie, for having that affair with him. If she hadn't, there was a good chance I'd still be married to him. Just that thought made me shudder.

"Yeah, okay, Marcy and I will head over to the aunt's place in a few."

"And I want to know what they say," Jordan said, still staring at Angel and ignoring me.

"Sure," Angel replied. "Anything else?"

"Talked to IA. You didn't have to turn in that incident report. I wasn't planning to report it," Jordan bit out.

"I was just making sure a full view of the incident was reported in case you did," Angel said blandly as he gave Jordan a blank face.

"Whatever. Go do your job." With that, Jordan strode away without a glance in my direction.

All in all, it was probably one of the best interactions I'd had with him since the capture of Nick Pound. I smiled at Angel. "Guess it's back to the car."

"Looks like it," he replied, shifting his body and swinging back to the door of the office area.

Back in the car, I input Flora's address, which was also in the Beverly Crest area, and set off for the 101. From there we hit Sunset Blvd and then wound our way into the neighborhoods that took us up near Franklin Canyon. I pulled into the entrance to Flora's driveway and pushed the intercom button.

"May I help you?" a voice came across the speaker box.

"This is Detective Kendrick. I'm here to see Ms. Dixon."

There was no answer over the intercom, but the iron gates opened inward, and I drove through. "Fancy," I muttered.

Angel chuckled.

"Feeling better, I take it?" I glanced over at him in the passenger seat.

"Coffee helped."

I grinned and parked the car. A few minutes later I lifted the large brass door knocker and knocked on the door.

A man dressed in all black answered the door.

"Er, we're here to see Ms. Dixon and the twins if they've finished their session with the police psychologist?"

"Come in, madam, sir." The man held the door open wider.

We entered and stood in a long foyer. I glanced around, taking in the opulence of the home. It looked like Audrina wasn't the only one to inherit a good bit of the family money. It seemed Flora had done well for herself too.

"This way." He led the way to a room that was elegantly

styled with antique-looking furniture that probably cost more than my yearly salary. "Ma'am, these detectives wish to speak with you."

"Send them in," Flora replied.

Angel and I entered, and her gaze went immediately to him and his crutches. Her eyes widened as if she were surprised to see an injured detective. She stood and gestured toward the seats, which Angel took with a grateful smile.

"Thank you," I murmured as I sat. "Where are the twins, Ms. Dixon? It was my understanding they were here with you. They are here, aren't they?"

She nodded. "They are here, but they are with that psychologist the judge sent over." She glared at me.

"I see. That is routine in a case like this," I shared, with a glance at Angel.

"The boys have been through enough; I don't see why you people are harassing them like this. They've just lost the only parent who really cared about them."

"So their father doesn't care about them?" Angel asked. "He did fight for custody, even won it for a while, didn't he?"

Flora huffed; a look of anger crossed her face. "That man," she spit the words out, "didn't deserve those boys. You know he experimented on them, gave them drugs? The things he did were awful, and we're only just now scraping the surface of the abuse he inflicted on their impressionable minds."

The twins entered the room a moment later, their faces downcast, their bodies moving in a lethargic way, almost dragging as they headed toward their aunt.

Dr. Zahir Patel, our LAPD psychologist, entered the room behind them. He gave me and Angel a tight smile and headed in our direction. "Ms. Dixon, I believe the boys might need a few moments before speaking with the detectives. Would you kindly sit with them while I have a quick discussion with the detectives?"

"Of course." She turned to the two young men. "Boys, let's go over here. Shelby will be bringing treats in a few moments." She herded the boys to the far end of the room, which put them about thirty feet from us, as it was a massive room.

"What was that about?" I asked, looking at Dr. Patel.

"Good to see you, Detective Kendrick, Reyes. Why don't we step out of the room so we can discuss this?" He gestured to the hallway we'd just come from.

I nodded and followed him back out of the room. "Well? What's your diagnosis?" I asked, opening my notebook to take notes.

"Both boys, who their aunt says go by the names Gary and Mike, show signs of extreme post-traumatic stress."

"From this incident, or—" Angel asked.

"That I can't determine exactly, but in my opinion, someone has terrorized the boys into silence." Dr. Patel paused and looked as if he was trying to choose his words wisely. "I believe the boys are currently suffering from peri-traumatic dissociation from what they experienced during and immediately following the attack on their mother. I believe they are in a derealization state with dissociative amnesia, emotional numbness, and that they are experiencing altered time perception. This is the body's natural instinct for self-preservation."

"Do you think it's permanent, or will it fade, and they'll be able to tell us what happened?" I asked.

He shook his head. "It's too soon to know. Some people

never recover those memories and continually suffer from PTSD from the trauma-related incident."

I rubbed my forehead and around my eyes, trying to focus my thoughts. "So, what do you recommend?"

"A lot of therapy with a psychiatrist who specializes in this kind of trauma in children."

I gave him a wry look. "I meant pertaining to us speaking to the boys."

The look he returned was stoic. "I recommend not pushing them and being gentle. As I said, I think someone has terrorized those boys over a long period of time."

"Their mother did say their father was doing some kind of mental experimentation on them," Angel put in.

Dr. Patel looked taken aback. "That would do it, but whether he's the one who's keeping them quiet..." He let his words trail off with a small shrug.

"Thanks, Doc. We'll go see what we can get from them."

"Gently, I hope?"

"Of course."

As Dr. Patel followed the butler to the front door, Angel and I returned to the room where Flora and the boys were waiting. We joined them in the seating area, taking seats across from them.

"Hello, boys. I'm Detective Kendrick, and this is Detective Reyes. We're very sorry for your loss. We'd like to talk to you about the day of the fire, if that's all right with you?"

Neither boy said a word, nor made any sort of movement of consent. They had identical looks of fear in their eyes. I saw the same, almost haunted appearance that spoke of years of mental and physical abuse in their young gazes. As if all hope was lost, and they had nothing left in them. Even their body language gave the impression they were cowed.

They were folded in on themselves, trying to make themselves smaller, nonthreatening. Aside from that, there were a couple of faint scratch marks on Mike's cheek, but I couldn't tell if they were self-inflicted or from someone or something else. I knew it was Mike because he had frosted blond tips, and Gary had blue ones.

I glanced at Angel, and he shook his head. I gave him a slight nod and turned back to Flora. "I'm not going to push them. Can you tell me if you know a man named Eddie Jakes?"

Flora frowned and seemed to think about it. "No, the name doesn't ring any bells."

I glanced at the boys to see if the name would draw a reaction from them, but they stayed silent and seemed as if they weren't mentally present. It was like their bodies were just empty husks occasionally taking a bite of a cookie or a sip of water. It was almost robotic, as if they'd been programed to do that. I had to stop the involuntary shiver I felt at the thought.

"All right, what do you know about their days leading up to this?" I specifically left out the reference to their mother's death.

"I know that both boys were diagnosed with anxiety and depression years ago, and when they were with Audi, their moods improved. However, the moment their dad got his hands on them, they backslid, and it took months and months of intensive therapy to stabilize them again. The last time they were with him was three months ago." Flora had a look of anger on her face, but she kept her voice soft and even as she spoke, and I could tell it took effort to do that.

"I see. And have they been attending therapy since they returned?"

Flora nodded. "They seemed to be doing better this past week, but now?" Her voice broke as she stroked Mike's hair. "They're broken." She glanced over at me, tears in her eyes. "He did this. I know he did. I don't know how, but he's behind it," she said vehemently.

"Ms. Dixon, I know you'd like to believe that, but I checked his alibi myself," Angel said, his voice soft. "He was in his office the entire time. His secretary can corroborate that. And about ten minutes before the incident, he was on a Zoom call with a patient; there is a log of the call. He couldn't have gotten across town in time to make that happen even if he did somehow sneak out past his secretary."

"I don't care. He's to blame." She was adamant, her jaw tightening as she looked at the two of us, almost ready to go to war with us if we dissuaded her from her belief.

"If he is behind this in some capacity, we will find out. For now, we'll be on our way. Please let us know if you think of anything, or if the boys start speaking and recall what happened." I stood.

Angel did the same, picking up his crutches from the side of the chair he sat in. "Thank you for your time."

"Shelby will show you out," Flora said dismissively.

11

STONEWALLED
ANGEL

I couldn't help but think Pfeiffer was rotten and somehow involved in this despite the fact he had an airtight alibi. Could he have paid a killer to do his ex-wife in? It wasn't unheard of for people to hire hitmen.

"I think we should dig more into Pfeiffer," I said as Marcy drove us back to the precinct. "Maybe check his finances closer. Look for any kind of strange withdrawals or payments."

She glanced at me and then back toward the traffic in front of us. "You're thinking hitman?"

I shrugged. "It's not entirely out of the realm of possibilities, right? Maybe he even hired this Jakes guy to do it."

"Definitely better than the alternative," she replied.

"Those two boys didn't strike me as homicidal," I said, feeling so much anger in my chest knowing what they'd been through. "I've never seen someone so young looking so... I don't... there aren't even words to describe how empty they looked."

"Yeah," she agreed. Her grip tightened on the steering

wheel until her knuckles turned white, and then she flexed her fingers. "We need to set up an interview with him. Can you see if you can make that happen?"

"Sure." I absolutely would.

I stole another glance at Marcy, her chestnut brown hair had gotten a little longer than she normally kept it, and it brushed against her cheek. There were streaks of light brown and auburn highlights that were natural and brought out by the sun. I wondered if she would cut it back to the chin-length bob she generally favored, or let it grow. I didn't ask, but I hoped she'd let it grow out a little more. She looked great either way, but I liked it when her hair fell to her shoulders, as it was now.

"What are you thinking so hard about?" she asked, her blue eyes meeting mine.

I snorted.

There was no way I was answering that. We might be close, and I might have feelings I shouldn't, but I wasn't going to act on them, no matter how much I wanted to. Firstly, she'd been traumatized by Henry's death. Secondly, she'd been married to Jordan, our new lieutenant. We'd been friends back before he'd cheated on her, and I realized what a misogynistic bastard he really was.

"Nothing important. Just considering what to have for dinner," I lied. I didn't lie often, but this was more of a little white lie to protect our relationship. We were friends and partners. We both liked it that way.

"Got a hot date?"

"Oh yeah, these crutches draw the women right to me. Got them lined up around the corner." I laughed heartily at her teasing.

"Then how about we hit Jimmy's and watch the game?" she asked.

"Who they playin'?" I liked baseball but not enough to know who the Dodgers were playing.

"Rockies."

"Colorado, yeah?"

"Yep. It should be a good game," she replied as she pulled into the precinct.

It was nearly five, so we didn't have long before we'd be heading back out again. "Sounds good, then."

She dropped me at the door and went to park as I headed inside. I hobbled my way toward my desk and sat down.

By the time she returned, Jordan was marching toward us. "I thought I told you to report what they said to me," he fumed, getting in Marcy's face.

I watched a muscle in Marcy's cheek tick, which it often did when she dealt with Jordan. "We—" I started, but Marcy put a hand up to stop me.

She was the senior officer, and she needed to answer, but I would have done it just to get her out of Jordan's line of fire. Protecting her was what I did. Even if it was from his wrath.

"We just got back, and I was headed to your office after I put my purse down." Her voice was calm and reasonable. "We spoke to Dr. Patel and the aunt. We tried to speak to the boys, but they are too traumatized."

Jordan grunted. "What did the doc say?"

"He says the boys are possibly suffering from PTSD and peritraumatic dissociation. Meaning they've got a form of trauma-induced mutism and amnesia. The aunt informed us they have a history of anxiety and depression, and I can tell you those boys are... God, Jordan, they were barely there. Their bodies were, but their minds were gone."

"Could they be on drugs? Faking?"

"I don't think they are on any drugs that aren't prescribed. If they were faking it, then they need a Hollywood agent asap because that was more believable than Russell Crowe in *Gladiator*, and he won the best actor Oscar."

I had to swallow a chuckle at the reference. Jordan was a fan of *Gladiator*. Marcy used to complain it was the only movie he would watch repeatedly.

"Fine, I want them tested for other drugs," he demanded. "Did you get any leads?"

"We've got a couple of angles we're working. The security guard and the possibility of a hitman."

"A hitman," Jordan scoffed. "Hired by who?"

"Her ex. He's a piece of work."

"Dr. Pfeiffer? I thought his alibi checked out?"

"That doesn't mean he didn't hire someone. We want to interview him."

"Prove he had any connection first. Look closer at that guard." With that, Jordan turned on his heel and left us, heading out of the building.

Marcy turned back to me. "I'll jump on Pfeiffer's assets. I want to know everything. But I don't care what Jordan says, I want that interview too."

"I'll call and see if we can get in to see him." I picked up the phone and started dialing.

"Dr. Pfeiffer's office, how may I help you?"

"Good afternoon, my name is Detective Reyes of the LAPD. I'd like to speak to Dr. Pfeiffer, please."

"I'll see if he's available to take your call, Detective, one moment," his secretary answered, putting the phone on hold.

I waited as the worst Muzak played over the line. She kept me on hold for fifteen minutes, and I was just about to hang up when she finally returned.

"I'm sorry, Detective, but Dr. Pfeiffer has left the office for the day. May I take a message?"

I glanced at the clock. It was ten after five. "Yes, would you please have him call me back first thing in the morning? It's very important that I speak with him."

"I will be sure to let him know of your request. Have a pleasant rest of your day." She hung up.

I turned my chair and looked at Marcy. "I think he avoided the call by leaving the office, and the secretary kept me on hold long enough so he'd be long gone by the time she came back on the phone."

Marcy sighed. "Fine, we'll pick this up tomorrow. So far, I'm not seeing any large cash withdrawals or suspicious payments, but I'm just on the surface right now. We'll see what happens when I dig deeper."

I nodded. "You ready to go, then?" I was looking forward to a plate of Jimmy's hot wings and an ice-cold beer.

Ten minutes later, I was seated in Marcy's car, my leg throbbing. It had been a long day, and I was ready to relax a bit. It took another half an hour to reach Jimmy's and ten more to get a table where we could watch the game on the TV.

Marcy ordered a West Coast IPA, and I got a Belgian IPA, which had more of a sweet, bready flavor than the fruitier and more bitter West Coast. We each also ordered hot wings and unlimited fries. Instead of discussing the case, we watched the game and talked about baseball stats with a bunch of other patrons who were also there to watch the game and cheer for the Dodgers.

At the end of the night, the Dodgers had won 7 to 2, and Marcy took me home with the promise of picking me up in the morning. I'd be glad to get the use of my leg back, and off these damn crutches. I wanted my own car back too, but that wasn't happening. I'd have to buy a new one. I hated that she had to be the one to drive us everywhere. Not that she was a bad driver, but it wasn't the same as me driving.

I woke up the next morning feeling pretty good, showered the best I could sitting on the medical stool the rehab clinic had given me for the purpose of being independent, and dressed for the day. Marcy picked me up at seven thirty.

"Your coffee," she said, handing it to me.

I smiled. "Thanks. You've gotten coffee the last week. I should treat you to lunch today."

"Don't worry about it," she said, shrugging it off.

"Still, my treat today."

"Okay, sure," she said, sounding distracted.

"What's up?" I asked, concerned.

"Just thinking about the case." She paused, and I thought maybe she wasn't going to say anything else. "I'm afraid that if there wasn't a hitman who somehow managed to get in and out of that penthouse unseen, without leaving a trace, and if Jakes also didn't do it, then we're left with the twins as our suspects."

I nodded. I knew where she was going with this. "And considering the heinousness of the crime, they'll be tried as adults despite the fact they're fourteen."

"Yeah," she said, her voice cracking.

"We can't worry about that right now. Let's just work the

case, and maybe something else will open up and give us another avenue to pursue."

She took a breath. "You're right. If Pfeiffer doesn't call by nine, call him back. I want that interview."

"I'll be all over it. I'm also going to keep digging into the sister while we're waiting."

"Good idea."

When we got settled at our desks, I did just that. I kept an eye on the clock, but my phone stayed silent. At nine, I called his office only to get the runaround from the secretary again. She claimed he was not available. Eventually, I found a cell phone number listed for him and called it. He didn't answer and didn't return my call after I'd left a voicemail. I began calling the number every fifteen minutes and planned to continue doing that until Marcy and I headed out for lunch.

At eleven fifteen on the dot, I called again, prepared to listen to it ring and click over to voicemail, but he finally answered. "Dr. Pfeiffer?"

"Detective, you are persistent, I'll give you that."

"I am. I would like to schedule a time for me and my partner to come speak to you about your ex-wife—"

"I have nothing more to say on the subject of my ex-wife, her death, or anything else for that matter. I've given my statement, and you've got my alibi. Anything else and you can speak to my lawyer." He hung up.

Frustrated, I set my phone down. "Bastard."

"What happened?" Marcy asked, turning toward me, tucking her hair behind her ear.

"He's refusing."

She tilted her head and frowned. "That's suspicious, don't you think? I mean, if he didn't have anything to hide, why refuse?"

"Right."

"I'll see if Jordan can get us a court order."

I froze for a moment. "Just remember, stay calm. He's trying to get you fired."

She nodded, but I knew this could blow up in her face if she handled it wrong. "I know."

"If he asks, do we have enough info to move on Jakes?" I asked.

"Some, he's got some gambling debts; he could be working with Pfeiffer. And we'll be going to see him tomorrow. I spoke to his supervisor, and they've assured me he'll be on duty." She stood up. "You coming?"

With a sigh, I grabbed my crutches, and we headed for Jordan's office. I hoped my presence alone would be enough to restrain Marcy's temper and keep things on an even keel, but Jordan was unpredictable. Marcy knocked on the door and waited for Jordan to call out for us to enter. She opened the door, but didn't go inside. We just stood in the entryway, looking in.

"What is it? Did you get a break in the case?" Jordan glanced up from the stack of papers on his desk.

"We need a court order to bring in Pfeiffer."

Jordan looked surprised. "The man has an airtight alibi; you can't be serious."

"He's avoiding talking to us; he's hiding something," Marcy argued.

"He has an alibi," Jordan repeated, staring daggers at Marcy.

I put a hand on her arm and said, "We think it's possible he could have hired someone, like Jakes, to murder his ex. He didn't come out of the marriage very well, and she did. There's reason for us to talk to him."

"And he's the only adult with access to those boys we haven't spoken to. He could give us insight into their states of mind and tell us whether they're actually capable of murder." Marcy's words were calm and reasonable.

Jordan stared at us. "Did you find any link to him possibly paying someone to do this? Have you proven that anyone other than the boys and Ms. Dixon were even in that penthouse?"

Marcy drew a sharp breath. "We're still digging—" she started.

"And Jakes has the code and access to the video surveillance; he could have faked the tapes or substituted the tapes," I added.

Jordan ran a hand through his hair. "Fine. I'll get you your court order."

"Thank you." Marcy turned and strode down the hall.

I wobbled as I tried to follow.

"Reyes," Jordan called.

I glanced over my shoulder to see Jordan jogging to catch up to me. "Yeah?"

"Do you really think Pfeiffer hired Jakes to do this, or is she just avoiding charging those boys?"

"I don't know, Jordan. Pfeiffer is hinky. Something about the guy is just off. And those boys." I shook my head. "You didn't see them. They are clearly traumatized by something. If they are behind this, then someone put them up to it."

Jordan gave a single nod and turned back to his office.

Sighing, I headed to my desk.

12

BAD SEEDS
MARCY

I dropped Angel at his place and then headed home. Once I was inside, I kicked off my shoes and changed into something more comfortable. After pouring myself a glass of wine, I dialed Shine View's number and put in my brother's extension.

A moment later, he answered. "Hey, Marce."

"Hey. Just thought I'd check in. Your fish are fine, by the way."

"Thanks. Did you clean the tank?"

"I did yesterday after the game; were you able to catch it?"

"Yeah, it was a good game. So, how's the case going?"

I really didn't want to talk about it with him because I knew he was recovering, but I needed to vent to someone who wasn't a cop. "It's not looking great," I muttered.

"What do you mean? Don't you have a suspect yet?"

"Kind of. I mean, we've got a perp we want it to be, one it could be and… two I'm afraid it might be," I answered reluctantly.

"Spill, why are you afraid?"

"They're just kids."

"You think the sons did it?"

"Maybe. But you should see them, they are so traumatized, Stephen. Worse than we were after Mom's death. I mean, they're practically catatonic. I think they were abused, not like you were," I rushed to put in, "but mentally, maybe physically too, and it just sucks."

"Any kind of abuse sucks, Marce." Stephen's voice was quiet.

"Damn it, I wasn't trying to diminish what you went through. I would never do that. I can't explain it; it was like they had just mentally checked out, completely void of emotion. I don't even know if it is possible for someone to kill another person in that kind of state. If they're a danger to others." I sighed. "If they did do it, I'm a hundred percent sure it's because someone traumatized them into it, and it wasn't of their own volition or because they're bad seeds or whatever."

"You do realize that most killers have some sort of mental illness or past trauma, right? A lot of them start out pretty young mutilating animals and the like. Do these boys have that in their past?"

I hadn't thought to check. I added it to my list of things to do. "I don't know, but you're right, I need to find out."

"And you need to remember, you're on the victim's side. Not anyone else's. It's your job to find whoever did it and make sure they pay for the crime, right?"

I nodded, knowing he couldn't see me. "Yeah, you're right. This one is hard though. Hard not to revisit what we went through watching Mom die, knowing they could have watched theirs die too, you know?"

"I get that, but there's a very real possibility that they did it, Marce, and you need to be prepared for that reality."

"Yeah," I replied, hating to admit he was right. "So, how's things going there?"

"Fine. I'm good."

He sounded a bit sharp in his answer, and that had me concerned. "Are you sure? Do you need anything?"

"No. I'm fine. You don't need to worry about me," he rushed out. "Listen, I need to go. I'll talk to you in a few days."

I blinked as the line suddenly went dead. That was a bit troubling, and I half wanted to call his doctor to make sure everything really was okay, but I knew I needed to back off. This was his treatment, and he was in the right place for getting help. I just needed to trust that he was.

I set my phone down and picked up my wine, finishing it. It was still early, so I decided to watch a movie and then go to bed.

The next morning, after picking up Angel, instead of heading to the precinct, we went to Beverly Crest. It was Saturday, but Jakes was supposed to be back at work, and I wanted to get the interview with him done as quickly as possible and find out if he was actually a viable suspect. Besides, with a case like this, we rarely took a day off. Too much could be missed if we did.

"You're quiet this morning," Angel murmured.

"Just worrying over shit that I can't control," I said, tossing him a wry look.

"Like?"

"The case, and Stephen," I admitted as we pulled into the parking lot.

"What's up with your brother?"

"I don't know. I spoke to him last night. He's still at Shine View. He seemed off. Lucid, but off. Like he wasn't telling me everything."

"That could be for any number of reasons. Maybe there's someone there he likes, or he's embarrassed for being there, or who knows?"

"You're right. It doesn't have to be anything awful. And I told myself that his doctor would let me know if there was an issue or concern."

"So stop worrying."

"Easier said than done." I smiled. "Come on, let's go talk to Jakes."

We headed into the building and made for the reception desk. Angel was getting much better at maneuvering on those crutches and could almost keep up with my normal pace.

A brunette with blue streaks in her hair sat behind the desk. She smiled as we approached, but the smile was merely pasted on her lips and didn't reach her eyes. "May I help you?"

"Yes, I'm Detective Kendrick; this is Detective Reyes." I flashed my badge at her. "We'd like to speak with Edward Jakes, please."

The woman picked up the phone and hit a button. "One moment," she said to us, then spoke into the phone. "Mr. Jakes, the police are here to speak to you." She paused and then flicked her gaze back to us. "Yes, I will send them back to the security office."

I waited patiently for her to hang up.

"He's back in the security office; if you go down that hall, it's the third door on the left." She directed us with a tilt of her head.

"Thanks." I turned and let Angel go first.

When we reached the door, I knocked.

"Come in," a deep, husky voice called.

I opened the door and stopped, taking in the scene. Eddie Jakes was indeed in the office, seated behind the wall of TVs, watching the video feeds. The problem was that he was in a wheelchair, and his right leg was in a hip-to-ankle cast.

"Mr. Jakes?"

He turned his head. "Come in, Detectives."

"We're Detectives Kendrick and Reyes. We'd like to ask you some questions about Ms. Dixon's death."

He nodded, a somber look on his face. "So horrible what happened to her. She was such a beautiful woman."

"Yes. Can you..." I stopped, wondering how to ask this man what his alibi was. "Look, I understand that Ms. Dixon nearly got you fired?"

Again, he nodded. "She did, but it was my own damn fault for gawking at her. I made her uncomfortable. I expect you'll be wanting to know where I was?"

"Yes, please," I agreed.

He banged his fist against the cast on his leg. "It was my day off, and at the time of... well, I was at the hospital. I'd been up on my roof, and coming down the ladder, the damn dog hit it, sending me flying fifteen feet to the driveway. I'm lucky I didn't hit my head, but I landed on my leg pretty badly. Broke it in a couple of places." He glanced at Angel. "Looks like you know a thing or two about leg injuries yourself."

"Car accident," Angel replied with a slight nod.

I pursed my lips, knowing he had to be telling the truth, but still, I needed to verify everything. "Do you have your admittance and dismissal paperwork from the hospital?"

"Sure, Detective." He rolled the wheelchair back and moved over to a second desk, shuffled a few things on the desk, pulled out some paperwork and handed it to me.

I took it and looked it over. It looked legit. Still, I said, "Mind if I take a picture of these for our records?" I also wanted to call and verify with the hospital that they weren't fake.

"Go ahead."

"Thanks." I pulled out my phone, set the papers down and took pictures of each page, then handed them back to him. "We won't take up any more of your time. Thank you for being cooperative, Mr. Jakes."

"Sure. Have a good day, Detectives."

Leaving the security office, I huffed. "Well, there goes that theory."

"Yeah, no way he did it. And... gotta say, even if he weren't in that wheelchair and cast... he really doesn't seem like the type to light a woman on fire and push her over a balcony to her death," Angel murmured.

"No." I shook my head. "That was my gut feeling too." I sighed. "Check his story with the hospital anyway, but let's move on to Pfeiffer."

Angel nodded and climbed into the car as I opened the door for him.

I hurried around the car and climbed behind the wheel. I wasn't looking forward to telling Jordan what we'd found out. I had a feeling he wouldn't be happy. We'd wasted valuable time pursuing a man who couldn't possibly have done it. He'd probably accuse me of not asking the right questions at the murder scene about Jakes, or even at the time we'd thought he was a viable suspect. His boss surely knew he couldn't possibly have done it. Looking back, I probably should have asked why he wasn't at work, and that was on me. I just didn't need Jordan pointing it out.

Frustrated, I drove us back to the precinct.

13

HOPES DASHED

MARCY

I bit the bullet and went straight to Jordan's office to inform him about our interview with Jakes. I didn't want to put it off and wait for him to blow up at me. However, when I reached his office, he wasn't there. Frowning, I looked back toward the detective pool.

"You looking for Brasswell?"

I turned my gaze to Hummel, who was coming down the hall. "Yeah. You seen him?"

"Sure. He's at a meeting with the deputy mayor, the chief of police and the captain."

I sucked in a breath. "Oh. Thanks." I turned on my heel and headed to my desk.

"That was quick. And quiet. I didn't hear any raised voices at all," Angel said with a smirk.

"Yeah, he wasn't there. Meeting with the brass."

"You think it's about this case?" Angel arched a brow.

I nodded. "Probably. Her death has been all over the news for the past three days since the press finally figured out it was her. I'm gonna bet the mayor and chief are pushing for an arrest."

"Probably," Angel replied. "I'll get started on that call to the hospital."

"Thanks."

As I sat down, my desk phone rang, and I picked it up. "Kendrick."

"Marcy, it's Damien."

"Hey, Damien, you got something new for me?"

"Yeah, but you aren't going to like it."

"Probably not. Lay it on me."

"The debris under the victim's nails? It was skin tissue. It matched the twins, but because they are identical, there's no way to say which one's skin tissue it is."

"Well, that's just great." I grunted in frustration as I rubbed my forehead and tucked my hair behind my ear. "Anything else?"

"Nope, that's all I've got."

"Okay, thanks for the info." I sighed and hung up before turning to Angel. "Well?"

"Who was that?" he asked.

"Damien. The report on the debris under Audrina's nails was skin tissue matching the twins. What about you? What did the hospital say?"

"Jakes' paperwork checks out. At the time of Audrina's murder, he was sitting in the ER getting his leg x-rayed. He was there about an hour before her death and didn't leave until the day after. There's no way he was involved."

"Figured as much after talking to him." I sighed. "That leaves Pfeiffer hiring someone else, or the boys, unfortunately—" I stopped as my desk phone rang, and I held a finger up for Angel to hold that thought as I answered it. "Detective Kendrick."

"Detective, this is Ken James, from Channel 24 news. I understand you're the one working the Dixon case?"

My teeth slammed together, and I immediately said, "No comment," and hung up the phone.

"Press?" Angel questioned.

"Yeah." Before I even got the word out, his phone rang. I closed my eyes and banged my head softly on my desk.

"No comment," Angel said into the phone and hung up. "This is going to be fun," he deadpanned, looking at me.

"Should have known it was coming since Hummel said the brass were meeting with Jordan. This is the only high-profile case right now. The press is going to sensationalize it."

My phone rang again.

I answered and said, "No comment."

"Wait! Before you hang up, Detective, can you just confirm that you suspect that Ms. Dixon's death was indeed murder?"

"No comment."

"Can you confirm that her sons were at the scene when her death occurred?"

"No comment."

"What can you comment about, Detective?"

"All I can say is that this is an ongoing investigation, and when we have something to share, Lieutenant Brasswell or Chief Robinson will let you know. Goodbye." I hung up.

"About time you got something right, Kendrick," Jordan said.

I looked up to see him about two feet from my desk and flinched. "Look—"

"Save it. How did the interview with Jakes go? Did you make an arrest?"

I shook my head. "The guy is in the clear. He was in the hospital with a broken leg at the time of the murder."

Jordan glared at me. "How did we not know this prior to wasting all this fucking time—"

"I know, okay? I know." I held my hands up to stop his rant. "Reception didn't tell us that he'd been in the hospital; they only said he was off for a few days. We didn't question why, and we should have. I should have spoken to his boss. I got that."

Jordan looked taken aback at the fact I was admitting I'd dropped the ball. He seemed speechless about it, and I wasn't about to look a gift horse in the mouth.

"So we're still digging into Pfeiffer to see if he could have hired someone, and we're waiting on that court order to get that interview with him. Also, Damien just informed me that the debris under Ms. Dixon's fingernails was skin tissue belonging to one of the twins, but because they're identical, there's no way to know which twin it belongs to, how long it had been there, or why it was there in the first place."

"Okay." Jordan paused, nodding as he appeared to be thinking things over. "I want you two to go back over there and try to get those boys to talk, maybe find out if they'll admit to how that tissue got under their mom's nails."

All in all, it was a pretty civil conversation for us. My phone rang again, but I ignored it. "Sounds like a plan."

"And don't talk to the press," Jordan ordered before heading back toward his office.

"Wasn't planning to," I muttered. I turned to see Angel on his feet, the crutches under his arms. "Ready to go?"

"Yup. Wanna grab some dogs on the way?"

"Sure. The truck out there?"

"Saw Vance come in with a couple a few minutes ago."

"Let's go, then." I grabbed my purse, and we headed out the door. "Wanna wait in the car while I get them?"

"Not really, but I won't be able to carry them anyway." Angel frowned, clearly frustrated with the crutches. "Do you mind?"

"Not at all."

He reached for his wallet and pulled out some cash. "Here, it's my treat." He handed it to me.

"Okay." I pocketed the cash, opened the car door, and helped him in, leaving his door open as I tossed the crutches in the back. He sat sideways, his feet on the pavement. "I'll be right back."

Ten minutes later I returned with four hot dogs smothered—two for each of us—and a drink carrier with a couple of sodas. We sat in the car and ate the dogs with the doors open. Afterwards, I tossed our trash, and we were on our way.

"Think they'll talk?" Angel asked.

"I don't think so. Not judging by how they were the other day."

"Me either."

Due to traffic on the 101, it took nearly an hour to reach Flora Dixon's home. I pressed the button for her to let us in.

"May I help you?" Flora's voice came across the intercom.

"Good afternoon, Ms. Dixon, this is Detective Kendrick. We'd like to come in and speak to the boys again if we may?"

"You may not."

"Ma'am?" I said, surprised.

"I've been advised by my lawyers and their doctors that for their mental health, I need to keep them from being questioned by both you and the press, so that is what I'm going to do."

"Ms. Dixon, this is a murder investigation. Those boys are at best witnesses; at worst they're the perpetrators—"

"Are you accusing these boys of murdering their mother?" she shrieked over the intercom.

"Ma'am, we are trying to determine th—"

"You'll need to come back here with a warrant!" she shouted.

I flopped my head back against the headrest of my car seat. "Very well, Ms. Dixon. We'll see you soon." I backed the car out of the drive and pulled out onto the street, headed back toward the station. "Well, that went well."

"Yeah, that wasn't how I expected it to go."

I drove silently for a few minutes as I thought about the case. I went back to the beginning, when we first arrived, and pictured the scene. After a moment I said, "I wanna talk to the paramedics who treated them at the scene."

"Why?"

"Audrina got that skin under her nails somehow, and I don't know if you noticed or not, but Mike had faint scratch marks on his cheek. I want to know if they were fresh when they were seen by the paramedics. I also want to know if they treated either of the boys for burns."

Angel nodded. "I didn't notice, but that is a good question."

"And I want to get Jordan to get that warrant." I paused and then added, "And the court order on Pfeiffer."

Two and a half hours after we'd left our desks, we were back at them. Angel made the calls to emergency services to track down the medics who had treated the boys while I went to talk to Jordan. I knocked on his open door.

"Come in, Kendrick."

I headed in hesitantly. I hated being alone with him, but I was a big girl, and this was my job. "Sir," I started, trying to be respectful, "Flora Dixon's lawyered up and won't let us speak to the boys. I was hoping you could get us a warrant to force her to allow it?"

"Done. Anything else?"

"We're going to go speak with the medics who treated the boys at the scene. I want to know if either had fresh scratch marks on their person, and if they had any burn marks. It wasn't in the CSI report."

"Okay. If the medics confirm that, I'm getting the warrant amended to putting them on house arrest, pending further investigations." Jordan looked up at me. "The press are all over this, demanding answers. Keep your mouth shut."

I nodded. I was hesitant to leave, so I just stood there.

"You can go, Kendrick."

He didn't have to tell me twice. I left without another word. By the time I reached Angel, he was already on his feet and headed toward the doorway. I grabbed my purse and joined him. "What did they say?"

"They're headed here to meet us in the lot."

"Oh, guess I didn't need my purse."

Angel grinned. "Nope. I offered for us to go meet them, but they said they were close and would swing by."

We didn't wait long for their ambulance to pull up to the curb. Two medics got out and walked over to us. "Detective Reyes?" one asked.

"That's me; this is Detective Kendrick."

"Hi," I said with a wave. "Appreciate you coming to us. We won't keep you long."

"Thanks. So, you said you had questions about the boys we treated out in Beverly Crest?"

"Yes. What can you tell us?"

The two exchanged looks and then said, "We can only tell you superficial stuff. Nothing specifically medical because of HIPPA."

"What if I ask a question, can you confirm it?"

The medic hesitated and winced as he said, "Depends."

"Okay, we'll just see how it goes, then." I frowned in consternation. "Did either of the boys have fresh scratch marks on them that you treated?"

They again exchanged looks. "Yes."

"Was it Mike? I noticed he had faint scratches on his cheek." I pointed to my own cheek where I'd seen the marks on Mike.

"Yes, it was Mike, and I did treat marks on his cheek right about where you pointed."

"Thank you. Now, did either boy have any burn marks?"

The two medics turned to each other and moved away from us. They had a heated, whispered conversation that I couldn't exactly overhear, but I did hear them mention the 911 call. Once they were done, they turned back and walked over to us again. "Since we were called in because there were victims of a fire who had both minor burn injuries and smoke inhalation, we can confirm that as well. There will be a phone recording of the 911 call into the station with that information."

"Can you confirm where the burns were? Were they on their hands?"

"Yes. They weren't to any degree near what the deceased incurred though."

"Okay, thanks. That helps."

"Was there anything else, Detectives?"

I shook my head. "No. Thanks for coming over here. Saved us a trip."

"No problem. We should get back on the road though. We've got a grid to cover."

"Sure."

They got back in their truck and drove off as Angel and I returned to the building. I headed to Jordan's office again and knocked once on the open door. Jordan waved me in, but he was on the phone.

"Look, I have to go. I'll be home when I get home." He paused. "I don't know. Just do what you have to. I have to go." He hung up and looked up at me warily. "What is it now, Kendrick?"

"Just spoke with the paramedics. Mike—Milgram had the fresh scratch marks, and both boys had minor burns on their hands."

He nodded. "House arrest it is, then. And I don't want them going to the press either, so I'll see if I can get a gag order."

"I still want to interview their dad. There's something not right about all of this."

"You think?" Jordan deadpanned. "I've put in the request. Now we just have to wait."

"That's the worst part."

He smirked. "Go home, Kendrick. You and Reyes. Get some rest. You can pick this back up tomorrow. Maybe the orders will be in then. And no talking to the press."

"Got it." I nodded and quickly left his office, wondering who had replaced Jordan with this reasonable clone. I wanted to thank them. Maybe with a fruit basket or a nice bottle of wine.

"I think that's a record," Angel said when I reached my desk.

"What are you talking about?"

"No yelling. No arguing. No Jordan stomping around the building demanding shit... what did you do?" He stared at me with fake suspicion, but his quivering lips gave him away. He was trying really hard not to laugh.

"Shut up. Don't jinx it. Whoever that clone is, I don't want them taking him back." I grinned. "Come on, let's get out of here," I added just as my desk phone rang.

Angel started to reach for it when I didn't, but I stopped him with a hand on his arm. "What if it's important?"

"They'll leave a message with the service, but it's probably the press, and Jordan said we are to keep with the no comments."

"Okay then." He nodded and leaned back in his chair, a smile gracing his lips. "Look at you being reasonable where Jordan is concerned."

I laughed. "Hey, I can be reasonable when he is." Grinning, I grabbed my purse from the top of my desk where I'd laid it. "Dinner?" I questioned.

"Sure. Tacos or burgers?" He pushed up to his feet and pulled his crutches to him, settling them in place under his arms.

We left the building, went out to the parking lot, and once we were in and buckled, I pointed the car toward our favorite Mexican joint.

14

BLOOD IN THE WATER
ANGEL

When Marcy and I reached the precinct the next morning, we were intercepted by the captain, who called us into his office. I had a physical therapy appointment scheduled for ten, so I hoped it wouldn't take too long.

We were kind of at a standstill with the case, waiting on the court order so we could talk to Dr. Pfeiffer, or for the boys to break their silence about what had happened. On top of that, the press were circling like the sharks they were. There was a group of them camped outside the precinct, who had shouted at us as we made our way in. It was like they could smell blood in the water.

I followed Marcy into the captain's office and noticed Jordan was already in there and seated in one of the two guest chairs.

Marcy moved to stand behind the other chair. "You sit. You spend too much time on your feet with the crutches," she said, giving me a look.

I knew I couldn't argue with her, but I didn't like sitting

when she couldn't. Still, I sat, but I sent a glare at Jordan. He should at least get up and offer his chair to Marcy. He didn't, of course, and sat there oblivious to my glare.

"Bring me up to date," Robinson said as he took his own seat.

"Sir, we've exhausted nearly every avenue we've got. The boys aren't talking, but it's looking more and more as though they might be involved," Marcy started.

"There was skin tissue beneath Audrina Dixon's fingernails that we believe belonged to Milgram because he had fresh scratch marks on his face, and both boys had burn marks on their hands."

"Have you arrested them?"

"Not yet, sir," Marcy said, glancing at Jordan.

"I've put in the warrant to compel them to speak to us, and I've asked for house arrest, pending further investigations," Jordan said, jumping in.

"And we're still waiting on a court order so we can speak to their father, Dr. Matthew Pfeiffer."

"What's the holdup?" Robinson asked.

Marcy shook her head. "I don't know, sir."

I glanced at Jordan, who looked decidedly guilty for some reason. I'd seen that look on his face before, usually when he'd been out fucking around on Marcy, and I'd caught him. "You did put in for the court order, didn't you?" I stared at him hard.

Jordan shifted in his seat, looking uncomfortable. "Well—"

"Jordan! You sat in your office just last night and said you'd already put it in and that we were just waiting on the judge to approve it," Marcy exclaimed.

"I may have exaggerated—"

Robinson glared at him. "Get the order and expedite it. I don't care whose dick you have to suck, get it done."

"Yes, sir." Jordan's neck flushed red.

"See that you do." Robinson's lips pressed into a thin line, and he seemed to be counting, judging by how he tapped each of his fingers against his thumb as he took deep breaths in through his nose. "Now, Kendrick, Reyes, I want you to try again with those boys. Get them to talk using any means necessary," he said when he'd calmed down some.

"Yes, sir, we can certainly try." Marcy nodded.

"Good." He gave her a smile that barely quirked his lips up before his expression turned serious again. "One other thing. I'm sure you noticed the gaggle of reporters outside."

"Yes, sir," I answered and glanced up at Marcy out of the corner of my eye to see her nodding.

"We did, yes."

"Someone, we don't know who yet, has leaked that we are definitely looking at the socialite's death as murder and that the boys are viable suspects. They are out for blood. I don't want another word of this investigation breathed to them. Is that clear?"

"Yes, sir, but neither Reyes nor I have spoken to the press in any detail. When they called, we said either no comment, or that it was an ongoing investigation and that you or the lieutenant would give them information when you were able."

"Well, someone is talking, and I want it to stop. The press is going to speculate and insinuate until we make an arrest. It's not our job to protect anyone from those speculations and insinuations, do you understand, Kendrick?" Robinson looked up at her.

Marcy didn't even blink. "Of course, sir. I wouldn't dream of setting the record straight with the vultures."

"Good. Maybe their stories will stir something up and get those boys to talk to us sooner rather than later. We need a break in this case. I have the police chief and the deputy mayor breathing down my neck. They want this solved. It doesn't look good to not have made an arrest yet."

"I understand that, sir," Marcy said.

"Then go get busy, find us something to work with. And, Brasswell, I want that order for Pfeiffer in Kendrick's hand by lunch."

"Yes, sir. I'll take care of it." Jordan stood, but he couldn't move because I was still seated and blocking him.

I took my time getting to my feet and getting my crutches under me. The more impatient he seemed, the slower I went. It was what he got for dragging his feet on that court order. The bastard. I maneuvered my way out of the captain's office, and once I was out the door, Jordan pushed past me and headed for his office. I chuckled.

"That was fun," Marcy said, watching him hurry down the hall. "Looks like we have to go back to the Dixon place in Beverly Crest."

I sighed. "I've got therapy at ten." I normally wouldn't go on a Sunday, but my physical therapist was making accommodations for me being on the job, and this was the only time available that worked for both of us.

"Crap," she murmured, then hesitated in the hallway. "Let me talk to the captain, see what he wants us to do. Give me a sec." She turned and went back into his office only to emerge about a minute later. "Okay, he told me to take you to your appointment, and then after, we're to go to the Dixon place."

"I'll cancel my Uber, then." I leaned on my crutch and good leg as I pulled out my phone and clicked on the app I'd used to order the car, then canceled it.

"I'm going to see what I can find on the boys while you're at your appointment. My brother mentioned something the other day that's been niggling at me, and I want to check it out."

"Okay, sounds good."

"And I'll make sure to grab the house arrest warrant from the courthouse too."

"Good thinking," I said with a smile.

Two hours later we were back in the car and headed toward Beverly Crest with the warrant in hand. I was sore as shit from the therapy session, but I wasn't about to complain. "Thanks for driving my ass all over the place," I said with a chuckle.

Marcy smiled at me. "Well, who else is going to? Unless you're hiding some hot nurse back at your place?"

I laughed harder. "Nope, no hot nurses for me. I'll be happy when they finally let me get off these crutches."

"What'd the therapist say?"

"I'm improving. I can start putting more pressure on my leg, just an hour or so at a time to start. But it's a beginning."

"That's great. Do the metal pins hurt?"

"Aches more than hurts. It's a weird feeling."

The doctors had to replace part of my femur, the thigh bone, with a metal rod made of titanium, and my kneecap with a 3D rendered titanium kneecap as well. So far everything seemed to be looking good, and I didn't have any swelling or infections. The doctors told me that titanium was the most biocompatible metal, and that it would be significantly less stiff than steel. It also lasted longer than other metals used. I was glad to hear that because I didn't want to go through surgery again to replace them.

I'd also broken both the tibia and fibula in my lower leg. The doctors were able to do a bone graft with a couple of metal pins to repair those, but they were wary of me putting too much stress on it too soon and breaking them again. That was why I was still going to physical therapy.

"I bet so," Marcy replied. "You know, I hadn't thought about it until now, but if you ever need me to pick up groceries or anything for you, I can."

I smiled. She was always doing things for the people in her life. I didn't want to be a burden to her. I was her partner. I was supposed to be at her side, helping and protecting her. Not depending on her to do shit for me. "I know. I appreciate that, but it's not necessary. I have them delivered. Thank God for the internet, yeah?"

Marcy glanced at me and tucked a piece of hair behind her ear. "Yeah, that's true."

"So, did you find anything on the boys? What was it your brother mentioned that was bugging you?"

"Oh, yeah. He'd mentioned killers with abuse or trauma in their past usually starting on animals and that maybe there was a pattern with the boys acting out their abuse. But I couldn't find anything to suggest the boys had any kind of instinct to kill, not even animals. I looked into missing pets in the area while they were growing up, but there was nothing there."

"Well, that's good, I guess."

She turned into Flora Dixon's neighborhood, and as her smile left her face, her eyes lost their sparkle. She'd put her mask back on. The one she hid her emotions behind. Marcy was a master at hiding behind that mask. I had a harder time at it, but knowing this was serious, I schooled my expression into the hardened detective mask I had to practice to achieve.

"Ready?" she asked when we reached Flora's driveway. She pushed the button and waited for the intercom.

"Yes?"

"Ms. Dixon, this is Detectives Kendrick and Reyes. We have a warrant; please open the gate."

I watched and waited, and a moment later the iron gates creaked open. "Do you think it was the 'please' that did it?" I quipped as she drove in.

Marcy gave me a sardonic smile, but didn't answer. She parked the car, and we got out, heading for the door, which opened before we even got there. That was a bit surprising.

"Ms. Dixon," Marcy started as the woman came out on the step, her arms folded.

"Where's the warrant?"

Marcy pulled it from her pocket and handed it to her. "We'd like to speak to the boys."

Flora looked at the warrant and then smirked. "They're not here."

"Where are they?" Marcy exclaimed.

"Safe. Any questions you have for them can go through our lawyers' office." Her smirk stayed in place. "If you have nothing further, I suggest you be on your way. There's nothing in here that says I have to let you into my home. It merely says I am compelled to allow you to speak to them. Which I'd be happy to do *if* they were here, which they are not."

I watched Marcy's fingers clench in a fist, and I nudged her before saying, "Ma'am, safe is not an answer, and you'll need to be more specific about where the boys are. As to questioning them through the lawyers, that is not how it works. Your lawyers are, of course, welcome to be there when we speak to the boys, but they cannot speak for them."

The smirk fell from Flora's face, and she sighed. "Fine. However, they really aren't here. Those reporters won't leave us alone, so I have them hidden in a safe house near my lawyers' offices with Shelby there to care for them."

"Great. Where is that?"

"I don't know that I have to tell you that. I'll speak to my lawyers, and I'll let you know when the boys will be ready to speak to you, unless you're arresting them?"

Marcy shook her head. "No, we aren't arresting them at this time, but we were going to ask that they be sequestered and to not leave the premises until further notice."

"Too late for that." Her smirk was back.

"We'll be back, Ms. Dixon, and if we have to, we will arrest the boys, as well as you for obstruction of justice."

"We'll just see about that. Good day, Detectives." She went inside and shut the door.

"I'm getting really tired of driving out here for nothing," Marcy practically growled. "We need to find those boys."

I couldn't have agreed more. "I'll start digging into properties she might own, or any payments she's making to somewhere she could have stashed them."

"Good idea," Marcy said as she tossed my crutches back in the back seat. "Let's go."

15

POSSIBLE SORORICIDE?
MARCY

I was completely frustrated with this case. I wasn't a hundred percent sure that the twins were guilty. It didn't feel right, but it also didn't feel as though they were completely innocent either. I knew they had to have seen something that would break this case wide open, but I was being stymied at every turn. I knew Flora was just trying to protect them, but I wasn't sure she was protecting them because she knew they were guilty, or if she thought she was protecting them from us because she thought we'd hinder their recovery. I also wondered if that protection extended to their father, whom I knew she had no love for.

And speaking of their father, I was still waiting on that court order. The captain had demanded we have it by noon, but still we had nothing, and it was nearly three. I headed to the captain's office to find out if he knew what the holdup was now.

"Hey, Jason, is he in?" I asked, stopping at the captain's assistant's desk.

"Hi, Detective Kendrick, no, he and the lieutenant were

called into a meeting with the chief of police and the mayor." Jason leaned forward, looking left and right, then back to me. "I'm pretty sure it's about that court order the lieutenant was trying to get."

I frowned, completely puzzled. "Why?"

"I heard the captain cussing, and he said something about it. And he mentioned Dr. Pfeiffer's name. That's connected to your case, right?"

I pinched the bridge of my nose and sighed. "Yeah." I shook my head, too frustrated to even elaborate at this point. "Thanks, Jason."

"Sure. Want me to tell the captain you were looking for him?"

"No, that's okay. Thanks." I headed over to my desk and flopped down in my seat.

"What's up?"

I rolled my head to the side and looked at Angel. "Something's up with the court order. I don't know what Jordan did to fuck it up, but we don't have it. On top of that, the captain and Jordan are meeting with the police chief and the mayor."

Angel sucked in a breath through his teeth. "Better them than us."

"True, but in the end, we're the ones screwed."

"Don't borrow trouble. We don't know what's going on with it yet; could be something else," Angel suggested, and then he tapped his notepad. "While you were talking to Jason, I did some research into the family holdings and found a place where I think Flora might have stashed the boys. Want to go check it out?"

I grabbed my purse and stood up. "Yup. Let's go." As we headed for the car, my stomach grumbled, and I realized we'd skipped lunch. "We'll swing through a burger place on our way."

"Sounds good. I could go for a double burger."

Back in the car, which I felt I'd spent nearly the entire day in, I said, "Where are we going, anyway?"

"Actually, not too far. Wilshire Blvd." He handed me the address.

I nodded, plugged it into my phone and headed for the 110. "We'll hit the Jack in the Box on Pico and Hoover."

After grabbing our food, I continued on Hoover toward Macarthur Park, then made a left onto Wilshire. By the time we arrived at the luxury apartments, I'd finished my burger and drink. I parked the car, grabbed a napkin, and wiped my mouth, then checked the mirror to make sure I didn't have any food on my face.

I glanced at Angel and smiled. "Ready?"

He nodded as he too wiped his mouth on a napkin. "Yep."

Getting out of the car, we made our way slowly toward the building. I would be so glad when Angel was done with his crutches. We entered the lobby, and I pushed the button for the elevator to take us up to the fourth floor. The doors opened, and we got in the car to ride it up. It didn't take long. The doors opened on a wide carpeted hallway. I found the right apartment and knocked on the door.

Shelby opened the door with a glare. "They aren't here. They've been taken to the hospital."

I frowned. "Why? What's happened?"

"They both had panic attacks that caused them to become combative. They've been admitted to the psych ward," Shelby explained.

"Is Flora here or with them?"

"Ms. Dixon is awaiting the doctor at the hospital."

I sighed. It looked as though we were going to have to make a trip to the hospital now. "Thank you."

He gave us a sour look and shut the door in our faces without another word.

"Well, that was fun," Angel said wryly.

I shook my head. "Come on, we'll catch Flora at the hospital, hopefully. I want to know what's going on with those boys."

Once we were back in the car, I looked over at Angel, who was leaned back against the seat, his eyes closed. I turned the car on and started out of the parking lot. Taking another glance at him, I frowned. He looked exhausted. I was sure all this in and out of the car and walking was wearing him out.

"You okay?"

"Yeah, I'm okay, just getting my exercise today," he replied.

"You and me both. I feel like we've been chasing the boys all over the city today. It's been like a wild-goose chase." I rolled my eyes as I turned the corner.

"That it does." He nodded. "I've been thinking..."

"Oh?"

He didn't say anything, just stared out the window.

"Angel? You care to elaborate?"

"Huh? Oh sorry. I was thinking what if we're looking at this wrong?"

"What do you mean?"

"Maybe Flora is the one who killed Audrina."

I frowned. "Why?"

"Maybe she did it so she'd get custody of the twins and the rest of her and Audrina's parents' fortune?"

"But why? Have we looked into her finances?"

"Not yet. But I've been thinking that maybe she's the only one in those boys' lives who really is stable. Maybe she's attached to them and resented her sister. I don't know, it's just a thought."

"No, it's a good theory, let's put a pin in it and see what she has to say when we talk to her. And we'll definitely look into her savings and investments, see if she's solvent. It's an avenue to pursue while we're waiting on that court order."

Angel nodded and looked out the windshield, then pointed toward the hospital. "You'll want to go around that way."

I did as he said, and soon we came to the section of the hospital that was dedicated to mental health services. We parked in the visitor area in a space reserved for police officers, which was right next to the handicap spots and worked out well for Angel. It took a few minutes, but we soon found ourselves walking down the hall toward the waiting area. There were a few rooms available to family members awaiting word on their loved ones, and in the third, we found Flora sitting and reading a magazine.

"Ms. Dixon."

She looked up and was immediately pissed off. "This is all your fault," she accused. "They're having nervous breakdowns because you won't leave them alone."

"Ma'am, this is a murder investigation. The boys are at best witnesses to their mother's murder. We need to speak to them."

"They're fragile and shouldn't have to relive Audrina's death."

I pinched the bridge of my nose and tried to remain calm. "Look," I said, holding up a hand to stop her protesting, "I understand your frustration, and I know you want to protect them."

She folded her arms over her chest and stared at us mutinously. "Have you even spoken to their father yet? Have you asked him what his former job was?"

"We're waiting on a court order," I admitted. "Speaking to him is on our agenda, I promise you. But you have to understand, those boys were there; they may have seen something very important to the case. Something that will help us catch the person who murdered your sister. That's what you want, right? To find the person responsible?"

"It was Pfeiffer." She glared at us.

"And maybe it was, but without speaking to the boys to confirm whether they saw their father in the penthouse, we can't do anything. Our hands are tied. There is no video evidence that he was there. Believe me, we looked."

"I don't know how he did it, but I. Know. He. Did." She was adamant that he was responsible. "You need to question him about his former job."

"You said that before; why do you want us to question him about a job he used to hold?" Angel asked, a look of confusion on his face.

I was sure my expression matched. I didn't know what kind of connection she was trying to make between Pfeiffer's previous job and her sister's death. What did one have to do with the other?

"I'm not going to say any more. You just need to do it." There was a stubborn set to her jaw. "I'll talk to the boys' doctor about allowing you to speak to them again. But it might be a day or two. I don't know how long they'll be here for. It all depends on if they can recover from the panic attacks."

Some of the tenseness I felt in my shoulders left. At least she sounded open to letting us question the boys again. I hated waiting, but we needed to make sure they were mentally okay before we interrogated them again, even if we planned to do it gently. The boys were, as she'd said, fragile.

"All right. Please keep us informed on the boys' progress." I handed her my card with my cell number on it. "Call me anytime, okay?" I murmured.

She took the card and looked at it, then back to me. "Fine."

"Thank you for your time, Ms. Dixon," Angel said as we left the room.

"Well, that went about as well as I expected."

"She didn't seem like she was purposely trying to keep the boys from speaking to us," Angel said as we made our way out of the building and to the car.

"No, she didn't. She did seem pretty adamant about us looking into Pfeiffer's occupation before he opened his practice. Did anything come up in the preliminary report on him?"

"I honestly didn't look at anything prior to him opening his practice. I'll add it to the list of things to do."

"Good. I can't help feeling we're missing something," I said as I pulled out of the parking lot to head back to the station.

16

FEELING GUILTY
MARCY

The room was soot covered, but I could see that it had once been a place of relaxation and peace. There were remnants of glass tables and bowls of crystals and the shattered remains of oil lamps scattered about. The white furniture was blackened and decaying.

I folded my arms and stared at the scene where it all started to the balcony where Audrina had gone and fallen to her death. Henry stood at my side. "I think the boys know more than they're saying. I can't help but think they're involved in some way."

"Shame on you, Marcy. Blaming those kids for their mother's death. What child could do such a thing?" Henry's voice was harsh to my ear.

I looked at him with surprise. "But you of all people know that children are capable of terrible things too; you profiled some of the worst of them."

He shook his head. A look of disapproval on his face.

"Henry, come on, you know I have to question them—"

He continued to shake his head as his body faded into the ether.

"Henry!" I cried. "Don't leave me! I'm sorry! I'm just doing my job; please don't go!"

He didn't return.

"Henry?" I called out as the room caught fire again from out of nowhere.

Flames licked up the walls, spreading across the crisp furniture and over the floor as if it followed a pool of liquid toward my feet. I backed up out of the doorway, farther onto the balcony. My back hit the railing, but the fire kept coming.

"Henry! Help!" I screamed.

There was no answer.

"Henry!"

"Henry!" I cried out as I woke up.

I sat there crying as I thought back over the dream I'd just had, though calling it a dream was generous. It was more a nightmare than a dream. I couldn't get over the feeling of guilt I had of having to investigate those boys. I couldn't understand it though. I'd never felt guilty for investigating anyone before. But something about those boys was messing with my head. And to add Henry to the mix made me feel like I was going crazy. I felt as though I was being haunted by his ghost, or maybe not his ghost, but some demon using his form to destroy my mind because the real Henry would never do such a thing.

I shook my head and wiped a hand down my face, drying my tears. I needed something to distract me, so I decided to call Stephen and see if he was awake. He might not be, seeing as it was only six thirty in the morning, but I was sure that the medical staff at Shine View would be available to let me know if he wasn't. I dialed the number for Shine View and waited.

"Shine View, how may I direct your call?" a voice asked.

"Hi, this is Marcy Kendrick. I'm calling to see if my brother, Stephen, is awake yet? I didn't want to ring his room if he was still asleep."

"Oh, Ms. Kendrick, I'm sorry to have to inform you your brother had another breakdown last night."

"What? Why didn't someone call me?" I asked in frustration.

"I'm sorry if you weren't informed. Would you like to talk to the night nurse who was on duty?"

"Yes, please, that would be helpful, thank you."

"Just one moment and I'll connect you with Maria."

The line clicked, and I was put on hold. I sat there for ten minutes listening to the Muzak version of "Paradise City" and various other rock songs from the eighties. I was just about to give up when it clicked again.

"Hello?" I said hesitantly.

"Ms. Kendrick? This is Maria Delacourte. I'm the night nurse on your brother's hall. I apologize for not calling you; it's been a very busy twelve hours. I don't know if it was the full moon or what, but it was a bit of a chaotic night."

"I understand; can you tell me what happened?"

"Yes, of course. Stephen began having pain in his chest and shortness of breath last night at about ten thirty. Dr. Faulkner had him admitted to the hospital for some tests because we thought he was having a heart attack. However, I want to assure you he's fine. It turned out to be a severe panic attack, not a heart attack."

"I'm glad it wasn't a heart attack. Do you know what brought on the panic attack?" I asked, concerned.

"No, ma'am, not at this time. Right now, your brother is sedated and resting comfortably, but he's not lucid and probably won't be until at least this evening."

"Oh," I murmured, sniffling.

"Ms. Kendrick, have you been by here to visit your brother?"

I shook my head, but knew she couldn't see me. "No, he said he didn't want me to come see him there."

"I can understand why you would want to follow his wishes. However, I've been doing this job for about ten years now, and I can tell you, our patients recover faster if their loved ones actually do come visit and don't listen to the patient's instructions not to. You see, many times they are too ashamed of being here getting treatment to want anyone seeing them, but that is actually what they need. They need to know that you support them no matter what."

"Okay, I didn't think of that, but it makes sense." I frowned. I should have thought of that. I should have realized what was bothering Stephen, but I'd been so caught up in my own head, my own drama, and this case, that I hadn't been a very good sister. I should have known he needed me. "I'll come by as soon as I can."

"Just remember, he probably won't be lucid until this evening, and then he'll need a session with Dr. Faulkner before he can see anyone."

"Yes, I understand. I may try to come by this week, give him time to do that."

"That would be nice."

"Thanks again, bye," I said, and then hung up. With a sigh, I rose from my bed and got ready for work. I was early, so I did a quick check-in with Katrina, sending her a text message.

> Hey, I know it's early, but I wondered if you wanted to get lunch later?

I didn't know if she was awake yet, so I didn't wait for her to text me back. I just grabbed my purse and my keys and headed out, locking up behind me. I hadn't stopped by Stephen's last night, so I went there to do a quick dust and vacuum and to feed his fish again. "Sorry, little guys, I know you must have thought I forgot about you." I tapped on the glass and smiled as they blew bubbles and started to devour the food like they hadn't eaten in a year.

While I was at Stephen's, I sent Angel a text.

> I'm up and about early, wondered if you want to eat breakfast out, or if you want me to pick it up and bring it to you? Or just coffee?

As I locked up Stephen's apartment and headed to my car, my phone buzzed. I pulled it from my pocket and looked at a text from Katrina.

> Sounds good, call me when you're ready.

> Perfect, see you later.

I was just about to pocket it when Angel replied too.

> Pick me up. We'll eat out.

> On my way.

I re-pocketed my phone and got in my car. I made the drive to Angel's place, and as I went to get out and help him, he came out of the house in just a boot and a leg brace. No crutches. "Are you okay to be doing that?" I arched a brow at him.

He laughed. "Already talked to the doc. The crutches

were driving me crazy; they're getting in the way and cumbersome. Therapy's going well, and as long as I wear this for most of the day, I should be okay. Still can't run, but I can move faster now, and I don't need help in and out of the car."

"As long as the doctor says it's okay, then I guess I'll allow it," I teased. "Just don't want you having any setbacks."

"Me neither. I wouldn't chance it if I didn't think I could handle it though," he replied with a smile as he got into the car on his own. "Where to?" he asked once I was behind the steering wheel.

"LA Café?"

"That sounds good," he replied.

As I headed downtown, I said, "Stephen had a major panic attack last night and had to be sedated."

"Is he all right?" Angel questioned, looking at me with concern.

"Yeah. They thought he was having a heart attack. The nurse I spoke to said that I should come visit him."

"You haven't yet?"

I shrugged. "I didn't want to go against his wishes, but she said I should anyway. What do you think?"

Angel scratched his cheek and said, "Maybe? It might be good to see a friendly face. One who's not a doctor or nurse, you know?" He paused, then added, "I know being in the hospital sucks. Seeing friends and family helps."

"I should have thought of that. I just didn't want to intrude." I sighed.

"You're his sister; you're not intruding." He smiled at me and patted my shoulder. "Don't be so hard on yourself."

I gave a half laugh. "How did you know I was feeling bad?"

"It's all over your face, Marce."

I glanced at him and smiled as I pulled into the restaurant parking lot. We headed in, and after looking over the menu, I ordered the crispy breakfast tacos while Angel had the Belgian waffle with strawberries and whipped cream.

An hour later, we were back at the station, working the case again. Angel pulled up Flora's financial records while I tried to dig into Dr. Pfeiffer's previous job history, but I kept hitting roadblocks. There was nothing available to find, which I found extremely odd.

"Hey." Angel rolled his chair next to me. He had his notebook open. "So, this is what Flora's accounts are sitting at." He showed me the rather high figures. "And she's got multiple investments in property and in stocks. Plus, she has her own trust from their parents. So I'm thinking money wouldn't have been a motive if she's the one who killed her sister."

"No, she'd have no need for Audrina's money, so probably not the motive unless she's excessively greedy, but she didn't strike me as being that."

"Me either."

"Did we ever check her alibi?" I asked, leaning back in my chair.

Angel frowned. "Nope, don't think so. We weren't really looking at her. Want me to call and check?"

"No, I'll do it. See what you can do with Pfeiffer. I'm running into trouble pulling stuff up on him."

"Sure thing." He rolled back over to his own desk.

I picked up the phone and dialed Flora's home number. I wanted to talk to her about the boys as well as check her alibi. I waited a few moments, listening to the phone ring, thinking I might have to hang up and try her cell, but a second later, someone answered.

"Dixon residence."

"Hello. Shelby, right?"

"Yes, ma'am. May I ask who's calling?"

"I'm sorry, this is Detective Kendrick. I was hoping to speak to Ms. Dixon. Is she available?"

"Yes, ma'am, she's right here," he replied.

I heard the phone change hands and Flora murmur to her butler. A moment later, she came on the line and said, "Detective, I hope you're calling to tell me you've asked that bastard about his previous occupation and what he did."

"Hello, ma'am. No, we're still having an issue with the court order," I answered, though I had no idea what was going on with that since I hadn't seen the captain at all today, and Jordan had only been out of his office to give orders to everyone except me and Angel. It was like he was avoiding us, which was actually kind of nice, and I didn't want to disturb that peace by questioning it, even though I really needed to know.

"I see."

"Ms. Dixon, I wanted to ask some more questions about the boys. You seem to know what their life was like prior to these events. I wondered what you could tell me of their everyday home life when they were with their mother? Were you involved in their upbringing at all?"

"Not per se, no. I have always been there for them, of course. I saw them often, and Audrina and I would vacation together with the boys. However, most of their childhood they had a series of nannies and housekeepers who looked after them. Especially when Audrina was away. I made sure to go and see them when she was gone, but it wasn't the same as having their mother there, as I'm sure you're aware."

"Of course, that makes perfect sense. Could you possibly

provide me with a list of those former nannies and housekeepers? I'm trying to build a full picture, and it would help a lot to speak to them."

"I don't know that I remember all of them, but I feel sure that Audrina has an address list and former employee documents in her office. I'll look for you. Is that all?"

"Oh, um, just one more thing. Can you tell me where you were at the time of your sister's death? It's just routine, we have to ask everyone, and I forgot to get yours the other day."

"Of course, I was at Ciel."

I paused, unsure of what she'd said. "Could you repeat that?"

"Ciel Spa in Beverly Hills. I was on the massage table at the time my sister…" She let her voice trail off for a moment. "I was getting a hot stone massage. Work has been rather tense lately, and I needed to de-stress."

"Will they have a record of you being there?" I asked, knowing the answer would be yes.

"Of course. They are located on La Cienega Boulevard, but I can give you the number if you need it."

"That would be very helpful, thank you."

Flora reeled off the number as though she knew it by heart. "Is that everything, then, Detective?"

"For now, thank you for your time, Ms. Dixon."

I hung up and immediately dialed the number she gave me. It didn't take long to find out she was telling the truth. She had been there when she got the call about her sister. There was absolutely no way she could have been the one to light Audrina on fire and shove her over the balcony.

I turned to Angel. "She's got a solid alibi."

"Well, damn."

"I still think she knows something though. It has something to do with the boys' father, but she's not going to come out with it. She is pushing hard for us to talk to him. Did you find out anything?"

"Nope, you're right, it's like certain aspects of his life for a number of years have been wiped from existence." He shook his head. "I've not seen anything like this except for in witness protection cases, a few military cases and—" He stopped and frowned.

"And?" I prompted.

"Government jobs."

"Huh. Wonder which category our Dr. Pfeiffer falls in."

"That's a good question."

17

BEWILDERED AND BEMUSED
MARCY

Angel and I broke for lunch, and I headed to meet Katrina at Mima's Mediterranean while he decided to stay close to the station. I'd invited him along, but he'd declined. We caught up while we ate our chicken shawarma wraps. Katrina shared about her week, and then I told her what had been going on with me. It was nice to talk to someone about the dreams I'd been having and be reassured that I wasn't actually being haunted or that I was crazy.

"I really thought I might be losing my mind," I said with a grin.

"It's normal to see people we care about in dreams, and our subconscious can often substitute their voice or use their image to get things we're worrying about out in the open. I think it's because we sometimes don't listen to ourselves, but we'll listen to those we care about." Katrina shrugged.

She wasn't wrong. This case was preying on my mind, and I didn't want to traumatize those boys more than I had to. I ate a few more bites and then glanced at the time. I needed to get back. After wiping my mouth, I waved to the waiter and asked for a to-go box.

"This has been great," I said. "I appreciate you being able to meet me. The group is nice, but I like this one-on-one stuff better."

"Me too, honestly," she replied with a laugh.

We paid our bill and headed out. I made plans to get together again in the coming week and, of course, to see her in our group therapy. After giving her a hug goodbye, I drove back to the station. I'd finally decided I needed to beard the dragon in his cave. Meaning I needed to see Jordan about that damn court order and find out what was going on.

I waved to Angel as I entered, but instead of going to my desk, I went straight to Jordan's office. The door was shut, so I knocked and waited for him to call out for me to enter, then opened the door and glanced in.

"What do you need, Kendrick?" he grunted from behind his desk without looking at me.

I didn't bother closing the door. I didn't want to get yelled at, and there was a better chance he'd keep his temper if the door was open. "I wanted to know what was going on with our court order. We were supposed to have it yesterday."

"Yeah, well, Pfeiffer's lawyers put in injunctions and tangled it all up in a bunch of red tape. That was why the captain and I were meeting with the chief and the mayor yesterday. Turns out Pfeiffer has friends in high places, and we got our asses handed to us." He looked up and glared at me for a minute, then went back to the paperwork in front of him.

"So, what, we just aren't going to get it?"

"We're working on it, Kendrick," Jordan practically

growled. "In the meantime, find another avenue to pursue. Don't make me do your job for you! Now go."

I shook my head and turned on my heel, leaving him to his grumpiness. I retreated to my desk and sank down in my chair. As I put my purse in my desk drawer, I looked over at Angel. "No luck with the court order. Pfeiffer's tied it up in court."

"Well, crap. In that case, maybe we start calling this list of nannies and housekeepers Flora brought in?"

"She came by with it?" Color me shocked.

He nodded. "Dropped it off about ten minutes before you got back. How was lunch, by the way?"

"It was good. Talking with Katrina helped."

"I'm glad. You look… lighter. Like a weight was lifted."

Nodding, I said, "Yeah, kind of in a way."

"Wanna split the list with me?" he asked, holding it up.

"Sounds good. Are there phone numbers included, or do we need to look them up?"

"She included both addresses and phone numbers."

"Great. Saves us time."

"She also added in their pediatricians and tutors with their information."

"They had multiple?"

Angel glanced at the list, then back to me. "About six pediatricians and nine tutors over eight years."

"Wow. That seems excessive on both counts. I wonder why."

"We should probably ask," Angel suggested. "How about I take them, and you take the nannies and housekeepers?"

"Perfect." I took my half of the list and started dialing. "Hello, I'm looking for Miss Kara Lawrence?"

"This is she," a woman answered.

"Ms. Lawrence, my name's Detective Kendrick. I'm calling in regard to the Dixon-Pfeiffer boys?"

"Are they all right?"

"Yes, I'm sorry, I didn't mean to worry you; you've heard about their mother, I assume?"

"Of course, so tragic," she murmured.

I went on to ask a series of questions, and she explained that she'd been fired because according to their parents, she'd coddled them. She'd hated having to leave them, and they'd sobbed as she'd been pretty much thrown out of the house when they were five.

"I see," I replied, feeling awful for those boys. "Well, thank you for your time."

"Please, if you see the boys, tell them that I think of them often, and I still have the trinkets they gave me, and I treasure them."

"Of course, I'll do that," I replied and then hung up and called the next name on the list. Unfortunately, it was pretty much the same story as Miss Lawrence had shared. She got too close to the boys and was tossed out like yesterday's garbage. Phone call after phone call played out nearly the same until I came to one of the housekeepers, Mrs. Caruthers.

"Ma'am, I was hoping you could tell me a little bit about the boys' lives while you were with them?"

"Such a shame what those two did to those boys." She made a tutting sound as though she was scolding them. "That father, doing experiments on those boys. I wanted to throttle him, I can tell you that."

"Experiments?" I asked, sitting up straighter in my chair. "Can you explain?"

"Yes, he would give them pills he called supplements, but

they were nothing good, I can tell you that. Made those boys all kinds of bewildered and just... bemused. There were days they couldn't tell up from down. Walked around the house in a complete daze with glassy eyes like a zombie. It was creepy and disturbing."

"Were either of their parents violent toward them?" I asked, taking notes, putting a question mark by the word supplements on my notepad.

"Not that I ever saw, but the potential was there. He always seemed as though he might strike one of them at any moment. Not the mother, she often took some of the same pills he gave the boys. At least her bottle looked the same as theirs, and I know they came from his office. Despondent is how I would describe her at the time."

That was interesting. I hadn't even considered that Audrina might have been taking those supplements too. However, she was the victim here, and I needed to know about the boys. "Were either of the boys ever violent?"

"Not that I recall. Mostly they were in bad moods, but it was more because they couldn't remember things that had happened hours previously. It was as though chunks of their lives were gone from their brains. They would black out and not remember they'd eaten their dinner, or going outside to play. It would just be gone from their memory."

"That seems odd," I murmured. "When was this?"

"It was a few years ago, they lived with their mother of course, that was who I worked for, but their father was always sending those supplements for them to take, and Ms. Dixon would always give them to the boys, believing they were some sort of special vitamin formulated specifically to deal with the boys' mental health. I told her she should stop, that it was clearly making the boys worse, but she just dismissed my words. Eventually she dismissed me. She got tired of me questioning her about it."

"I see. So let me go back to the boys for a moment. In your opinion, could either of the boys be violent?"

"No, those boys were sweet as pie when they weren't on those pills, and when they were, it was as I said, they were zombie-like. Not violent, just confused and out of sorts."

"All right, well, thank you for your time, Mrs. Caruthers."

"I hope I was able to help you, Detective. I feel bad about those boys and how things have gone for them. I hope they're finally getting the help they needed all those years ago and they're well away from that father of theirs."

At that point, I couldn't help but agree with her.

18

CHILDREN OR FERAL DOGS
ANGEL

I hung up the phone, having just gotten done with the last physician's office. I had a headache from dealing with them because not one would cooperate and just give me the information I was looking for, quoting their HIPPA oath as the reason to stay quiet. A few said if I wanted the information, I'd have to get a court order. They wouldn't answer any questions at all pertaining to the Pfeiffer twins. Not even why they changed doctors like they changed their underwear.

The tutors had been a little more forthcoming. It seemed many of them left the Dixon-Pfeiffer residence because they couldn't get the boys to retain anything beyond the basics. It wasn't that they were mentally challenged. Not like you would normally think of a mentally challenged person. They'd describe periods where the boys would be missing chunks of time and information. It would just be gone from their brains, and no amount of patience, or threatening even, could draw it out of them. They weren't being obstinate; it was as though they'd never heard or learned what was taught. It was extremely frustrating to say the least, according to several of the tutors.

I turned to Marcy and smiled as she twirled a strand of hair around her finger while she was on the phone. She paused and wrote something down, then went right back to twirling. I doubted she was aware she was doing it, but I thought it was cute.

"All right, thank you for your time, Mrs. Caruthers," Marcy said into the phone and then paused. She listened for a moment longer, then added, "Take care now," and hung up.

"Learn anything?" I asked, rolling my chair over toward her.

Marcy nodded and glanced down at her notepad. "How about you?"

"A bit." I shook my notepad. "You go first; what did the nannies and housekeepers have to say?"

"Most of the nannies said they were dismissed for being what their father termed 'overly affectionate' with the boys, but was really just the normal amount. And apparently their mother just went along with what Pfeiffer said about the boys' care. It seemed he wanted no affection shown to the boys at all, even when they needed that kind of nurturing, according to those I spoke to, at any rate." Marcy shook her head and had a disgusted look on her face.

"Were they raising children or feral dogs?" I asked, frowning. "Who doesn't want their child shown love and affection?"

"I don't know, but the more I hear about this father of theirs… it's a good thing he doesn't have custody at all."

"Was there more?"

"Yeah, the last housekeeper I spoke to, she had quite a bit

to say. I'm starting to wonder if their father was providing some psychedelic kind of drugs to those boys. Mrs. Caruthers had called them experiments, and they'd lose chunks of time and be in bad moods. Never violent, but they'd have blackout periods where they wouldn't remember things."

"Huh, well, that jibes with what I learned from the tutors. Most left because the boys were difficult to teach; they kept losing lessons, chunks of learning were just gone from their memories was how they described it."

"Wow, what the heck was he giving those boys?" Marcy asked.

"I wish I knew. Their former doctors all refused to answer questions, said we'd need a court order."

Marcy made a sound of disgust. "I'm so sick of trying to get those on this case." She shook her head and then sighed. "I feel like we're missing something."

"Aside from speaking to the man who had to have been a major influence in all their lives?"

"Yeah, aside from that." She nodded.

"Wanna re-look at the crime scene?"

"Yeah, maybe. Where's the photos?"

"I've got them." I rolled back over to my desk, sifted through the files I had scattered there, and pulled the manila folder out that held the pictures. "Want to pin them up? Look at them all together?"

"Yeah, let's take them to an incident room." She rose, and we headed to one of the rooms that we used for major crime cases that was currently empty. "This will work."

Corkboards covered in pale green cloth—to make the room more aesthetically pleasing to the eye I supposed—took up two walls in the room. There was also a whiteboard wall and then a glass wall that looked out onto the detective pool.

I opened the file and started pinning the pictures up on one of the corkboards. I put them in order, following the numbers in the pictures.

Marcy started writing details about the case on the whiteboard. She put up the victim's name, then taped a picture of her under her name. Then she added the boys and their pictures, Flora, and Dr. Pfeiffer to the board. She put notes under each, stating their alibis and any notes we had as well as questions we needed answered.

As I was pinning the last of the images up, she made a timeline starting twenty-four hours prior to death to a few hours after death, just to get an idea of where people were and what they were doing.

"Okay, I'm ready." I leaned against the table, staring at all the images from the crime scene.

Marcy put the cap on her marker and walked over. She turned and leaned back against the table next to me. "So it starts with where our victim was doused with the fire, correct?"

"Yes, that's the spot where the fire chief determined it all began." I pointed to the first image. "It progressed here, here, and here, and we can see how she must have hit the glass, dropping the lamp, which broke and also shattered the table, sending the crystals scattering everywhere."

Marcy nodded. "Wait, is that the victim's phone?" She pointed to the picture with the number seven on it.

"Hang on, let me check the notes." I turned to the folder and pulled out the paper to see what it said. "No, it's Milgram's—Mike's."

She frowned. "Why was his phone found there, that close to where his mother caught fire?"

"That's a good question."

"Has crime scene unlocked the phone? Do we know who he was talking to? Maybe that will give us something?"

"I don't know; want me to call Lindsey?"

"Yeah, see if they've even looked at it yet." Marcy moved over to the whiteboard, writing down *Mike's Phone* and that it was found close to the victim.

I picked up the desk phone on the conference table and hit the button that would connect us to the crime lab.

"Lindsey Stone," she answered.

"Hey, it's Angel. Marcy and I are going over the crime scene photos from the Dixon murder."

"Yep, what do you need from me?"

"Have you looked at the phone?"

She paused, and I could hear her flipping through some paperwork. "Milgram's phone? Yes, looks like one of my team finished going through it this morning. Have you not gotten a copy of what we found yet?"

"No, sorry, haven't seen anything."

"Okay, I'll get it sent up to you, but there wasn't much on it. A few memes and pictures of him and his brother. The Google history showed he mostly looked up gaming information, various TV shows and videos. He spent a lot of time on TikTok watching gamers."

"Who was he calling and texting?" I asked.

"There were calls with his brother, his aunt, a few friends, and his father. In fact, there was an incoming call logged in from his father that lasted about three minutes just prior to the murder."

"Really? Do you have Gary's phone too? Did he surrender it?"

"It was actually found in the hallway just outside the room of the fire. We bagged it, and I think my tech guy is going over it now. Let me see if he's done, one sec."

I could hear her walking, her heels clicking on the tile floor. I covered the mouthpiece of the phone and said to Marcy, "Mike spoke to his dad just prior to the murder."

She nodded and added that to the board. "How long was the call?"

"Lindsey says three minutes."

She added that to the board as well.

"Angel?"

"I'm here."

"He's looking at the call logs now; doesn't look like Gary had any calls come in or go out around the time of the murder. His last use was a text to someone named Ethan the night prior to the murder."

"Okay, was the text message between Gary and Ethan of any importance?"

"It looks like they were planning to meet up to play *Fortnite* online the evening of the murder. There's a couple of additional texts from Ethan asking where Gary is and why he wasn't there, but then we already know why, and he hasn't had his phone to reply."

"Yeah, that Ethan kid probably thinks Gary ghosted him." I sighed. "Guessing he'll hear about what happened soon enough. Can you have the information on both phones sent up as soon as possible?"

"You got it."

I hung up and turned to Marcy. "So it doesn't look like Gary got a call from dear old dad, just Mike."

Marcy frowned. "I wonder why that is."

"Do you think the call was Pfeiffer telling Mike to kill his mom?"

"God, I hope not," she said, but then added, "It does kind of look that way, doesn't it."

"So do you think it was just him? He did it without Gary's knowledge?"

"Or they did it together at their father's bidding."

"That's possible, but why kill their mom?"

Marcy stared at the whiteboard and then said, "Remember what the housekeeper said about experiments and drugs he was giving them? What if he somehow coerced the boys to do it, and they can't remember doing it?"

"Then we could charge him as well. The boys wouldn't be off the hook, they'd still be responsible, but damn, I hate thinking they played a role."

"Me too." She nodded. "But it really looks like they did; now we just have to figure out how and why."

19

CONTROLLING THE MIND
MARCY

Yesterday Angel and I went over everything Lindsey sent up on the boys' phones, and then called it a night. Today we were going to start fresh, looking into the *good doctor* Pfeiffer. Just the thought of him gave me the creeps. What kind of father did experiments on his own kids?

Before, when I'd looked into Pfeiffer, my internet search had brought up his bio, which was basic and barely touched on his life prior to him starting his practice. But there were a number of years where it just glossed over, barely talking about anything but the fact he'd married and started a family, nothing about his work. There were a couple of things that came up that I hadn't really looked at.

It turned out Pfeiffer had written a number of books and co-written many others. He had about thirty-three credits to his name on the website. I decided to read the reviews and descriptions of the books while Angel was at his physical therapy appointment. He'd taken an Uber, still not able to drive. Of course, I'd offered to take him, but he'd told me to stay and keep working the case.

I pulled up a book called *Hallucinogens and the Brain* and read over the description. There was another called *Therapeutic Derealization* and a third called *Creating a Fugue State*. Those were just the tip of the iceberg, from what it looked like. I clicked on the "look inside" option for *Therapeutic Derealization* and found the information I'd been looking for. It listed the good doctor as having worked for a pharmaceutical research company called California Medico during the years that were missing from his bio.

I opened another tab and typed in the company name and found that it heavily focused on the effects of various pharmaceuticals on the human brain. Their main focus was on three classes of drugs: sedatives, hallucinogens, and amnestics. I looked those up and found they were often used to create fugue states during which a person is left with no memory of their experiences or actions.

I leaned back in my chair, thinking about everything I'd learned in this case. What I was reading about now was a reflection of what the housekeeper had said. "That motherhumper," I murmured under my breath. "He was using his boys in his research."

Glancing at the clock as my stomach growled, I decided to grab lunch from one of the food trucks that tended to set up down the street, then come back and look deeper into some of these books he'd written. I turned my computer monitor off, grabbed my purse, and headed out of the department. The day was nice, mild temperatures and sunny. It felt good to get some fresh air as I made the short walk down the street.

Within minutes I was headed back to the precinct with a

lobster roll, some lobster mac and cheese and a large lemonade. It smelled so good my mouth was watering by the time I got to my desk and dug in. As I ate, I clicked my monitor on and started reading the available pages of the books that were allowed on the *look inside* part.

It seemed most of these books talked about certain sedatives and hallucinogens that could be used to create suggestibility and docility. He'd written a few that talked about how several drugs were used on various patients with different disorders and what outcomes were achieved by each of the drugs.

"What are you reading so intently?" Angel asked, appearing at my side. "Is that lobster mac and cheese?"

I glanced up at him. "Yes, Lobsta is down the street; you want me to go grab you some?"

He hesitated, but then shook his head. "Naw, I shouldn't, just had a burger and fries. If I'd known they were here, I'd have waited."

"I could get you some to take home for dinner?"

"Maybe? First, what are you reading?"

"I figured out where Pfeiffer was during those missing years." I grinned at him smugly.

"Where?"

"He might have scrubbed them from his bio, but it's still listed in a couple of his books. California Medico."

"Wait, I know that name... weren't they linked to the CIA?" Angel sat down in his seat and rolled it over next to me. He grabbed my fork and took a bite of the mac and cheese.

I paused. "That makes a lot of sense. And stop that. I'll get you some if you want it." I shook my head at him.

"So good." He had a look of pleasure on his face that was adorable.

I smiled. "Give me a minute." I grabbed my purse and made the quick trip back to the food truck and ordered two more of the deliciousness and then hurried back to my desk. "Here."

"Thanks. I was just looking at some of these books you pulled up. This all sounds a whole lot like they're used for mind control. Didn't the CIA have a program for that? Something Ultra." He started typing in a new tab, and it came up. MK Ultra. "Yeah, look at this. It says they conducted hundreds of clandestine experiments on people. I bet it was more than hundreds." He shook his head as he kept reading.

"And look at that," I said, pointing out a section. "The CIA had a chemist and poison expert named Sidney Gottlieb. Isn't that an interesting name?" I pressed my lips in a firm line.

"He named his son after a CIA poison expert!"

"You know, Stephen mentioned one of the guys there with him was a real conspiracy nut. He was pretty vocal about MK Ultra, now that I recall. What if they didn't stop?"

"Who? The CIA?"

"Yeah, what if they just said they stopped the program? What if they're still doing this stuff?"

"Maybe we should talk to an expert?" Angel suggested.

"That might be a good idea. How do we even begin to find one though?"

Angel closed the tab and opened a new one, he started typing, and after a minute, he pointed to a name. Dr. Oscar Glenn. His bio said he was a renowned psychiatrist and psychotherapist trained in hypnotism, who'd authored several books on programming and deprogramming the human mind.

"Look, it says he has knowledge about conspiracies like MK Ultra and other mind-control programs. And that he works with a lot of cult survivors," he pointed out.

"Give him a call; see if he's open to talking to us."

"Sure thing." Angel picked up the phone and dialed the number of the man's clinic.

I finished off my lunch, saving the second mac and cheese to take home for dinner. I closed out the tabs on my computer as Angel spoke to the receptionist.

"Thank you." He hung up and turned to me, saying, "Okay, we've got an appointment to meet with him the day after tomorrow at his office downtown."

"What time?" I tossed my trash in the waste bin.

"Four thirty."

"That works." I nodded as something niggled in my mind. "You know, it's kind of a coincidence, don't you think, that Flora works as a biochemist. Wouldn't she know about all these pills he was supposedly giving the boys?" I had learned that when I'd done our initial background check on everyone involved in the case.

"Maybe."

"I'm thinking we might want to ask her about that," I murmured.

"Kendrick, Reyes, you're up!" Jordan called from the hallway. "Shooting on Adams Boulevard. Two vics en route to the hospital."

I grabbed my purse, and Angel stood too. Grabbing the note from Jordan, we headed out of the station. I hated leaving the case, but crime didn't stop just because we were working on something else. Angel and I still had to pull our weight on the everyday stuff that came in.

I put the siren on the dashboard, and once Angel was in and buckled, we took off.

20

SLIPPERY AS AN EEL
MARCY

We'd lost the entire afternoon dealing with the shooting on Adams the day before. The victims had passed away en route, and we'd had to spend an exorbitant amount of time combing through security footage from various businesses to get a proper ID on the shooter. We'd tracked the guy down, but it had turned into a stand-off where he took his girlfriend hostage. In the end, he'd ended up shooting himself, but we'd saved the girl, thankfully, not that she appreciated it.

There was just no reasoning with some people.

Once it was over, and we'd gone back to the precinct to write up the reports, it was late, so Angel and I had called it a night and planned to start fresh again in the morning.

I pulled into Angel's driveway and watched as he wobbled his way to the car, still wearing the boot and brace on his leg. He was really getting around much better, and his therapist had said he could remove them soon. I knew he was looking forward to that.

"Hey, did you get any sleep?" I asked once he was in the car. He looked like he hadn't even been to bed, though he was wearing a fresh suit.

"Not much. My leg was pretty sore."

"Too much walking on it, you think?"

"Naw, I think it was mostly from the therapy session yesterday. We pushed it really hard. Just going to take time to build the muscles back up."

"Coffee?" I asked, as I hadn't picked some up on my way to Angel.

"Sure."

We hit the coffee shop drive-thru and then headed for the station. Jordan was waiting for us as soon as we walked in. My steps faltered as I steeled my spine for a confrontation, but there wasn't one forthcoming.

"Court order has finally come in with prejudice. So you'll have to stick to certain topics. It's in the documentation, so look it over. I talked to Pfeiffer's receptionist; he's got an hour opening in"—Jordan turned his wrist and looked at his watch—"thirty-three minutes. Get over there and talk to him."

Angel took the paperwork, and we headed back out the door without a word. He started reading through the paperwork once we were back in the car, then grunted and sucked his teeth.

"What is it?"

"We have to stick to questions about the case only. Nothing about his background is allowed."

"So we can't ask him about California Medico? Or even his current practice?"

"Nope."

"Great."

Twenty minutes later, we pulled up to a futuristic building with a tasteful sign that read Pfeiffer Elite Psychiatric Institute. I parked in the well-kept parking lot, and we entered the building. Following the signs, we headed for Pfeiffer's office. It looked as though he had a few other psychiatrists working there as well, but his office was on the top floor of the building. I assumed it was because he thought that meant he was the most important.

We stepped out of the elevator into an aesthetically appealing reception area where a woman sat behind a curved desk in the center of the room. There were black leather couches set up around the room with plants between them and coffee tables with magazines in front of them. Angel and I headed for the desk.

I flashed my badge. "Detectives Kendrick and Reyes to see Dr. Pfeiffer."

"Please have a seat, Detectives. I'll let him know you're here." She directed us to one of the couches with a hand flourish and then picked up the phone.

We chose a couch and sat down as she murmured into the phone. It was another ten minutes before her phone buzzed, and she looked up at us with a pasted-on smile that didn't quite reach her eyes.

"He'll see you now." She nodded toward a doorway where the door clicked open.

Angel and I rose and headed for the door. I took in the room we'd entered. It held a plush light-brown fainting couch and two comfortable chairs placed in a group setting in one corner near the huge glass windows. In the far corner was a large, dark wood desk, where Dr. Pfeiffer was seated in an ergonomic office chair.

"Detectives, please have a seat." He gestured to the hard chairs in front of his desk.

"Good morning, Dr. Pfeiffer. Thank you for seeing us," I said as I sat.

"You didn't give me much choice." His voice was snide and cold.

"Yes, well, this is a murder investigation, and you were married to the victim, sir."

"Be that as it may, I haven't been involved with her for quite some time, as I am sure you're well aware. And thanks to her Dixon magic, I don't even have access to the twins anymore."

"Yes, about that. You do still speak to the boys, correct?"

He glared at me. "I am permitted phone calls, yes. However, that is all I am allowed."

"Sir, we wanted to ask you about the twins—"

"As I've just said, Detective, I don't see them."

"Yes, I'm aware." I nodded. "What my partner was going to ask was whether you believe the twins are capable of murder."

He shrugged, acting rather disinterested and matter-of-fact about the question, as though the twins were objects instead of people. "I don't know what they are or are not capable of. They are not my problem anymore. I've washed my hands of them. They are that bitch's problem now."

I arched a brow at him. His behavior and words left me surprised. I had imagined him being outraged at the question, but that wasn't the reaction we'd gotten. "Were they a problem before?"

"Look, Detective, the boys had many issues when I was allowed in their lives. I did my best to help them. However, my former wife and her sister interfered, and as I said, my parental rights were taken away with their legal witchcraft." He glared at us with a self-satisfied smirk on his lips.

"Sir, we are aware that you spoke to Milgram just minutes prior to Audrina's death. Can you tell me what that conversation was about?"

"No."

"Excuse me?" I stared at him. "Sir—"

"The conversation was just one of those typical calls, Detective. Me trying to connect with him, and his rebuffing me as only a fourteen-year-old can. There was nothing of substance to it, and therefore nothing for me to say."

I pursed my lips. The man was as slippery as an eel and danced around everything I'd asked.

"Sir, what can you tell us about their aunt?" Angel asked.

I glanced over at him, wondering what he was up to.

"Who? Flora? That bitch always has her nose where it doesn't belong. She's the reason Audrina and I divorced in the first place. She spread lies about me and my business, poisoned Audrina against me. The boys too for that matter. She wanted them for herself, and now she has them."

"You do realize that if we charge the boys with their mother's death, they'll be tried as adults and face, at minimum, life in prison? They'll grow up behind bars," I said, trying to gauge his reaction.

He shrugged. "If they did kill their mother, then perhaps that is what they deserve. Maybe it will finally straighten them out."

How could a father convince his children to commit murder, then deny the fact that he's behind it all? The only explanation was the man was cold-hearted and evil. I knew I shouldn't, but I had to explore what the housekeeper had told me. "Sir, what was in those 'supplements' you gave the boys? What experiments were you doing on them?"

I'd thought his face was a mask of condescension before, but after a flash of anger—which honestly surprised me given the fact he hadn't shown any emotion before, his expression was more of a sneer. Looking down his nose at us, he rose from his seat. "This interview is now over. Get out."

Angel and I rose from our seats as the door clicked open, Pfeiffer standing there with a look of disgust as we silently left the room. Neither of us said anything until we were out of the building and back in the car.

"Well, that went well," I said, a sarcastic bite to my words.

Angel chuckled. "Let's go grab some milkshakes, yeah?"

"Yeah, good idea." I sighed and turned the car on. "Mel's?" I asked, giving him a sideways look.

"It's over in Hollywood—sure, why not." He grinned.

I pulled onto Santa Monica Boulevard and headed toward Highland. "He was lying," I said.

"Yeah, I picked up on that. There was something about that phone call he doesn't want us to know about."

I nodded as I made the turn on Highland toward Hollywood Boulevard. "But what could he have on those boys to get them to murder their mom?" I shook my head. "It doesn't make sense."

"I wish we could talk to them."

"Me too." I pulled into Mel's parking lot.

We both ordered thick, old-fashioned milkshakes and drank them in the car. I couldn't help but think about those boys and everything they'd been through with a father like Dr. Pfeiffer. How he'd drugged them, possibly with hallucinogens and various other controlled substances.

"Flora's a biochemist, right?"

Angel nodded as he sucked on his straw. "Yeah."

"And Audrina presented evidence that Pfeiffer was abusing the boys, possibly that they were drugged?"

"Yeah, that was in the court records, the abuse I mean, I didn't see any allegations of him drugging them, though."

"But if she and Audrina did think they were being drugged, did Flora run blood tests? Is that how she knows what Pfeiffer was doing to them?"

"Maybe so, but then why not report it?" Angel questioned.

"Maybe because Audrina used it to blackmail him into giving up custody?" I looked over at Angel. "You heard him say they used 'magic' and 'witchcraft' to get their way... What if he's really saying they forced his hand with proof of what he'd been doing?"

"That is a definite possibility. How does it help us though?"

"What if those drugs did something to their brains?"

"We really need to talk to Dr. Glenn to see if that is even possible."

"Yeah, what time are we supposed to meet him?"

"Tomorrow afternoon, four thirty."

"Wish it were today. I feel like we're losing time." I frowned. "Like the waters are getting muddier the longer this drags out."

Angel nodded. "You're not wro—"

The police radio on my dashboard crackled to life. "All officers in the Central Hollywood vicinity, we've got a possible code 187 at North Cherokee Avenue and Fountain."

I grabbed the radio, knowing that it would come to homicide anyway, as that code meant a possible murder.

"Detectives Kendrick and Reyes checking in; we're in the area and en route."

"Copy that, Detective Kendrick."

I set my shake in my cupholder while Angel pulled the siren out and set it on the dashboard. I pulled out of the parking lot and switched the siren on as we made our way to the scene.

21

STALKER OR PARANOIA

MARCY

Angel and I spent most of the day chasing down the man who'd murdered three people at a boutique over some credit card charges. An argument had escalated and turned into a shooting, resulting in the death of two employees and the man's wife, who had started the whole thing. There were days when I thought this world was going to hell in a handbasket; tempers were just in the red all the time with so many people.

By the time we'd returned to the station, it was after five, but we still had to file our report. After that, we decided to call it a night. I dropped Angel at home and then headed to Stephen's to take care of his fish and water his plants before driving home. It was still light out, so I decided to go for a run. I hadn't been in a while, so I changed into my workout clothes, moved my Glock to a concealed holster beneath my T-shirt, tied on my running shoes, grabbed my phone and my keys, and headed out of my apartment building.

I looked around as I stretched, taking note of my

surroundings. A woman could never be too careful. I started with a jog and then transitioned into a run. When I crossed the street, I noticed a white sedan with a man in dark glasses driving past me. A couple of minutes later, I passed by the same car, as it had pulled into a parking space on the opposite side of the street.

I kept running, enjoying the burn in my muscles. I traveled a couple more blocks, finally letting some of the stress of the day, of the week, go. As I ran toward the street I was going to turn into, the white sedan passed me again. I frowned and turned the corner, but it kept going straight. Five minutes later, I saw it again. This time coming toward me. It must have gone around the block and turned back.

I was starting to get paranoid. Was I really seeing the same white car? Or was my brain playing some kind of game with me? I decided if I saw it again, I'd check out the license plate and make a mental note of it. That would tell me if I was actually being paranoid or if I'd suddenly acquired a stalker.

I had a sense of unease when the car returned, coming up from behind me, then holding steady alongside me, moving slower than regular traffic. I did my best to pretend that I wasn't paying attention to them. When the car passed, I noted the plate number, memorizing it by repeating it in my head multiple times. Once they were much farther away, I pulled out my phone and typed the number into a memo, saving it.

Putting my phone away, I decided to take a circuitous route to my apartment building, zigzagging my way back, running forward and doubling back on a few streets, hoping to throw off whoever this person was. I didn't see the car again for the next twenty minutes and thought I'd been mistaken.

There were a crap ton of white sedans in California, so seeing them wasn't unusual. I was just seeing several that looked alike, that was all. It was all a coincidence, and I was being paranoid. I started to relax again, running and enjoying the burn. However, the tenseness and paranoia returned as I approached my building and saw the very same white sedan parked on the curbside. The license plate matched the one I'd noted.

A chill raced down my spine. I slowed to a fast walk and pulled my phone from my pocket and snapped a picture of the car and its license plate. As I did so, the car pulled out, and the driver took off as though the hounds of hell were after them, going about forty miles over the speed limit. I watched as they swerved around other cars, then disappeared.

I paused outside and looked around again as I stretched, just to be sure they hadn't returned or left someone else out here to watch me. When I was sure they were gone, that I wasn't about to be kidnapped or robbed, I headed inside. My body was exhausted, as was my head, so I took a shower and put on my loungewear before going to the kitchen to fix something to eat.

I vegged in front of the TV for a while, but after eating, all I wanted was to sleep. I turned the TV off and headed to my room, setting the alarm on my phone to wake me for work in the morning. Sliding beneath my sheet and comforter, I let myself relax.

I woke to a shrill sound, groggily looking around in the dark. I realized it was my phone, but it wasn't my alarm. It was a call, but from a ringtone I didn't recognize. I glanced at the clock, seeing it was after one in the morning. Who the hell would be calling me from an unknown number at this hour?

I reached for the phone and hit the answer button. "Hello?"

"Ms. Kendrick, listen to me very carefully—"

I sat up, suddenly wide awake. "Who is this?" I asked, a feeling of ice sliding down my back.

"Never mind who I am. You don't need to know that—"

"Are you the man who was following me earlier?"

"Ms. Kendrick, it is vitally important that you listen to me. Stop investigating Dr. Pfeiffer. Stop looking into his past. If you continue down this path, you are not going to like the results."

"Are you threatening me?"

"I'm only warning you that this path you're on could be fatal to your career, so watch your step, Ms. Kendrick."

"Why are you protecting Dr. Pfeiffer?" I demanded.

"He's not the one I'm protecting. Find another avenue to pursue, Ms. Kendrick. This is your last warning." The man hung up.

Frustrated, I started to dial Angel, but then thought better of it. It wasn't an emergency, and it was nearly one thirty in the morning now. I put my phone down and lay back, hoping to go back to sleep, but it wasn't working. I kept hearing the man's raspy voice in my ear every time I closed my eyes.

By the time the sun rose, I was frustrated and angry. How dare he threaten me. How dare he tell me what to pursue and not pursue. It only made me more determined to follow the line of investigation Angel and I were on. I was up, dressed, and out the door about thirty minutes before I usually was. If this person followed my routine, I was going to change it up as much as possible.

As I headed for the car, I looked around for the white sedan or anyone suspicious, but I didn't see anything out of the ordinary. Even as I drove, I kept an eye out for the sedan. Just in case, I went to a different coffee shop before taking a different route to Angel's.

Once he was in the car, I pointed out his cup in the holder, then pulled onto the street and turned in the opposite direction to the station.

"Where are we going?" he asked as he picked up the cup and looked at the logo. "Did you go somewhere different this morning?"

"Yeah." I pulled my phone from my pocket and handed it to him. "Pull up the pictures."

Angel set the cup down and opened my photo gallery. "What's this?"

"That car was following me last night, and then I got woken up after one a.m. this morning by that guy calling me." I slid my glance toward him. "On my *unlisted* phone number."

"What did he want?"

"Warned me to stop investigating Pfeiffer."

Angel chuckled. "Well, that was the wrong thing to do if he wanted to get you to stop."

I grinned sardonically, my lips twisting up into a smirk. "Right?"

"That was like a dog whistle. Now you're just going to dig your heels in and go deeper."

"You got it. I want to know what Pfeiffer was doing to those boys. I want to know what kind of pills he was giving them. I want to know the effects each pill had on them, and what the long-term effects are of them."

"So do you think this guy was working for Pfeiffer?" he asked.

"I don't know, and I honestly don't care, but I have a feeling he doesn't. There was something off about him. He reminded me of a government spook."

"You're thinking CIA?"

"Maybe." I nodded. "I haven't seen the guy this morning, but it doesn't mean he's not around." I stared into my rearview mirror. "He was pretty damn obvious about tailing me while I was on my run last night. It was like he wanted to put a scare into me. I think that's the same reason he called after one a.m., to throw me off and freak me out."

"You sure you want to keep pushing, Marcy? I mean what if the CIA has a reason for not wanting us to dig into this?"

I swung my head toward him. "This is a murder investigation. The man literally used his sons to murder his ex-wife."

"No, I agree, I am sure he's guilty, but maybe there's another way to go about getting the answers?"

I shook my head. "I want to know everything. I'm not stopping, Angel. This jerkoff isn't going to stop me investigating what needs to be investigated."

"Okay, just checking. You know I've got your back." He took a sip of coffee and made a face as though the coffee was bad. "Next time you're being followed by these guys, call me, okay? I don't like the idea of you out there vulnerable."

"I had my Glock. They weren't going to take me down without a fight." I smirked.

"Don't get cocky, Marce. You know as well as I do what can happen when the shit hits the fan."

I relented and gave him a real smile. "I know. I promise I was careful and extra vigilant. They wouldn't have gotten close to me."

"Good. Still don't like that they followed you though."

"You and me both." I pulled into the precinct, parked, and we headed in to start our day.

22

DISAPPOINTED
MARCY

As we walked in, Jordan was making his way toward our desks. I heaved a sigh. He was the last person I wanted to deal with at the moment. I glanced at Angel and wondered if I had enough time to escape and if he'd mind if I did.

"Kendrick, Reyes, what did you learn from Pfeiffer yesterday? I haven't gotten your report," Jordan accused as he stared at us darkly.

"We got caught up with that triple homicide and didn't have time to write it up. I'll get on it now," I answered with a long-suffering sigh.

"You should have stayed and gotten it written up last night." Jordan was seething. "The chief is all over me on this one. They want answers; they want arrests, Kendrick. What's the holdup?"

"Look, I understand, but we're working the case just like we would any other. We're not cutting corners. Everything at this point is circumstantial, but I hope to have some more answers soon. As to the meeting with Pfeiffer, the guy is hinky. He's hiding things from us, and we are doing our best to uncover what those things are."

Jordan huffed. "End of the week, Kendrick. You have until then to get this wrapped up."

"But—" I started to complain, knowing he was giving me barely a day.

"I don't want to hear it. I want an arrest on the books by end of the day Friday."

I glanced at Angel, and we both nodded. If I needed more time, I'd go above Jordan's head to the captain. I wasn't going to let Jordan dictate things. Especially on this case with two young boys' lives hanging in the balance. We needed to find out exactly what happened and how.

"And I want that report on my desk in an hour," he said over his shoulder as he headed back to his office.

I sank into my chair and turned on the computer. "I'll start the report; can you look up the license plate of that sedan?" I asked, looking over at Angel.

"Sure, give me your phone?"

I passed it to him, then got busy typing up the report on our meeting with Pfeiffer, adding in all the questions I had since leaving his office, and what we'd be looking into further. I wondered if the boys were still taking the pills their dad had supplied them with. And if they were, why? Did they even know what they were taking? Did anyone?

I hit save and then print on the report. Getting up, I went to the printer to grab two copies of it. I handed them to Angel to look over and sign. "Anything I need to add or change?" I asked.

"Looks good to me." He signed them with a flourish, then handed them back. "The sedan is registered to a Mark Atwell, a CPA who lives in West Hollywood. It wasn't reported stolen, nor is it missing. He claimed it was sitting in his driveway, where he parked it after work yesterday morning, and it was there when he got up to go to work this morning. Nobody borrowed it either."

"Well, somebody was certainly driving it yesterday, unless—" I stopped and looked at him. "Did he check to see if the license plate was actually his?"

"You think someone switched plates?"

I nodded. "Can you check?"

"Sure, but it might not help."

"Why?"

"Because if the plate is correct, then we have two options. Either his car was stolen and returned, which seems unlikely, seeing as he didn't think it had gone missing at all, or his plate was stolen and returned."

I sighed, feeling disappointed. "You're right. Either way, we won't know who was following me."

"Which makes me believe we are dealing with someone connected," Angel replied.

"Probably so." I paused, report in hand, trying to figure out my next move. "Okay, keep digging into Pfeiffer. Research California Medico, see what he did for them, and if any of the projects were for the CIA or any other government project. I also want to know what drugs he was working on or with."

"You've got it." Angel nodded and turned back to the computer.

I set one of the reports on my desk, signed the other, and headed toward Jordan's office to drop it off. Knocking on the door, I said, "Here's the report you asked for," and held it out to him.

"Just put it there." He nodded toward the inbox on his

desk and then looked up at me. "Just got a call from the officer we put on the hospital. The twins have been released. I think you need to set up another interview. Find out what they know."

"Great. I'll call the aunt and get that set up." I turned and walked out of his office.

Back at my desk, I picked up my phone and dialed Flora's home number. Shelby answered, and a moment later, Flora came on the line.

"What is it now, Detective?" she asked, sounding exasperated.

"Ms. Dixon, I understand the boys are back home now?"

"Yes, but they're very fragile, Detective."

"I am sure they are, Ms. Dixon. However, we still need to speak with them. We've had more questions pop up, and it is necessary to pursue them. You do want to know what happened to your sister, right?"

"Yes, of course I do." She sighed. "Very well, we can set up an interview for next week sometime."

My jaw locked. I wanted to speak to them today or tomorrow at the latest. "Can we not do this sooner?"

"Detective, as I said, they are still fragile; they aren't speaking. They barely acknowledge me. Please, give them some more time."

I knew Jordan wasn't going to like it, but we needed these answers. I just had to hope I could talk to the captain and get him to see things my way. "Very well. We'll set up a time for next week. Would Monday suit?"

"No, they have therapy on Monday, maybe Tuesday?" she asked.

"Fine. Tuesday." I knew I was going to have a fight on my hands with Jordan and probably everyone else higher up, but I couldn't push this. There were extenuating circumstances that I needed to sort out prior to making any arrests, namely how Pfeiffer managed to get the boys to do his bidding. For that, I was going to need to talk to Glenn.

I hung up and turned to Angel. "That didn't go as planned."

"What happened?" Angel asked over his shoulder.

I relayed what she'd said.

Angel turned toward me, his lips pursed.

I nodded, already knowing what he was going to say. "I know."

"He's going to be pissed."

"Yeah. I know that. But we've got to figure this out, and if the boys can't answer the questions, and we charge them, they're going to get off on mental deficiency charges. I want their puppet master, and again, if we charge them now, without having that information, we'll never get it."

"I'm the choir you're preaching to; you need to justify it to Brasswell." Angel started to turn back to his computer just as his phone rang. "Reyes," he said as he picked it up. He looked over at me and pressed his lips in a hard line. "Yeah, that is too bad. I'm sorry to hear that. Does he know when he'll be back?"

A feeling of dread filled me at those words. I wasn't sure whom Angel was speaking to, but I knew it wasn't good.

"Okay, we'll want to see him as soon as possible on Monday; can you squeeze us in?"

I wondered again whom he was speaking about, but the only name I could come up with was Dr. Glenn. Were we being cancelled on?

"Yes, that will work." Angel hung up and looked at me. "Glenn had to cancel on us for today. His brother was in an accident down in Santa Monica. He's gone to help his sister-in-law for the weekend and is supposed to be back in the office on Monday. His secretary is going to get us in between patients."

"Well, that's just great." I squeezed the bridge of my nose. *Can this day get any more disappointing?* I wondered.

"Sorry, Marce."

"Not your fault; it is what it is. We'll just have to keep working the case as best we can until we get the answers we need. I do have one option I can try," I murmured, considering what Stephen had told me.

"What's that?"

"My brother mentioned a guy at the facility who knows something about all this mind-control stuff. I'm thinking maybe he can enlighten me about some of it."

Angel looked at me skeptically. "You want to discuss mind control with a person who's had a mental breakdown?"

"Stephen said he's ex-CIA, or he at least claims to be ex-CIA. Maybe he'll have worked with Pfeiffer."

I could see the look of doubt on his face, and I knew before he spoke what he was going to say.

"I don't know, Marce, it doesn't sound like a good idea. Not only could you be hindering the guy's recovery, but you could also be muddying the waters of the case."

"I'm just going to talk to him. See what he can tell me. I'm not saying I'm going to give his name to the DA to call as a witness, Angel." I rolled my eyes. "I just need information that I can't find online, and Glenn isn't available until next week. I feel like I need to be doing something. I want to nail that bastard Pfeiffer to the wall, and right now I don't have the evidence to do it because I'm not sure what I need to be looking into."

"Just be careful, Marce, that's all I'm saying." With that, Angel turned back to his computer.

Sighing, I picked up the phone and called Shine View. I hit the extension to connect me to Stephen's room and waited for him to pick up.

"Hello?"

"Stephen, hi," I said.

"Oh, hi. Aren't you at work?"

I smiled at his surprise. "Yes, but I wanted to call and give you a heads-up. I'm coming by to see you after I get off."

"What? No. Marcy, that's not necessary."

"It is, Stephen. I spoke to your nurse. I know you're ashamed about being there, but you shouldn't be. You're getting the help you need, and that's what is important. I am your sister, and I love you. I want to support you. I also miss you, so I'm coming by to see you and give you a hug. I don't care what you look like, and I don't care if you aren't your normal self. And I'm not taking no for an answer. Besides, there's something I kind of need your help with."

"Okay. It's not like I can stop you, I guess." He sighed.

I laughed. "You're right, you can't. I'll be by in a few hours."

"I'll see you then."

23

THEY'RE WATCHING
MARCY

I managed to avoid Jordan for the rest of the day, mainly because he was called away to a meeting with the captain and deputy chief of police. Better them than me. I really had to wonder why exactly I'd wanted Jordan's job in the first place. It seemed all it had done was turn him into a bigger asshole, and he spent all his time in meetings and wrapped up in paperwork. He hardly ever got out on the job and rarely visited any crime scenes.

I was more of a hands-on kind of person. I wanted to be in the thick of it. I wanted to find and catch the bad guys. Which included Pfeiffer, who I knew was guilty of this murder, even if he wasn't physically there. Every fiber in my body told me the man was behind it, but I had no proof. Every thread I pulled, I ran into a knot that I had to unravel, and that took time. Time Jordan didn't want to give me. I could feel the pressure closing in on me to complete the case, but I was doing everything I could to push back and make sure I did it right.

My reason for visiting Stephen was kind of twofold. First,

I could check on him and see for myself how he was really doing. Phone calls just weren't enough. He could fake those. Make me think he was doing better than he was. He couldn't do it in person so much. Second was so he could introduce me to the conspiracy-theorist guy he was there with.

I pulled into Shine View and went through their visiting process at the clinic. Fifteen minutes later, I was led to a common room, where Stephen was brought to meet me. It was a nice large room that held a few tables and chairs, a couple of sofas and chairs arranged together so that family members could sit and talk with their loved ones, as well as a section set off around a television, where several residents sat watching a movie that looked like a Disney cartoon.

I'd taken a seat on one of the sofas instead of at a table. It looked as though the tables were used for various activities like board games, puzzles, and crafts. There was a nearby bookshelf with boxed games, puzzles, and crafting supplies. I didn't want to take up space there if someone wanted to come in and do one of those things.

Stephen entered the room. He looked embarrassed as he stepped forward and opened his arms for a hug. "Hey," he murmured in my ear. "You look good. Stressed though."

I sighed softly as I hugged him back. He felt skinnier than I could ever recall him being. I pulled back and looked at him again. His eyes were clear, and he didn't seem as manic as he'd been in the past. "You look good too."

He gave me a wry smile. "No, I don't. I've lost weight and muscle tone."

"Maybe, but you seem less stressed and anxious. You can build that muscle back up. Don't they have a gym here?" I asked, looking around.

Stephen shook his head. "No, I'll have to go to the gym

when I get out of here. Doesn't help that the chef keeps the food so bland that I don't want to eat it."

I frowned. "Why bland?"

"Because there's so many food allergies and different tastes here, I guess. So they just make it all gross; that way we all have something to complain about," he said with a laugh.

I laughed too, then smiled at him. "Come sit and tell me how you really are."

He joined me on the sofa, and we talked for a little while about his therapy and how he was doing. I asked him what had happened to trigger his panic attack, and he finally said, "I had a dream about Mom. It felt so real..." His voice turned to a soft whisper, and he looked down at his hands folded in his lap.

I reached over and put my hand on top of his. "Stephen," I murmured, "what Mom did to you wasn't your fault. You know that, right? You were a kid, and she should never have touched you. I hate that she did that to you. That she was a... pedophile." I choked on the word, but I got it out.

I hadn't known Mom was abusing him. He'd kept it from me until recently. I'd always put Mom on a pedestal, sure, she was a hooker, but she'd treated me like a princess, and I'd thought she'd hung the moon. It really sucked when those we loved the most were found to be monsters. It made me never want to trust anyone ever again.

"I know," he murmured without looking at me, keeping his voice low. "I never wanted you to know. I thought I could just bottle that shit up and keep it from you, keep you from knowing how awful she was, but—"

I squeezed his hand. "No. I'm glad I know. You've always been there to protect me, but I'm a grown-up, and I needed to know, and I need to be here to help you. I want to be here.

If Mom were alive, I would throw her ass in jail for what she did to you. She doesn't get a pass because she gave birth to me."

Stephen's lips quirked up at that. "Mind if we talk about something else? I mean, I get enough talking about this crap with Dr. Faulkner and the group, really don't want to rehash it all, you know?"

I smiled. "Yeah, I get it."

"How is work? Have you made an arrest on the case you were working on?"

I shook my head. "I haven't yet. In fact, that's actually one of the things I wanted your help with. Remember when you were talking about the guy in your group who says he's ex-CIA?"

"Watson? What about him?"

"I was hoping you could introduce me to him."

"You know he's not really ex-CIA, right? He's delusional, Marce."

"Yeah, I didn't think he actually was, but some of the stuff you mentioned has come up in this case, and if he's that deep into the conspiracies, I thought maybe he'd know some stuff that I haven't been able to find. I'm meeting with a guy next week who is versed in deprogramming cult members, but I need some information now. This case is driving me up the wall. I keep running into roadblocks." Not to mention the probably real CIA who were trying to get me to stop digging into Pfeiffer, but I wasn't going to mention that to Stephen. I didn't want him to freak out on me over it.

"Okay, he's over there, the paranoid guy who keeps looking around the room as if he's being watched." Stephen nodded toward a thin, very pale, high-cheekboned and spindly-fingered man with red hair and blue eyes. Stephen stood up and walked over to the man, leaned down and spoke to him, then looked over at me.

I waved and tried to smile at the man, but he was looking at me as though I were there to kill him. I dropped my hand back to my lap and waited.

After a very hushed conversation, Stephen returned to me with Watson a step or two behind him. "Watson, meet my sister, Marcy. Marcy, this is Watson."

"Nice to meet you," I murmured, holding out my hand.

Watson stared at it as if I were trying to poison him. Then folded his arms and shoved his hands under his armpits. He gave me a nod, but looked distrustful.

"Please, will you sit and talk to me for a moment?" I asked.

He looked around the room and then chose the plush seat next to the sofa. "He says you're a cop."

"Yes," I acknowledged. "Would you like to see my badge?"

"They can be faked."

"Probably so, but mine's real."

"That's what you'd say if it was faked." He stared at me.

I nodded. "True. How about this, do you have a phone?"

"No. They can track you on those."

"Right. Okay, I'll pull it up on mine, and you can watch me do it."

"What are you pulling up?" He looked at me suspiciously, his eyes narrowed in distrust.

I smiled. "LAPD Homicide Special Section Unit personnel photos." I turned the phone so he could see what I was doing; then I showed him my picture. "See? Detective Third Class Marcy Kendrick, and that's my picture."

Taking the phone, he looked at it and then me. He gave me a nod. "Okay, I believe you."

I took my phone back and swallowed the smile I was trying to hide. "Thank you."

"Why do you want to talk to me? I could get into a lot of trouble for talking to you." He kept his voice soft as his eyes darted around the room, as if looking for someone or something.

"My brother mentioned that you know a lot about MK Ultra and about mind control. I wanted to ask how it works. This case I'm on, it has been proposed that the perpetrators might have been under the influence of some sort of mind control, and I don't know if that's even possible, or if they are responsible for their actions. I want to make sure all those involved pay the price for the crime."

He nodded and seemed to think about what I was saying. Again, his eyes darted around the room with suspicion before he leaned in toward me. "I can tell you that one of the processes the CIA has been striving to perfect since the days of MK Ultra is mind control."

"So this is still going on? They didn't drop it after MK Ultra came to light?"

He shook his head. "No. They've pursued it under various different names, but their ultimate goal is to create soldiers they can control to do whatever they want."

"How are they doing this?"

Watson looked around the room again, his eyes darting in every direction as he leaned forward even more as though what he was about to say was top secret. "Subjects' personalities are either destroyed or temporarily pushed aside by a fugue state they are conditioned to enter into when a command phrase is used. The subject is then what they call a *tabula rasa*. The CIA can program them to do anything: spy, steal, sabotage, or even kill."

"So they're using these subjects to spy? To kill people?" I asked in disbelief.

Watson looked at me intensely, his blue eyes shining in a manic way as he nodded. "All the time."

"But how do they achieve this kind of thing? How do they set it up to trigger the subject to do their bidding? I mean when they want them to do whatever they are programed to do?"

"They use both drugs and mental conditioning to achieve their goals. It's triggered by a word or phrase that their controllers have. It's not something likely to be used in their everyday lives; it is usually something obscure."

I wanted to ask more, but Watson seemed to grow visibly agitated and jumped to his feet. "Watson," I started, trying to calm him down.

"Can't say any more. Shouldn't have said anything." He fidgeted as he spoke, his words coming out in a hiss. "They're watching. I've got to get out of here." With that, he rushed from the room, looking over his shoulder as if a ghost were after him.

I glanced at my brother. "Well," I began, "that was... informative." And it was, but also very odd. "He's a bit of a strange fellow."

"Yeah, I tried to warn you. The guy is paranoid. Thinks the CIA is here watching him twenty-four seven."

I scratched my head and slid my gaze back to him. "I kind of understand that feeling, seeing as I've had an agent watching me." It felt like I was being watched right at that moment, and it made me feel uneasy. I let my gaze travel the room before landing back on Stephen.

"You've what?" Stephen stared at me, shock on his face.

I wished I could take the words back, but it was too late now. "Sorry, yeah. I'm pretty sure there's a CIA agent following me, or maybe just taking an interest in the case, I'm not sure. But I was followed, and he's called me, warning me away from this aspect of the case," I explained, hoping he'd let it go.

"Marce, promise me you'll be careful. These guys are nothing to mess around with."

I smiled and patted his hand. "I know that. And I'll be careful. Promise."

I just hoped I could actually keep that promise.

24

RANDOM OR NOT-SO-RANDOM EVENTS

MARCY

As I exited the Shine View building and walked to my car, the hairs on the back of my neck and my arms rose. I felt a prickly sensation over my skin, as though something or someone was watching me. I quickened my pace, my keys in my hand as I moved across the parking lot. I hit the button to unlock the doors and scrambled into my car. Once inside, I hit the button to relock it. My hand shook as I fumbled with the key, trying to get it in the ignition.

I could feel my heart racing in my chest. I had no idea what was spooking me, but that was what it felt like. As though I were being haunted. I turned the car on and sat there for a moment, trying to get my breathing under control. I needed to calm down. I was safe, and nothing was after me. I had no idea why I suddenly felt as though I was in mortal danger. It didn't make any sense.

I'd been in grave danger before. I knew what that felt like for real. This was just paranoia, wasn't it? All from my talk with Watson. Perhaps I was picking up on some of his suspicions. Maybe somehow, they'd bled into me, and I was just reflecting how he must have felt when he rushed from the room. After a few deep breaths, I was able to back out of the parking spot and pull out onto the street.

It wasn't quite dark yet, but it was getting there, and many drivers had put on their headlights. As I turned the corner, I noticed the car two car lengths behind me did the same. Not a big deal, it was a popular roadway, still... something was bothering me. Just to test my paranoia, I made a random left turn, then watched my rearview mirror. The car made the same turn.

That freaked me out.

I pressed on the gas, picking up speed, my eyes on the rearview mirror instead of on the road. I switched lanes without signaling, swung a right and then another left. The car stuck with me. I was panicking now. I stared at the headlights of the car behind me as I pressed even harder on the gas. I was well over the speed limit now, not paying particular attention to where I was going. I was just making random turns, trying to lose this guy.

That was when it happened.

I heard the crash before I felt the airbag explode in my face, though it all occurred within milliseconds of each other. I slammed forward into the airbag, then into the back of my seat. My body hurt, and I felt the breath get knocked out of me. Everything in me screamed in pain. My legs felt like they'd been jarred back into my hips. My hands and arms had flown back along with the rest of me upon impact, my left hand hitting the window with enough force to be slashed open on the broken glass that had shattered in the crash. I could feel pieces of it embedded in my forearm and hand.

"Ma'am? Are you alright?" a voice from outside asked.

I couldn't really answer that. I wasn't even sure if my voice worked at this point. I was still in a bit of a daze.

"The police are on their way, ma'am; can you move? We should get you out of there if we can," the same voice continued. "There's fluid leaking from under the car."

I realized he was thinking the car might explode. I wanted to do as he said and get out and forced myself to look at the man. He was young, maybe in his early twenties. He had blond hair and blue eyes and a concerned look on his face.

"I'm going to open the door and see if I can help you out, okay?" he said, his voice calm.

"Okay," I croaked, keeping my eyes on him.

The door opened, and I watched him pull a knife from his pocket. He sliced into the airbag, deflating it, and then shoved it out of the way, toward the dashboard.

I could feel the blood trailing down my arm. I had no idea how bad the rest of me looked.

"Do you think anything is broken? How is your neck?"

I blinked, trying to assess my injuries. I slowly turned my neck. "I think it's okay. I don't think anything's broken," I replied, but my voice was still craggy.

"I'm going to slip my arm behind you and wrap it around your waist. I'll help you out and bring you over to the curb where we can see how hurt you are."

I nodded and felt him do exactly what he'd said. A moment later, we were moving from my car to the opposite side of the street. He helped me sit down on the curb facing my car. I could see I'd run straight into another car, and I was terrified that I'd hurt someone. "Is there anyone in there?" I whispered.

"No, the car was parked. You came around that corner really fast and slammed right into it. It shouldn't have happened, the car was illegally parked, but you were going over the speed limit."

I tried to recall exactly what I'd been doing. I had been watching my mirror instead of the road... I'd been followed. I turned my gaze to the man. "Did another car follow behind me? Where did it go?" I looked around, hoping I'd see it.

"There was a white sedan that came around the corner after you, and they slowed for a moment, then took off that way." He pointed down the street.

"Where were you?" I asked, still trying to get a feel for what had happened.

"I was sitting on my porch, right there." He nodded behind me. "Saw the whole thing."

I could hear the police sirens as they made their way toward us. It wasn't long before a couple of patrol officers, a fire truck and an ambulance had joined us. I reached in my pocket and pulled out my badge, holding it up for the first officer who approached me. It turned out to be Officer Kim, and I smiled at seeing him, or at least I tried to. I wasn't quite sure if I was successful at it.

"Kendrick? What the hell happened?"

I explained that I had just left Shine View, where I'd been visiting my brother, and that when I pulled from the parking lot, someone started following me. "I was following procedure, trying to shake the tail, but I didn't see the parked car when I turned the corner."

"Why did you think you had a tail?" Officer Kim asked.

"It's this case I'm on." I looked around, once again feeling like I was being watched. Maybe I was. There were a lot of officers on the scene. The fire department was spraying down my car with something, I assumed to keep it from going up in flames, and the EMTs were loitering nearby. I was sure they were waiting to get the nod from Officer Kim that it was okay to come over and treat me.

"What about this case? Which case?"

"The Audrina Dixon murder," I replied. "I've been digging into stuff, and I think I've attracted the attention of the CIA."

Officer Kim scoffed. "You sound paranoid."

I shrugged and then groaned at the pain of it.

"Okay, well, your car's pretty damaged; you won't be driving it. You should probably go with the medics to get checked out." He waved them over.

I nodded.

"And I'll need a statement from you, sir," he said to the young man who'd helped me. "What's your name?"

"Liam Winters," the blond-haired guy answered. "I live right there."

"Ma'am, will you come with us?" one of the EMTs said, squatting down next to me. "Can you stand?"

"I think so," I replied as he helped me to my feet. I went with him to the ambulance, now out of earshot of Liam and Kim since we'd moved too far away.

After being assessed, they decided I did need to go to the hospital, but before we went, I made sure someone grabbed my purse and anything official from the car like my police radio and the siren. I'd need them for work. Kim arranged to have a wrecker come and pick up my car, then handed me my apartment keys, leaving the car key with the car. He'd also found the driver of the illegally parked car, gotten their insurance information, and ticketed them for their illegal parking job. Since they were illegally parked, technically the damage done wasn't my fault, and they'd have to take it up with their insurers. Unfortunately, even though it was a blind corner, I was still partially at fault for the damage to my own car. Kind of like hitting a deer, I was going to take a hit on my car insurance.

As I sat in the ambulance, I went through my purse. Thankfully, nothing in it, including my phone, had been damaged. We arrived at the hospital, and I was taken to the ER. As I wasn't exhibiting any signs of distress, I had to sit and wait my turn, which took about an hour. I was pretty sure they'd slid me in faster than they should have since there were other people more injured than I was, but I wasn't about to complain. All my test results came back; they pronounced me good to go and said they'd get my release papers ready.

I called and arranged a car rental, and they picked me up from the hospital. I would have called Angel, but he still couldn't drive, and there wasn't really anyone else I felt comfortable enough to call. Besides, I was going to need a car for work.

As I got behind the wheel of the blue Nissan Rogue, I thought about just driving and not stopping, disappearing from this life, going somewhere far, far away. Somewhere this CIA spook couldn't find me.

The problem was, I didn't know if there was a place that he wouldn't find me. The CIA seemed to have information that wasn't accessible to anyone else on the planet. And it didn't seem like they had any qualms about killing people. I didn't want to be one of these people, but I also didn't want to quit the case. I needed to see it through. I needed to get justice for Audrina.

I couldn't run away.

It was late when I finally got home. I pulled into my apartment parking lot and looked around for the white sedan. I didn't see it, but that didn't mean the driver wasn't there somewhere, waiting to ambush me. My whole body ached as I climbed from the car and limped toward the building as quickly as possible. I was one massive bruise, and all I wanted was to soak in a hot bath full of Epsom salt.

I locked my apartment door, dropped my keys on the table next to my purse and kicked off my shoes. I shrugged off my blazer and yelped at the ache that caused. Making my way to the bathroom, I turned the water on high in the bathtub, then poured in a generous amount of the bath salt.

As the bath filled, I remembered I'd left my phone in my purse, and returned to the entryway to get it. I switched my notifications on and realized I'd had a few missed calls from Angel. I dialed voicemail and listened to him telling me to call him as soon as possible, then headed back to the bathroom and shut off the water.

I finished undressing and sank into the tub before calling him.

"You heard?"

"Are you all right? Do you need me to come over there? Are you still in the hospital? What the hell happened, Marce?"

There were too many questions for me to answer, let alone keep track of. "I'm okay."

"Do you need me?" he said, his voice deep and growly.

"No, I'm okay, Angel. I hit a parked car; my airbag did its job. I'm sore though."

"I can grab an Uber and be there in twenty minutes."

"Thank you, but no. I'm okay. I even drove myself home. I'm in the bath, and nothing's broken. I'm just banged up."

"You're sure?"

"Yeah, I'm sure."

"What the hell happened?"

I sighed and explained. "It was just an accident. The car was parked illegally, too close to the corner. It was random."

"You could have been killed."

"I'm fine, Angel."

"I mean with that guy following you, why didn't you call it in?"

"I thought I was being paranoid," I whispered into the phone. "I mean, sure, he was following me, but—"

"It might not have been random, Marce; what if he was trying to spook you into doing something that would get you killed?"

I didn't know how to answer that.

"I'm just worried about you, okay?" His voice held concern and had an ache to it I'd never heard before. "I don't want to lose you, Marcy."

Sighing, I smiled. "You're not getting rid of me that easily, Reyes." I used his last name to remind him I was his partner, not his wife. We weren't going to pursue that kind of relationship. We were co-workers, friends. I didn't want to screw that up. I knew he didn't either.

"Good. I'd hate to have to train a whole new partner." He chuckled. "Get some rest, okay? And if you need anything, call me."

"Yeah, okay."

We hung up, and I leaned back in the tub, my eyes closed. I felt myself drifting, my muscles unwinding, unknotting.

I was on the edge of sleep when my phone rang, the shrill sound of a new number's ringtone blaring into the quiet of the bathroom.

I sat up, sloshing water around, but thankfully not onto the floor, and grabbed my phone. "Hello?"

"Marcy?" My brother's voice was shaking, and he sounded really upset.

I frowned. I hadn't recognized the ringtone when he called. I wondered what was going on and why he was upset. "Stephen, what's wrong?"

"It's Watson."

Suddenly I felt a chill race down my back. "What about him?"

"He's... he had to be admitted to the hospital. He had an episode; he went crazy... screaming about how they were coming for him," he explained.

"I don't understand; did something trigger that?" I asked as I sat shivering in the now cool water. "Did he have any visitors after I left?"

"No, but he did get a phone call."

"Do you know who it was from?" Another sliver of fear raced over me.

"Nobody knows. He just kept saying it was them. They are always watching, and he should have kept quiet. Marcy, I'm worried."

"He'll be okay. The staff at Shine View are the best; they'll take care of him."

"I know, but I'm worried about you. If he's right... Marcy, what if they come after you?"

I stood up and grabbed a towel, wrapping it around me. "I'm a cop, Stephen. I'm armed. I'll be fine." Even though I said it, I wasn't exactly sure I believed it. Still, I wanted him to believe it, so I kept my nerves from my voice. He didn't need to be worrying about me. He had his own demons to deal with, and I didn't want to add to them. "Promise."

25

WILD THEORIES
MARCY

Sleep didn't come till nearly four a.m., so when my alarm went off at six, I was not only achy, but exhausted. I rolled over and hit the button to turn the blaring sound off. I lay there, not wanting to get up, staring at the ceiling. The only good thing I could say about barely two hours of sleep was that I didn't have any nightmares. At least none that I could recall. No dreams either.

Henry hadn't visited me in my dreams; he didn't come to me and declare me guilty of getting him murdered; he didn't morph into some kind of zombified corpse and try to kiss me. He wasn't there accusing me of not doing my job. I hadn't seen his mutilated face or body. It was nice not having those kinds of things disturbing my rest. I just wished there'd been more of it. Especially after that accident the night before.

I thought back over what had happened. I had been going pretty fast when I'd turned that corner. I'd barely even realized it was a street when I turned onto it. I knew I'd been more focused on the headlights in my rearview mirror. I had been trying to get away from them. The corner itself had one of those large conifer trees on it, you know the kind that looked like Christmas trees? Large and bushy. There wasn't any way for me to have seen the compact car parked three feet from the intersection.

Besides that, the street was narrow. No cars should have been parked on the street. It was just big enough for two lanes of traffic and nothing else. I'd been so out of it that I hadn't even checked to see if there were no-parking signs posted on the street. I'd have to check with Kim. He'd know. It bothered me that I'd been so distracted by that white sedan following me that I'd gotten into an accident. I could have killed someone.

I took a deep steadying breath and willed away the tears that wanted to well up in my eyes. I hadn't hurt anyone but myself. Yes, it could have been worse, but it wasn't. I needed to be thankful for that. I could argue all day that I was following protocol, but deep down, I knew that if I'd hurt someone, killed someone with my reckless driving, I would carry that blame and shame with me forever. I vowed to be more careful in the future. Even if I was being chased all over the city by asshole CIA spooks.

I glanced at the clock again. Only a few minutes had passed since my alarm had gone off, but I needed to get up and start my day. My body felt stiff as I tried to push myself into a sitting position. I could feel every abrasion and bruise from the accident. My left arm itched from the cuts and whatever they'd put on them to close and heal. The bandages would need to be changed.

I grunted as I finally made it to my feet. I was going to

need some painkillers, so I padded to the kitchen and opened the cabinet where I kept various medications, including ibuprofen. I released two into my palm, grabbed a bottle of water from the fridge and downed them. As I headed back to my bedroom to get ready, my phone rang.

It was that unknown caller again. I didn't want to answer it at first, but decided I needed to. I needed to give this guy a piece of my mind. How dare he keep following me, and cause an accident—because yes, he too was to blame for it—and then scare the shit out of Watson.

"You!" I practically growled into the phone. "Who the fuck do you think you are?" The audacity of this man to continue harassing me after last night. I was livid.

"Ms. Kendrick—" he started, not even using my title, knowing full well I was a detective.

"No, seriously, who are you? Why the hell are you following me around the city? Why are you scaring some poor man who's just trying to get his life together? You have no right!" I demanded answers. I was seething with rage, and if the man were in front of me, I wasn't sure what I'd do to him.

"You can call me Agent White. And you didn't heed my warning. I told you to back the fuck off and find another avenue to pursue. Yet still, you are persisting."

"Listen here, Agent White, you are interfering in a murder investigation, and I take my job seriously. As to the avenue I am pursuing, that's up to me, not you. Dr. Pfeiffer is guilty. What kind of father encourages his kids to commit murder and not own up to it? Tell me that. He experimented on those boys, and it's looking more and more as though he used some sort of mind control to get them—"

"Ms. Kendrick, if you continue down this road, you are going to find yourself the laughingstock of the police department. I understand you've already got an enemy in your lieutenant; do you really want to give him another reason to have you fired? Because that's the trajectory you're on. You'll end up just like your brother. Living in a mental institution after a nervous breakdown. Is that what you want? Because I can make that happen." His voice was even, almost monotone, as he threatened me.

"He's guilty as sin and you know it. How can you let him get away with this?" I was so angry I was literally seeing red.

"Go ahead and try to get a coercion charge to stick, but every court in the country will laugh you out of the courtroom if you start bringing up mind control and conspiracy theories. You've got nothing. Your witnesses, if you can even call those boys that considering they're the ones who are the actual murderers, are two mute, psychotic boys, along with a delusional schizophrenic who writes a conspiracy theory blog and tries to kill himself every few months. None of them are credible. You'll get nowhere. No one is going to believe them or you."

I wanted to argue with him, but he did have a point about the boys and Watson. Still, I replied, "Be that as it may, if the CIA ends up with egg on its face, it's because Pfeiffer brought this on you all, not because I've done my job, which is to get to justice for what really happened for the victim."

"You could be right, but you still need to heed my warnings. Nothing you uncover is going to get the outcome you're after. You're going to end up harming yourself and your career if you continue."

"You don't know that—"

"I'm telling you straight out, Detective Kendrick, if you go public with your wild conspiracy theory that Dr. Pfeiffer worked on mind-control projects for the CIA, I personally will make sure everything I've said will happen actually does."

The line went dead, and I wanted to scream. "Fucking bastard."

I was so pissed off I was shaking. I knew Pfeiffer was guilty. Every bone in my body felt it. I had no doubt he had worked with the CIA and then used the knowledge he'd acquired to bend his sons to his will. He'd somehow forced them into committing murder. And not just any murder. He'd used them to murder his ex-wife. Their mother. That was some kind of Machiavellian shit. It was no wonder the boys were mute. They had been terrorized and traumatized by what had happened. They didn't deserve that kind of treatment from the person who was supposed to care about them.

I had to find a way to prove my theory. Even if it did go against the CIA. I didn't give a flying fig if they were shown to be the bad guys. It was obvious that they were in this case. Probably in a million others too. Agent White's threats did bother me though, I was worried he would make what he'd said a reality, but I couldn't let that stop me.

Audrina deserved justice. So did her family.

It was my job to make sure she got it.

I glanced over at the clock and realized I was now running late. It was nearly seven, and I still hadn't gotten ready. I rushed to the bathroom and quickly went through my morning routine in a quarter of the time it usually took me, despite the fact I hurt all over.

I ignored the pain as I dressed, put on my holster, and slid my gun into place. I hurriedly grabbed up my keys and shoved my phone in my purse, then ran out the door, locking it behind me. I didn't bother waiting for the elevator. Instead I took the stairs two at a time, which probably wasn't the best idea considering how much my body hurt, and ran to my rental. I was on the road by fifteen after seven.

26

DISCORD AND EXASPERATION
ANGEL

I didn't sleep at all. All I could see when I closed my eyes was Marcy crushed in a car accident because some asshole government agent didn't want her investigating this murder to the extent that she was. It scared the shit out of me. I wondered how it had even started, where he'd picked her up and started following her. She hadn't mentioned that last night when she'd finally called me back.

Getting that call from Kim last night telling me about the accident had turned my stomach inside out. It wasn't that long ago that I'd been the one in an accident that had upended my life, and to hear that Marcy had been in one... it about killed me.

Kim had said she was okay, she'd been up on her feet and moving around, but that didn't make it any less scary. It was funny that her doing the job every day, going after guys twice her size and three times as mean, didn't faze me, but this was seriously messing with my brain. I knew it probably had to do with the fact that I'd just gone through the same thing, well, near enough anyway, but I couldn't help how I felt.

It made me want to just do what the fucking agent was asking and close the case. Charge the boys and be done with it. I knew Marcy wouldn't be happy. I'd told her I'd have her back. Which I meant. I did have her back. I didn't want her fired. I didn't want another partner. I wanted her. For more than my partner, but I knew that wasn't going to happen. Didn't matter though. It was how I felt. That being said, I figured that having her back in this instance meant protecting her from this agent who was intent on destroying her career. I absolutely didn't want that to happen. She had worked hard to get where she was, and I'd be damned if I let some government spook take it all away from her.

The problem was, I knew Marcy. She was going to be pissed at me. We were going to have an argument. I could already see it coming. I scrubbed a hand down my face as I waited for her to pick me up. I hoped to avoid the argument for as long as possible, but I could feel it coming.

I heard the horn of her rental and hurried out the door. I was still in the boot, but I could take the brace off, so my movements were improving. I only had a few more days of the boot too, and I couldn't wait to be done with it. Right now, it only served to remind me of my accident, which led me to thinking of her being in one last night, which just stirred my anger.

I got into the car without a word, but noticed she hadn't stopped for coffee. Of all the mornings for her not to, today was a crappy day for it. I needed it. Still, I wasn't going to complain. If I opened my mouth about it, it would lead to us arguing sooner.

"You okay?" she asked as she pulled out of my driveway. Her voice sounded unsure, almost curious.

I glanced at her and grunted as I gave her a nod.

"Why do you sound how I feel?" She turned the corner. I knew she was heading toward our regular coffee shop, and I was grateful. "Leg bothered me. Didn't sleep." I was lying. My leg felt fine, but I wasn't about to admit worrying about her had kept me up.

"I didn't get much sleep either, honestly."

I didn't reply to that, and we rode in silence the rest of the way to the coffee shop. After getting the coffees, we stayed quiet as we let the caffeine do its job.

She pulled into the station, and we headed in. I could feel the tension between us. It was like we both knew there was a storm brewing, but I doubted she knew why. I was going to blindside her with it, and I hated that. The problem was, I didn't know how to avoid it. I just knew she would go ballistic the moment I voiced my opinion.

I'd just turned on my computer when she brought it up. "I had another phone call this morning."

I felt the worry and fear of last night fill me again, and I had a hard time keeping my voice calm as I asked, "What did he say?"

"Told me his name, or at least what to call him. Agent White. The bastard threatened me again. Said he'd turn me into a laughingstock if I tried to bring charges against Pfeiffer for coercion."

I clenched my fist in my lap. If I could beat the ever-living shit out of this guy, I would. Still, I had to consider the consequences of what she was saying. The guy had the power to do what he'd threatened. That had me by the nuts, and I hated it. I took a breath, trying to keep calm. "What set him off yesterday? You didn't speak to Pfeiffer again that I know of, did you?"

She shook her head. "I went to see Stephen and one of the guys he's at Shine View with. Remember I was telling you about the conspiracy-theorist guy? Well, he knows a lot about this mind-control stuff, and he confirmed some of the stuff we've been looking into."

I didn't say anything as I processed what she was saying. She spoke to a conspiracy theorist? A guy who thought he was ex-CIA? And then this real spook went after her? There had to be a connection. Maybe the guy really was ex-CIA? That had my stomach clenching harder.

"Anyway, after I got off the phone with you, Stephen called and told me that Watson, that's the guy at Shine View with him, got a phone call and then went a bit off his rocker and had to be admitted to the hospital. It was this Agent White who'd called him, can you believe that?" She swiveled in her chair toward her computer.

What the hell had this guy been up to? Did he threaten Watson? Fear gripped me, and I started breathing hard. "Maybe we need to listen to him and drop this, Marce." My voice was quiet, barely a whisper. I didn't want anyone to overhear.

Marcy whirled around, her chair turning toward me, her eyes wide. "What the fuck? No. I'm not going to drop my investigation at the say-so of this asshole! How can you even suggest such a thing?" she accused, her eyes narrowing into slits as she stared at me, looking as though I'd just betrayed her.

"Marcy, he practically ran you off the road yesterday! You could have been killed! This is not worth it. He'll ruin you, ruin your career. We've got nothing to tie Pfeiffer to the scene. All we have are the boys, and we know they committed the murder. They're guilty, at least partially, even if he did coerce them into it. We can't prove anything. They aren't talking. And getting theories from a paranoid schizophrenic isn't going to help our case!" I was on my feet, my voice rising as I spoke.

I was beyond pissed. I'd lost my temper, and I couldn't reel it back in. I was not only angry at this government spook, but at her for not listening to me and at myself for being angry at her when I knew she was right. And she was. I knew Pfeiffer was as guilty as they came. The problem was knowing it and proving it were two entirely different things.

She stared at me, exasperated, in disbelief. "You know we are clearly dealing with a man who doesn't love his children at all. He has done things to damage their psyches, and he's the only one with a clear motive for wanting to kill Audrina. Pfeiffer wanted revenge because he'd lost their long, bitter, divorce battle. He just bided his time before taking it," she said, poking her finger in my chest.

I knew she was right. Pfeiffer was the only one with a real motive for wanting Audrina Dixon dead. Still, that didn't excuse those boys from committing the act. And without proof of Pfeiffer's involvement, we were tilting at windmills.

I reached for Marcy, putting my hands on her biceps. "None of that matters; we don't have proof. There's no way to prove it since we can't get those boys to talk." I stared into her face, willing her to listen to me.

"What the hell is going on out here?" Jordan shouted, standing on the other side of our desks.

I sighed. I hadn't meant to draw him from his office. I dropped my hands from Marcy and looked over at him.

"Kendrick, get your ass in my office now!" he practically

screamed. His face was as red as a tomato, and he had spittle flying from his lips as he pointed down the hall.

Marcy's chest was heaving, and the look on her face was one of betrayal as she stared at me for another moment. I could see the hurt and anger that lay in her eyes. I regretted causing it, but I was actually trying to protect her. I wished she'd realize that, that I wasn't trying to hurt her. I didn't want to fight with her. I'd tried to hold on to my temper, to convince her, but my fear had gotten the better of me, and now she was going to get her ass chewed by Jordan, who wanted her out of the department. Hell, he wanted her kicked off the force entirely. He'd been gunning for her job since before they'd split.

He didn't care that she was a good cop, an excellent detective. He'd wanted her at home playing the sweet little domestic wifey. The kind who had no thoughts of her own and was subservient to him in all things. When she hadn't complied, he'd gone out and found a barely legal college girl he could bend to his will. Now he just continued as a way to punish her for not doing what he wanted.

Marcy was still staring at me.

"Now!" Jordan raised his voice even louder, seething with more anger than I'd felt toward that government agent. And that was saying a lot.

Suddenly, I was extremely worried about her going to his office. "Jordan—" I started to intervene.

"Shut your mouth, Reyes, not another fucking word." He turned his anger on me.

Fuck.

I looked at Marcy with remorse. I hadn't meant for our argument to draw his attention. If anyone deserved to have

Jordan's wrath aimed at them, it was me. I mouthed, "I'm sorry," to her.

Marcy shook her head and made her way down the hall, her head held high and her shoulders back as though she had every bit of confidence in the world. I admired that about her. No matter what was thrown at her, she always faced it head-on.

Damn, the woman drove me nuts, but I couldn't help but love her.

Jordan tossed me one last glare and then followed Marcy down the hall.

I sat down and dropped my head to my desk. I was an ass. Me letting my fear get in the way of us doing our job might have just cost Marcy hers.

27

BETRAYAL AND JEALOUSY
MARCY

I shook my head at Angel, then turned and strode down the hall without another word.

I was pissed. No, I was so far beyond pissed I didn't know what I felt except for let down, hurt, and disappointed. I couldn't believe that Angel had suggested we drop our investigation into Pfeiffer all because some jerk with the CIA was demanding it. I had tried to explain why I wanted to keep going after Pfeiffer, but Angel was putting up a decent argument. The problem was I didn't want to give up.

I could see Hummel and Vance watching me, as well as a couple of other detectives, as I made my way toward Jordan's office. Of course, they'd heard everything, including Jordan ordering me to his office like a naughty schoolgirl. I lifted my chin and kept my back ramrod straight as I continued down the hall. I turned into his office without a backwards glance.

A moment later, Jordan entered and slammed his door.

I knew it was coming, so I didn't flinch. I wasn't going to give him an inch of satisfaction. I needed to hold on to my temper here. I couldn't let him force me out of the job I loved.

"What the hell do you think you're doing having an argument like that in the office? This is a professional building, and you are acting anything but professional. We deal with the public here, Kendrick. You shouting like a shrew at your partner is not professional," he ranted at me.

I just stared at him, not saying anything.

"Of course, what the fuck else should I expect from you? You are insubordinate to your superiors and sloppy and unprofessional in your work ethic! You're a vigilante cop who doesn't think the fucking rules of the law apply to her! You're a disgrace to the profession, and you shouldn't even be here!"

He was on a roll now and shouting at the top of his lungs. I didn't bother to interrupt and correct him. I couldn't believe he was accusing me of being sloppy and unprofessional in my work ethic. I did nearly everything by the book. My reports were top notch and so was my work. I'd been cleared of every charge he tried to force on me because I actually was a good cop. I never once thought I was above the rules, as he'd accused. I always followed the law. I didn't go out looking for suspects to shoot, as he was alleging.

Internal Affairs had investigated every single shooting I'd been involved in. My record was scrutinized more than any other cop on the force, all because Jordan had a major grudge against me. I didn't even think it really had anything to do with me being a cop. It had to do with me having been his wife. He'd been jealous of my work on the job when we'd been married. He had wanted me to quit.

Of course, I hadn't. I loved my job. When I didn't comply, it had been the beginning of the end between us. He'd wanted a wife who would stay at home and repeat his every opinion and have dinner on the table the moment he walked in the door. A Stepford wife was what he'd wanted, and I was far from that. Then the last straw was finding out he had been cheating on me with Katie, who was half my age. I'd gotten a private investigator to get proof of his infidelity and then filed for divorce.

And then the real trouble between us started. We'd both been up for the same promotion, and Jordan had done everything he could to discredit me, to throw me under the bus at every turn. Turned out the brass didn't want to give a promotion to someone under IA investigation. Never mind that the allegations were unfounded. It was enough to get them to stop looking at promoting me and give the job to him.

I gave my brain an internal shake and tuned back in to Jordan, who was still ranting. It seemed my silence was making him worse. I stared at him, watching his face turn every shade of red.

"You sleep with fucking suspects and walk around here like a wounded puppy for weeks after your actions get them killed."

His words were like an ice pick to my heart. I was seething, but I wasn't going to explode. I drew in a sharp breath and expelled it, trying to calm myself down.

"I want you getting a psych eval before you fucking go mental and become violent like your fucking brother," he said, spittle flying from his mouth as he shouted in my face.

That was it. I'd had enough. How dare he disparage Henry and Stephen. I wanted desperately to punch him, but that would just fuel him and justify his rant at me, and I wasn't going to give him the satisfaction. I glared at him.

"You know what, Jordan? You deserved every bit of Stephen's anger toward you, and you know it. As for Henry, you need to keep your jealousy to yourself because that's what this is really about, isn't it? You talk about professionalism, but you're one to talk. Henry was never a suspect. He was a consultant with the department. He didn't deserve to be murdered, and how dare you try to use my grief at the loss of him against me." I kept my tone even and calm, but I wasn't nearly done.

Jordan sputtered, "You—"

I cut him off, holding up my hand as I moved closer, getting in his face, going toe-to-toe with him. "You know, if you really want to be envious of a dead man, I can't stop you. However, if you really want to be green with envy, it should be over the fact that I found him to be so much more satisfying in bed and a million times better at sex than you and your tiny problem." I held my fingers up to show about an inch and then, shifting backward, crossed my arms and continued glaring at him.

I didn't know that a person could turn so red they were nearly purple, but Jordan accomplished it. He turned from me and swept his arm across his desk, flinging everything into the wall. Glass from his picture frames shattered as they fell to the floor. Papers floated in the air; his phone and laptop computer slammed to the floor.

I didn't think I'd ever seen him so violently angry before, not even when we were married and I'd caught him cheating. But ever since he'd gotten this promotion, he'd become more and more volatile toward me. It was almost surreal watching him like this.

"You fucking bitch! You're nothing but a whore! How fucking dare you!" he shouted as he started toward me.

I stood my ground, but I had to admit there was a sliver of fear that raced down my spine at the look of absolute fury on his face. Still, I wasn't going to back down. If I cowered in front of him, he would think he'd won. He would think he could continue pushing me around and berating me in front of God and everybody without consequence.

He'd done it often enough to make me feel ashamed of myself for not standing up to him before. I couldn't allow that to continue. I wouldn't. He might be a higher-ranking officer than I was, but that didn't give him the right to speak to me or treat me any differently than any other officer. I didn't deserve it, and it wasn't fair.

Part of me wished I had thought to grab my phone before coming to his office. If I had, I could have recorded his rant and turned it over to Internal Affairs. Hindsight was always twenty-twenty, as the saying went, but I hadn't been thinking about that when he'd ordered me to his office. It only occurred to me now in the middle of all this.

"You're fucking finished! You will never work as a cop again! I will make sure you lose everything!" He raised his hands toward me as though he was going to come for my throat.

I nearly took a step back, but there wasn't anywhere for me to go. Moving backwards would put me against the chairs, and the last thing I wanted to do was sit. That would put him at a greater advantage against me.

A split second later, the door next to me flew open and slammed into the wall. Captain Robinson stood there, his eyes hard and angry. His jaw worked as he apparently tried to get words out through his clenched teeth. It took him a moment, but then he finally bit out, "That's enough! I will not have you berating another officer in this way! You're suspended, Brasswell!" His voice was harsh, his gaze directed right at Jordan.

My gaze flew from Robinson to Jordan, my jaw nearly hanging open from my shock at this turn of events. I hadn't expected an intervention.

"But—" Jordan's eyes widened as he stared at Robinson, clearly in shock himself. "Sir!"

"Save it, Brasswell! I heard every word from down the hall. Everyone did!" Robinson swung his arm wide, as if to encompass all of the detective pool. "I'd be surprised if they didn't hear you all the way down in the labs."

I couldn't recall ever seeing Captain Robinson so livid. And it was all aimed at Jordan. I felt my heart swell with pleasure. Not only had I held my temper, but I'd given Jordan a taste of his own medicine; he'd been the one suspended this time. I felt almost vindicated. It was an unusual feeling when dealing with Jordan.

Jordan gritted his teeth and glared at me, his seething anger back in his eyes. "Fine," he muttered as he brushed past me, moving toward the door.

I had a feeling I'd need to watch my back even more from now on, but even knowing that couldn't wipe the smile from my lips.

28

FORGIVENESS
MARCY

As Jordan stomped down the hall, I stood still, unsure what I was supposed to do now that he'd gone. In any other situation, I would have just gone to my desk and gotten back to work. However, Captain Robinson was between me and the door. I waited for him to say something, to tell me what he expected of me.

Part of me sort of assumed with Jordan gone, he'd turn his wrath on me for my part in the argument. If he'd heard Jordan's rant, he had to have heard my answer to him. I thought back over what I'd said and cringed a little bit. It certainly hadn't been work-appropriate commentary. He would be within his rights to suspend me as well for it. I hoped he wouldn't, which was why I stood there, not saying a word.

I just watched him as he took in the mess Jordan had left behind. His shoulders were heaving as though he'd just finished a hard workout or a boxing match. I could hear him breathing in through his nose and blowing it out like he was a bull in a ring.

I swallowed, patiently waiting for him to turn his angry gaze on me.

A moment later, his hand rose to his face, and he pinched the bridge of his nose as he closed his eyes. When he opened them again, he seemed calmer. He turned from the mess and looked at me. "I'd like you and Reyes in my office in ten minutes. I want a complete report on what you have on the Dixon case and what you're working on." His gaze slid back to the mess, and he shook his head. He bent down and picked up the phone, setting it back on the desk and hanging up the receiver. "He can deal with the rest of his mess when he returns."

I wondered about the laptop for a second, but considering the shattered screen, I doubted it even worked anymore. Still, it was LAPD property. I picked it up and set it next to the phone, closing the lid. It might not work, but I couldn't leave it there.

Robinson smiled at me. "Go on, Kendrick, get everything together, grab Reyes and meet me in my office."

"Yes, sir." I nodded and went out the door before him.

I could feel everyone's eyes on me as I made my way back to my desk. Angel was still there, scrolling through something on his computer. His eyes met mine, and I could see the sorrow there.

I sighed. I knew he wasn't to blame for Jordan's behavior, and that was what he was remorseful over. Not for the fact that we'd disagreed about the case prior to Jordan interfering. I was sure he'd had his reasons for disagreeing with me, and I wasn't going to fault him for his opinion. I still thought I was right, and I still wanted to pursue Pfeiffer for coercion. However, I did understand where Angel was coming from with his disagreement. We'd have to talk about it later though. Right now, we had to gather everything and get to Robinson's office.

I started shifting things around on my desk, putting things together. "Robinson wants us in his office to explain where we are in the case," I murmured.

"Okay."

I slid my gaze over him without turning my head. Angel began gathering his own paperwork, and then he stood and moved to my side. I gave him a half smile, and together we headed for Robinson's office, a seemingly united front despite our earlier argument.

Jason saw us coming and said, "He said to just knock and go in."

I gave him a nod and did as he said, rapping on the door and opening it. "Captain?"

Robinson looked up from his desk and then stood. "Come in, have a seat." He gestured to the chairs in front of his desk. "Close the door, Reyes."

Angel did as he asked as I moved to the farthest chair, leaving the closer one for him. I sat with my files on my lap. Angel sat down a moment later, and then the captain took his seat again.

"Alright, bring me up to speed." He nodded at me.

I glanced over at Angel. I really wanted to bring up the whole CIA angle, but I had no proof; it was only conjecture at this point. Aside from the threats directly from what I assumed was an actual CIA agent, but that wasn't proof of Pfeiffer's guilt. It was only proof that the CIA didn't want me bringing their mind-control projects out into the open for the public to get wind of. Because of that, I decided to stick to Pfeiffer's work in psychopharmacology and the statements from the nannies, housekeepers, tutors, and Flora, his sister-in-law.

"As of right now, we're fairly certain that the boys are guilty of starting the fire," I began, "however, it is the CSI team and the coroner's opinion that Ms. Dixon jumped from the balcony with the intention of trying to land in the pool, but missed. The burns on the boys' arms and hands are consistent with them starting the fire, but not with touching their mother once she was alight." I handed him the CSI report as well as the autopsy report from Damien.

Robinson nodded as he took them and quickly scanned them.

"That being said, we—" I glanced over at Angel again to make sure he was with me on what I was about to say.

He gave me a slight nod, telling me to continue.

"—believe that the phone call Milgram received just prior to the incident plays an important role in the events that led to them starting the fire." This was where it was going to get tricky without mentioning the CIA and the mind-control parts I believed had happened. "Before starting his psychiatry practice, Dr. Pfeiffer worked for California Medico. A couple of the nannies and housekeepers, as well as a tutor, all complained that Dr. Pfeiffer was giving the boys drugs that he called supplements and was performing experiments on them." I nodded to Angel to hand over the detailed reports from the tutors, and I did the same with the ones from the nannies and housekeepers.

"This is consistent with what we've learned from Flora Dixon, Audrina's sister. The staff as well as Audrina gave testimony during the divorce trial that Pfeiffer abused the boys, giving them medications that she later discovered weren't necessary and were causing the boys more harm than good. Of course, that was after firing a slew of those employees who tried to warn her. That was how she finally managed to gain full custody of the boys with no unsupervised visits with Pfeiffer. He was allowed to call them, but he could not be in their presence without another guardian figure present." I handed him my notes from our interviews with Flora, and Angel gave him the court records of their divorce decree.

Robinson sat quietly looking everything over. Once he'd gone through it all, he asked, "Have the boys spoken yet?" without looking up from the paperwork.

"No, sir. When we went to interview them the last time, they'd had another mental breakdown and been admitted to the psychiatric hospital. They are back home again, and we set up an appointment with them for next week. We've reached out to a specialist, Dr. Glenn, who works with people who have been—" I paused, wondering how to phrase what I wanted to say, but then there wasn't any other way to word it, really, so I just continued with what I knew. "With people who have been brainwashed, like those who leave cults."

He nodded. "Not a bad idea. He might have a way to get through to them." He flipped back to the crime scene photos. "Has he agreed to help?"

"Yes, sir, however, he's out of town at the moment. He got called away for a family emergency, or we would have made it happen this week."

"Alright, see when you can set something up."

"His secretary is getting us in on Monday to speak to him about the case," Angel put in.

"Keep me updated on that," Robinson said, going back to the file.

With that settled, I moved on to the next point of interest. "Sir, with the allegations in the divorce trial about his possibly using drugs on the boys, we were thinking perhaps Flora, who is a biochemist, might have had the supplements analyzed."

Robinson glanced up from the papers, a thoughtful look on his face. "Okay, that's a good question to pursue. Follow up on that."

I took a deep breath. I was about to take a chance, but I needed to ask. "Sir, we'd really like to get a warrant to search Dr. Pfeiffer's home and office."

He immediately shook his head. "No, not at this point in time. You have nothing concrete to get a judge to sign off on, at least not yet. Let me take the weekend to go through all of this you've brought me more thoroughly. Monday, you and Angel go interview Flora again. Ask about the supplements. While you're there, see if you can talk to those boys. Try to get them to talk."

"Sir, the boys have therapy on Monday. Flora asked if we'd wait till Tuesday to speak to them."

"I understand you are trying to be accommodating, Kendrick, but this is a murder investigation. I want this interview done."

"Yes, sir." I nodded, feeling deflated.

"For now, I think the two of you need to knock off early. Go enjoy your weekend, relax, and unwind. You've been putting in long hours, and with your accident last night and"—he glanced over to Angel—"you still recovering from yours, you both need to de-stress. Come at this with fresh eyes on Monday. The case isn't going anywhere, and as far as I can tell, no one else is at risk of being killed. We've got eyes on the boys, and they don't have their phones, so their father can't contact them."

He made a good point, but that didn't stop me from sighing over the fact I was putting things off for two more days. I knew there wasn't much I could actually do for the case over the weekend, except maybe make those interviews happen sooner, but maybe the captain was right, and we needed to come at it with fresh eyes and a new perspective.

"Thank you, sir," I murmured as I stood.

Angel stood and gestured for me to pass him to go first. "Thank you, sir. We'll see you on Monday."

The captain nodded, then said, "And Kendrick?"

I turned back toward him. "Yes, sir?"

"Stay away from Brasswell. I've spoken to the chief, he's on suspension for two weeks, and the chief is going to make him start taking anger-management classes. If you want to file a restraining order or bring a formal complaint against him, that is your right."

I shook my head. "I will stay away from him, sir. I won't be filing a complaint. I know things are a bit complicated with him being my ex-husband, and our conflict was brought into the work space when it shouldn't have been. I'll try to refrain from having it come up here again, sir."

Robinson gave me a slight nod, but then sighed. "It wasn't entirely about your former marriage, though I think you're right, him being your ex-husband isn't conducive with him now being your lieutenant. We'll see if we can't find a work-around for the future. For now, just stay away from him. You have any problems, bring them to me."

"Yes, sir."

Angel and I returned to our desks, and I grabbed my

purse from the drawer, then shut everything down. "Ready to go?" I asked, looking over at Angel.

Nodding, Angel grabbed his jacket from the back of his chair, and we headed out of the office and through the station doors. I clicked the button to unlock the Rogue and climbed in.

Angel got in the passenger seat and buckled his seat belt. "Let's go get an iced coffee. My treat."

I glanced over at him, arching a brow at him.

"Look, Marcy, I'm sorry. I didn't mean to cause a blowup between us or between you and Jordan."

"It's okay. I know you didn't." I put the key in the ignition but made no move to start the car. "I just felt like you weren't backing me. Like you wanted to give up on the case."

Angel sighed. "No, I'm just worried about you. That accident could have killed you, and this Agent White concerns me. I know you can take care of yourself, but this guy… he's a wild card, Marce, and getting Pfeiffer isn't worth your life."

I smiled and reached over, patting his hand. "Thank you for caring about me and worrying about me, but I'm a big girl, Angel. I can take care of myself."

Angel bobbed his head in acknowledgment. "I know that. Doesn't stop me from worrying about you. We're friends, and you're my partner. I'm always going to care."

I gave him a smile and turned the car on, then pulled out of the parking space. I headed to our favorite coffee shop. We ordered iced mochas with extra whip and syrup as well as a couple of pastries. Sitting down at the table, I started to giggle.

"What's so funny?"

"I was just thinking of how shocked Jordan looked when

Robinson slammed his office door open and told him he was suspended." My giggling turned into a full-on belly laugh.

Angel started chuckling. "He looked like an angry toddler as he stomped out of the office."

I grinned, my giggling subsiding. "Being made lieutenant hasn't been good for Jordan. He's gotten petty and mean. He yells at everyone, not just me." I sighed. "I wonder if the brass are now regretting giving him that promotion."

Angel shrugged. "Maybe so. And you're right, he's become a real ass since getting that promotion. Though honestly, I think he was on his way to true assholeness before he got that job."

It was my turn to shrug. "Well, that is why I divorced him." I smirked. "I just wish I'd seen it sooner." I shook my head, my smirk sliding from my face. "All that time I wasted with him. I don't even know what I ever saw in him anymore."

"Have to agree. Not even sure how I was ever actually friends with him."

"If he continues on this path he's on, he's going to cause a big mess for the department." My smile returned, and I looked over at Angel, feeling a little mischievous. "I kind of hope I'm around to see it happen."

He shook his head and laughed again. "Come on, let's go. I want to start my weekend." He grinned at me as he finished off his pastry.

"Got big plans, do you? A date maybe?" I asked, feeling a spike of jealousy that I tamped down with an internal shove.

"Naw, nothing major. Just planning to take it easy, get rid of this boot for good, and finally hit the gym for real."

"It's gonna be strange not seeing you hobbling about on it." I laughed again, teasing him.

He chuckled. "I don't even know if I will be able to walk normally without it yet. Still, I'm looking forward to driving again. In fact, I'll pick you up on Monday."

"You sure?"

"Yep." He popped the *p* and grinned at me. "I am anxious to break in my new ride."

"What, that huge suburban that's been hanging out in your driveway?" I teased. "I thought that was just for show."

It felt good to be back in sync with Angel, laughing and teasing each other. I hated it when we argued. It was too bad we weren't together in a romantic way. I'd bet the makeup sex between us would have been hot. However, I'd have to save that thought for my dreams because there was no way we were going to act on those kind of feelings.

Right?

29

RENEGADE
MARCY

After dropping Angel home, I headed to Stephen's place to take care of his fish. I ended up staying there for a while, not wanting to go home yet to an empty apartment. I cleaned, vacuuming and dusting, wiping down the kitchen and bathroom, just to waste time. When there was nothing left to clean, I got back in my car and just sat there.

I still hurt from the accident, and I knew I should probably go home, but I still wasn't ready. I pulled my phone from my purse and called Lindsey.

"Hey, are you still at the precinct?" she asked.

"No, Captain sent me home early," I replied, knowing she was going to ask why.

"I heard about your big blowup with Jordan and that he got suspended. Did he really call you a whore?"

I snorted. "Among other things. It wasn't pretty, but I think I held my own." I smiled as I recalled my comment about his small dick energy. "Wanna meet me for dinner? I'll spill the tea."

"Hell yeah," she replied.

We met up at our favorite Mexican place and spent a couple of hours eating and chatting. I even had a watermelon margarita. It had felt good to relax and share everything with a female friend who knew Jordan and what an ass he was. By the time I reached home, I was sleepy, and after washing up and changing into my pjs, I was ready for bed.

On Saturday, I spent the morning cleaning my apartment and then going to the grocery store to restock. In the afternoon I headed over to Shine View to see Stephen. I checked in with the front desk, and an orderly brought me to the same room we'd met in last time.

When he entered the room and saw me waiting there, he smiled and came over to give me a hug. "Hey, sis. I didn't know you were going to stop by."

"You look good," I replied, looking him over.

He really did look better. Like he was getting more sleep, and his head was clear. Almost like a weight had been lifted off him.

"Thanks. You still look battered though. You okay?" His voice was laced with concern.

"Eh, it's just some bruising. I'm fine, really."

"Good."

We sat down, and I asked, "How's Watson?"

Stephen's eyes dimmed a little, and he gave me a somber look. "He's okay. They brought him back from the hospital, but they keep him sedated for most of the day. It's really kind of sad, Marce."

I reached a hand out to him and squeezed his fingers. "It is. I'm sorry if I caused him some kind of trauma."

"It wasn't you. It was that phone call. I'm starting to wonder if maybe he wasn't lying. That maybe he was a member of the CIA," he whispered, leaning in closer, trying to keep his voice low so we wouldn't be overheard.

The way he looked around the room had me feeling a little paranoid as well. Was it possible that the CIA was here keeping tabs on Watson and perhaps me when I visited? I followed his gaze around the room, but I didn't see anyone or anything suspicious.

Instead of continuing with that conversation, I changed the subject, and we chatted for a good while about his own recovery. I was happy to hear he was doing so much better. I stayed for an hour and a half, and then when he was called to go to his group therapy session, I headed back to my rental.

My steps faltered though as I got closer to my car. There was a man leaning against it, one foot braced on the rear passenger door as he smoked. He glanced over at me, glaring. It was the same man who'd been following me. The man from the white sedan, which I could now see parked two spaces down from me. Agent White. CIA spook and all-around dickhead.

I'd been planning to take myself out for an ice cream sundae, but apparently that was now on hold. Gritting my teeth, I finished my journey to my car. I stopped a foot away, my hand going toward my hip where I wore my gun. I put it on the hilt, ready to draw if he made a move toward me.

"What are you doing here?" I practically growled.

He didn't say anything for a moment, his eyes on my hand, and then he flashed his gaze back to my face. "I see you haven't dropped your investigation."

I arched a brow at him. "No, I haven't."

He stared at me, trying to intimidate me, not saying anything.

"Who is going to make Pfeiffer pay for his crimes if not me? You certainly aren't. Your organization won't. He's your man."

"You need to trust me. Pfeiffer is never going to get another chance to hurt anyone."

I snorted at that. "Trust you? That's some funny shit right there. I'm not going to trust you. I'm going to do my job whether you like it or not. Your organization can't protect him forever."

Agent White gave me an exasperated look, pressing his lips into a thin, flat line as he stared at me. He pushed off my rental and moved toward me. "Pfeiffer is a renegade and a criminal who misused his research, and nobody else deserves to have that blow back on them." He gave me one more hard look before brushing past me and going to his sedan and getting in.

I stayed where I was until he pulled out of the parking lot and took off down the street. Shakily, I got in my car. As I sat there, I wondered if he meant the twins or the CIA when he said nobody else deserved to have that blow back on them. I scoffed. It was unlikely he was talking about the twins. The man obviously didn't care two shits about those boys. If he did, he'd be helping me nail Pfeiffer, not trying to keep me from investigating him.

I spent the rest of the weekend trying to relax, but my mind kept playing over the encounter with Agent White. By Sunday afternoon I couldn't take it anymore. I needed to get back to the case. I decided to call Flora. I had her number in my phone. I wanted to ask her about those supplements. I needed answers.

"Dixon residence," Shelby answered, I recognized his voice by now.

"Hi, Shelby, it's Detective Kendrick. Is Ms. Dixon in?"

"I will see if she's available, ma'am."

I heard him set the phone down, and the line stayed quiet for about three minutes. Then, with a huff, Flora said, "What do you want now, Detective?"

"I'm sorry to bother you on a Sunday, ma'am. I had a question about something that's come up in our investigation. We've been looking into Dr. Pfeiffer, as you suggested," I began, trying to win her over. "And we spoke to a number of the staff whose names you gave us."

"And? What of it?"

"That's what I'm getting to, ma'am. During the interviews, several of them brought up the supplements Dr. Pfeiffer was giving to the boys. They claimed the pills made them lose periods of time and act lethargic and forgetful. I wondered if you ever had the pills tested to determine what exactly he was giving them."

Flora sighed. "I never got the chance. The ones he had sent Audrina to give the boys were gone. I did do a lot of background research into what drugs could have been used though. The ones that caused the symptoms Audrina described like euphoria, nausea, distractedness, and the blackouts include LSD and mescaline. But we couldn't exactly prove that was what he was giving them. He wouldn't allow us to do any blood tests and got court orders to keep us from doing them. Then he managed to gain custody of the boys, and we knew they were taking the pills again while he had them. Audrina made threats about demanding tests, and by the time we had the boys back, it was too late. He'd stopped giving them the pills, and it was out of their bloodstreams, whatever it was that he was giving them."

"Well, damn. I was hoping we could use that," I muttered.

"Sorry."

"I suppose if it came to it, you would testify to your research?" I asked, feeling hopeful.

"If it helps nail that bastard, you can count on it."

"Great. Thanks, I appreciate your time. Oh, and just giving you a heads-up. My partner and I are coming by in the morning to try to speak to the boys again. Captain's orders."

"I thought we agreed on Tuesday?"

"We did, however, the captain is pressuring us to get this done tomorrow."

"Very well. You can try talking to them, but they aren't speaking. Please don't arrive before ten though. The boys don't wake until after nine, and I want to give them time to have breakfast before you interrogate them."

"Sure, we'll be there around ten a.m. then."

"I'll see you tomorrow. Goodbye, Detective."

She hung up, and I couldn't help but rehash what she'd said about her research. I wondered if there was any way I could use it to convince Captain Robinson that with Flora's testimony we could charge Pfeiffer with coercion or at the very least get the warrant for his home and office. He had to have notes about the experiments he'd done on those boys, right? The question was, where did he keep them?

30

A PICTURE IS WORTH A THOUSAND WORDS

MARCY

Angel and I walked into the precinct early Monday morning. He'd picked me up this time, now that he was given the all-clear to drive. It was kind of nice not having to drive. We'd gone through the drive-thru at the coffee shop, and I was able to just sit and enjoy my drink rather than concentrate on driving.

I told him about my conversation with Flora, and he agreed we should let the captain know, so we headed in to speak to him first thing after dropping my purse and blazer at my desk. I stopped at Jason's desk, and Angel stood at my side.

"Hey, is the captain in?"

"No, he's with the mayor; all hell has broken loose, apparently," Jason shared.

"What do you mean?"

"You didn't catch the news this morning?"

I shook my head and looked over at Angel, who shrugged.

Jason tapped at his keyboard and then turned his screen

toward us and hit play. We watched as the local news station reporter ambushed the mayor about our case. It seemed there was a public outcry over Audrina's murder and the fact that her killer or killers hadn't been arrested yet. I felt my eye twitch in irritation. He hit stop on the video and turned his screen back.

"After that, well, there were several calls put in to the mayor's office, all before seven a.m., and he was on the phone to the police chief and the captain by seven fifteen," Jason explained.

"Great." I started to turn away.

"Do you know when he's—" Angel started, but I elbowed him because I saw the captain coming down the hall. Angel turned and noticed him too. "Never mind."

Robinson saw us and pointed to his office without saying a word. His face was a mask of discontent. I was almost afraid to go into his office with him. I didn't think he was about to yell at us, but I could feel the irritation and anger rolling off him in waves.

Once we were both in the office with him and seated, I said, "Sir, Jason showed us the video clip of this morning's news. What did the mayor say?"

His voice was hardened and brooked no argument as he said, "He wants the boys arrested within the next forty-eight hours."

"But—" I don't know why I was going to try to argue. I knew it was pointless. Still, I wanted to try.

"Save it, Kendrick. I already know your argument. It's the same one I made to the mayor. That's how you've gotten a forty-eight-hour reprieve. You want to charge Pfeiffer with coercion, then get me some evidence, a witness statement, something that will prove enough for the charge to stick. If you can't, then the boys will be charged as the prime suspects and will be remanded to jail until the trial. The DA will ask that they be denied bail because they are a flight risk."

I nodded even though I disagreed about them being a flight risk. "Okay, sir. I did speak to Flora about the supplements. She wasn't able to test them or the boys' blood; it was too late. However, she did some research into what he might have been giving them based on their symptoms, and she's willing to testify about it. Do you think that's enough to get a warrant to search his home and business? He's got to have notes on his research."

Before I even finished speaking, Robinson was shaking his head. "No. The chief isn't going to allow it, nor will the mayor. Neither want to implicate Pfeiffer, nor tip him off if he is somehow responsible. They want concrete evidence prior to issuing a warrant."

"Great." I sighed.

"Did you arrange to speak to the boys?" he asked.

"Yes, sir. We're heading over there soon. And we're meeting with Glenn later as well."

"Good. Well? Anything else?"

"No, sir."

"Then get out of here. Go find me some evidence." He directed his eyes toward his door as though nudging us to get out.

I nodded, then Angel and I both headed for the door. As we moved through the detective pool, I pulled my phone from my pocket and checked the time. "Wanna head out early?"

"Sure." Angel nodded.

We grabbed our jackets, and I pulled my purse back out

of the drawer I kept it in, then headed back to his Suburban. I climbed up into it and settled in the seat. A minute later we were back on the road heading to Beverly Crest.

"Do we have time to stop at Barney's?" I asked, feeling my stomach rumble.

"Sure, I think so. We're not supposed to meet her until ten, yeah?" He looked at his dashboard clock, then back to the road. It was barely nine fifteen now.

We had just gotten off the 101 and were now on Santa Monica Boulevard. "Right. Though we didn't exactly set a firm time. She just said not to show up before ten." I shrugged.

A few minutes later he turned onto Holloway Drive and then turned into the alley that led to the parking for a couple of businesses. We headed into Barney's and ordered a couple of breakfast sandwiches and more coffee to go. It didn't take them long to prepare, and soon we were back on the road.

I finished mine off as we entered the Beverly Crest area. It was two minutes to ten when we pulled into Flora's gated driveway. I figured it was close enough to ten that she would be fine with it. Angel pressed the button.

Shelby's voice came over the intercom. "May I help you?"

"Detectives Reyes and Kendrick to see Ms. Dixon."

Shelby didn't answer, but the gate opened.

Angel drove in, and a moment later we were parked and walking toward the home.

Shelby must have been waiting for us because the door opened, and he gestured for us to enter. "Ms. Dixon will receive you in the salon."

I stared at the man, wondering if he was sending us into an at-home beauty salon. "And where would that be located?" I arched a brow at him.

"This way, Detectives." Shelby rolled his eyes and turned in the opposite direction of the room we'd previously seen her and the boys in. The room he led us to was larger and filled with multiple sets of furniture that all matched. They were put together in little sections, and I assumed they used this room for larger gatherings or parties.

Flora was there messing with a flower arrangement in a vase. Seated on one of the couches was a man in a slate-colored suit, his dark hair slicked back, his brown eyes intent on Flora. They both turned their attention to us when we entered, and then Flora gestured to the closest couch and chair arrangement, where the man was seated.

"Good morning, Detectives."

"Ms. Dixon." I nodded and took a seat next to the man.

"Good morning," Angel said, sitting next to me on the couch.

Flora nodded at the man, then turned her gaze to us again. "My lawyer, Jackson Declan."

"Good morning," he said, holding out his hand.

"Morning." I shook his offered hand.

Angel shook it as well and gave him a nod.

Flora took one of the chairs and turned to Shelby. "Would you have the boys join us in a few minutes?"

"Yes, ma'am." Shelby gave a nod and left us alone.

She turned back to us, her expression guarded. "The boys still aren't speaking. I'm not sure how much you're going to get out of them."

"Are they communicating in any fashion?" Angel asked.

"Nods mostly. Sometimes they can draw me a picture."

"Can we have some pens and paper brought in for them, then?" I asked.

"I'll have Shelby see to it." She rose and headed for the door.

I heard her murmuring, I assumed to Shelby, before returning to her seat.

While we waited, I decided I needed to let her know what we were up against. "Ms. Dixon, I wanted to make you aware, our captain has given us forty-eight hours to find a connection between Audrina's murder and Pfeiffer. If we can't, we have to charge the boys as the prime suspects in this case."

"That is absurd!" Flora said, jumping from her seat. "Surely you will see how traumatized the boys are. They aren't responsible for killing their mother."

The doors to the room had opened in the middle of her rant, and the boys stood there, eyes wide and looking frightened. Jackson rose as well and headed to Flora, as though to comfort her.

I stood as well, holding out a hand, trying to placate her and calm her down. "I know, and I agree, that is why we're trying to discover how Dr. Pfeiffer is involved. How he was able to accomplish the..." I hesitated as my eyes slid over to the boys before I continued. I didn't want to have them backslide in their trauma recovery. "Events that took place."

Flora had her arms wrapped around herself, and she looked pale. She gave us a nod and then looked at the boys and gave them a smile, but it didn't quite reach her eyes. "Boys, please, come in. You remember Detectives Kendrick and Reyes? They have some more questions for you. And Shelby has brought you a few things to help you answer."

Their haunted gazes and expressionless faces turned to me and Angel. They both gave us a single nod and then moved toward us, taking the empty chairs next to Flora.

Shelby handed them a clipboard with paper and a pen.

"Hello, boys. Thank you for allowing us to speak with you," I started.

Again, they gave me a single nod.

"I know this might be hard, but Detective Reyes and I are trying to help you. We need to know how this all started and what you can tell us of the events that took place in your home prior to you coming to live with your aunt. We need to know what happened to your mother. I understand if you are unable to vocalize your answers, but can you write it down or draw me a picture?"

The boys looked at each other for a moment, and it was as though they were lost in their own world, able to communicate with each other without words. Then they picked up their pens and began drawing. When they were finished, they handed the drawings to me.

What I saw was a little disturbing. Gottlieb—Gary had drawn three stick figures, two of them smaller, with their heads almost bent, and the third figure hovering over them with its hands on their heads, as though forcing them down. In the smaller figures' hands were boxes that seemed to be melting. I didn't know what that meant.

I pointed to the box and asked, "What is this? Can you draw it larger with a little more detail?"

Gary nodded and began to draw on another piece of paper, then frowned and looked at Flora. He tapped the pen and then to his shirt, which had a design of multiple colors.

"You need more colors?" she asked.

He nodded.

Flora got up and moved to the door again. When she returned, she said, "Shelby will bring you some colored pencils; it might be a moment." She looked over at me. "Perhaps look at Mike's drawing while we wait?"

I did as she asked. It was even more disturbing than Gary's. In it was a woman stick figure who seemed to be covered in flames. He'd added a cartoon speech bubble with screaming inside it. At the bottom of the page, he'd drawn two more stick figures holding something and a TV screen that he'd written the word games on. I pointed to what was in the hands. "Game controllers?"

Mike nodded.

"You were playing video games when this happened?" I pointed to the woman on fire.

Mike and Gary both looked confused, but then Mike nodded, and Gary shook his head.

"You don't know?"

They both gave us frustrated looks.

"You think you were, but you don't remember?" I asked.

They nodded, and Mike reached for Gary's paper and tapped the object in the small figures' hands as Shelby returned with the colored pencils.

Gary grabbed them and finished his drawing, then handed it to me.

I stared at it. It was clearly an iPhone, but it was dripping red stuff that seemed like blood. I looked from the drawing back to the boys.

Angel looked at the picture too and then at me.

"Boys, we know your father called Mike that day; are you saying that the phone has something to do with what happened to your mom?"

Both of them looked frightened. As though a monster had just shown up. Still, they nodded.

"Did your father tell you to do this to your mom?" Angel asked, pointing to the picture of the stick figure on fire.

Again, they couldn't make up their minds, one nodding, the other shaking his head, as if indecisive or as if they had no idea what had actually happened. They looked terrified.

I decided to reword the question in hopes they could give me a more definite answer. "Mike, did your father call you right before you found your mom on fire?"

He hesitated for just a moment, then nodded.

With that confirmed, I smiled. "Thank you, Mike. Can you draw me a picture of what your father said in that call?"

He shook his head, looking frightened again, and Gary burst into tears before jumping up and running from the room.

"I think that is going to have to be enough for today, Detectives," Jackson said.

Flora rose and directed Mike from the room. Over her shoulder she said, "Goodbye, Detectives." Then she and Mike followed Gary out the door.

I stared at the lawyer for a moment. "Have they drawn or written anything about their father?" I asked.

Jackson smiled that non-smile all lawyers seemed to have mastered. "If they had, I'm not sure I'd share it, Detectives, but they haven't. This is the first I've seen of anything that occurred that day."

"Okay. Thanks," I offered as both Angel and I rose.

31

CULTS AND DEPROGRAMMING
MARCY

Angel and I had returned to the precinct and spoken with the captain about our talk with the boys. I'd shown him the images they'd drawn, but he hadn't been impressed. I replayed the conversation in my head as we went to meet Dr. Glenn.

"This isn't enough to do anything with, Kendrick." Robinson had shaken his head as he looked at the pictures. "We can't put them on the witness stand against their father using pictographs and head nods."

"But, sir, they were able to confirm that their father called right before Audrina was set on fire. And they were terrified to say, write or draw what he'd said to them. Surely—"

"I'm sorry, Kendrick, it might make a jury sympathetic, but the DA isn't going to go for it. We need more. You're meeting with that doctor, aren't you? Maybe you can get him to talk to the boys, somehow deprogram them so they can actually speak."

"Yes, sir."

"Don't forget, the clock is ticking, Kendrick. You don't have much time to get this done."

I sighed.

"What's up?" Angel glanced over at me as he turned the corner.

"Just thinking about our deadline."

"Hopefully, Glenn will be able to help us out."

"Yeah." Unfortunately, I was running out of hope. On top of that, I felt as though I was being watched again. I glanced in the side mirror, but I didn't see any white sedans following us. It made me wonder if Agent White had gotten a new car to surveil me in.

Angel pulled into a parking lot next to a modest two-story brick building with glass front windows. The signage for the place was modest as well, just a small script sign next to the door that read:

Dr. Oscar Glenn, psychiatrist.

We headed in and found his receptionist behind a gray counter with a sliding glass window. She pulled it open and smiled at us. "Welcome. How might I help you?"

"Hi, we're Detectives Reyes and Kendrick. I believe I spoke to you last week about getting in to speak with Dr. Glenn?"

"Oh yes, I do remember. And he has about thirty minutes before his next appointment. I'll let him know you're here. One moment." She picked up the phone and spoke for a minute. Then with a smile, she pushed a button, and the door next to her desk clicked open. "Go on through; he's in the first room on the left."

"Thank you."

We followed her directions and walked into a small office that held a nice-sized desk with some filing cabinets behind it, and two comfortable chairs for visitors. The African-American man behind the desk was short and stocky. His head was shaved to his scalp. He had dark brown eyes and a neat, graying mustache, but he didn't look older than forty-five. He smiled, and his brown eyes lit up with golden flecks.

"Hello, come in," he said; his voice was gravelly and comforting at the same time. He held a hand out for us. "I expect you must be Detectives Reyes and Kendrick?"

"Yes, hello," I said, smiling as I shook his hand.

"Thanks so much for seeing us," Angel said, shaking his hand also.

"No problem. I understand you have some questions?"

I explained the situation about the twins and how they were unable to vocalize anything, and that they were having panic attacks. I then went into the history we'd learned from their aunt, housekeepers, nannies, and tutors.

"It does sound as though they've been through something similar to what cult victims endure." He paused. "I normally focus on cult victims, as I'm sure you saw on my website. However, I do also specialize in patients with PTSD and drug-induced trauma. Especially ones like Rohypnol, which I'm sure you've heard called the date-rape drug of choice. I've testified in court cases about how it can render a victim unconscious, suggestible, and/or amnesic. If it were coupled with brainwashing, it could certainly lead to what you're thinking Dr. Pfeiffer did."

I was glad he was validating my theory without me bringing up the CIA or his mind-control projects at California Medico.

"It's a shame their father was the inflictor of this behavior. I do have some techniques you can employ—"

I winced and then sighed. "Sorry, I don't mean to be dismissive, but we are on a time crunch. We have less than forty-eight hours before we have to charge them, and if we can, we'd really like to implicate their father, because we're pretty sure he's somehow behind all of this. The problem is proving it. We were hoping that you could see them?"

Dr. Glenn frowned, but he didn't say anything as he considered my words.

"I'm sure their aunt would be willing to bring them to you," I said. "She's anxious to make sure the boys are helped and that they don't go down for their mother's murder. They might have been party to it, but it was under duress. It's really not fair for them to spend the rest of their lives in jail. Not if we can find out what really happened."

He nodded. "All right. My office hours usually begin at eight a.m. It will take some time to work with them to discover what you need for the case." He pursed his lips and pulled out his calendar, glancing at it. "I can move my eight a.m. client and possibly my nine o'clock as well." He spoke almost to himself and then refocused on us. "Can they be here by six?"

"In the morning?" I wanted to clarify because that was earlier than I'd imagined.

"Yes. You said you're on a deadline and though sessions usually are an hour, I think we'll need a more intensive and lengthy session to draw these boys out."

"Yes, of course. I'll speak to Ms. Dixon and arrange it."

"I'll have my secretary reach out to my morning clients and get them shifted and then call you to confirm."

"Thank you so much, Dr. Glenn. I really appreciate this.

And of course, the department will pay you for your time as a consultant."

"That's really not necessary. I am happy to offer my consultation and work with these boys."

As Angel drove us back to the station, I called Flora. "It's Detective Kendrick; may I speak with Ms. Dixon, please?"

Shelby acquiesced, and a moment later Flora said, "What now, Detective?"

"Flora, we've arranged a meeting with a psychiatrist who specializes in working with patients who have PTSD and drug-induced amnesiac trauma. He is making time for the boys at six a.m. tomorrow morning. You know we're on a time crunch before we have to charge them, and I'd really like to avoid that if at all possible, so do you think you can have them there?" I spoke quickly, hoping to break down her arguments before she even began them.

"Who is this psychiatrist?"

"His name is Dr. Oscar Glenn. His office is in the Melrose Hill area."

"All right. We'll be there, Detective. Will you text me the address?" She proceeded to rattle off her cell phone number, though I already had it.

"Of course. Thank you, Ms. Dixon, we'll see you in the morning." I hung up as we pulled into the precinct.

We headed in, and just as we were about to update the captain on what we'd been working on, a call came in.

"Reyes, Kendrick, we've got a 10-71, multiple victims on-site, Old Bank District, patrol are en route, go."

Angel and I hadn't even put our things down; we just turned and ran out the door. At the Suburban we headed for the back end where Angel kept our gear. I pulled on a Kevlar vest, then rushed back to the passenger seat. I knew the captain would have dispatch update us once we were on our way. Sure enough, as soon as I stuck the siren on the dashboard and we pulled into traffic, the radio crackled to life.

"Detective Kendrick, what's your 10-20?"

I picked up the radio and clicked the button as I watched Angel drive. "Spring, crossing Third."

"10-4, Detective, proceed with caution. Possible multiple shooters in the vicinity." The dispatcher went on to update us with information as we headed for the hotel on Fifth Street and Frank.

The area was loud with multiple sirens from various patrol cars racing toward the area. We arrived, and Angel didn't even bother switching his SUV off before we were out of it and drawing our weapons, rushing toward the building. We stopped just outside the glass doors and pressed ourselves to the cement wall, then peered inside.

I could see two men with what looked like M16s. There were also a couple of bodies scattered over the lobby floor. "I see two."

"Same." Angel nodded. "Got a shot?"

"Tall one, blue shirt."

"I've got the green shirt."

"On three?"

He gave me a nod.

I aimed my gun and knew Angel was doing the same. I figured I had an angle of obliquity less than 15 degrees, and my target was about six feet away. I was taking a chance, so was Angel, but we were looking to put them down without any more casualties. "One." I took a breath as I calculated my aim. Despite my penchant for killing killers, if I didn't have to kill them, I wouldn't. Incapacitating them was just as good and preferable. But I could see the guy had his finger on the trigger. He had the gun pointed straight up though, so I hoped I could just disable him. "Two... three."

I pulled the trigger on my Glock, and the glass shattered. I lost sight of the gunman for a minute, and I heard his M16 go off. I used my elbow to break the glass so I could see. The gunman in the blue shirt was still on his feet, his gun now aimed toward me and Angel. My eyes widened, and I felt the bullet he fired hit my vest hard. Still, I was aimed at him as well and pulled my trigger the moment his bullet hit me.

Angel yelled, "Marcy!"

I staggered back, my breath knocked from me. I fell on my ass and backward onto the pavement. As I lay looking up at the sky, I tried to breathe. Angel dropped and started hovering over me. I heard him shouting, and I could see him waving his hands at someone. I know only seconds passed, but everything seemed to be happening in slow motion.

Another face appeared over me, and Angel disappeared. I tried to focus on the new face and realized it was Officer Liz Allen. Her icy blue eyes stared down at me with worry.

"I'm okay," I said, but my voice sounded far away.

"Just don't move, ma'am. Medics are on the way."

I shook my head as my breath was returning to normal. "The vest did its job. I'm fine; just feels like I was punched by Rockslide," I replied.

Liz gave me a funny look. "What?"

"You know, the X-men character? Rockslide? Part of the Hellions Squad?" She didn't seem to know whom I was talking about, and I sighed. "Never mind. Can you just help me up?"

She looked around, but hesitantly nodded as she gave me a hand up.

Once I was on my feet, I looked toward the hotel. I'd

flown farther than I'd thought with that hit. I was nearly in the street. I saw my gun on the ground a foot from me, where it must have fallen from my hand. I picked it up and started back toward the building.

"Ma'am? Detective Reyes went in, both shooters are down, and Officers Kim, Desmond, and Jenkins are in there."

"Thanks for the heads-up. Do we know if all the shooters are down? Were there more than two?"

"Only two were reported, ma'am."

I entered the building. "Reyes?" I called out.

There were people everywhere now. Medics were checking victims. Reyes was cuffing one of the shooters, the one who'd shot me. The one in the blue shirt was dead though. I didn't know if it was from my gun or Angel's.

"Yep, over here."

I headed for him and glanced at the shooter in the green shirt, who was now cuffed and being led out of the building by Desmond and Kim. "Got a name?"

"Gang related. The Vipers. Initiation shooting. Kid you downed"—he glanced at the body—"Brice Lawson, age seventeen. Rap sheet a mile long, multiple stints in juvie."

I sighed. "How did these two get their hands on M16s?"

"That would be a question for his brother Dison. The other shooter."

"They taking him to the hospital?"

Angel nodded. "So we have six victims headed to the hospital, three fatalities not including the shooter."

I blinked and shook my head. I must have been out of it longer than I'd thought, considering he had so much information.

"You okay?"

I nodded and pulled at my vest. "Hurt like a bitch, but I'm fine. Probably going to have another bruise."

"CSI team and Damien are here now. I'll release the scene to them. Why don't you head on over to the SUV?"

I nodded as he started toward Lindsey. I gave her a wave and got in the Suburban. A few minutes later we were headed back to the precinct. It didn't take long, but the ride hurt due to the seat belt pressing on the massive bruise I could feel forming on my chest.

As soon as we entered, the captain was waiting for me with his hand out.

I'd forgotten. With a sigh, I pulled my gun from its holster, took out the magazine, and pulled the slide to empty the chamber of the bullet. It hit the floor with a ping. I looked in the chamber to make sure it was completely empty, moved the slide back in place and handed it over to Robinson. "It was a justified shooting."

He nodded. "IA is still going to look at it, seeing as it's you." Robinson sighed. "You okay? Heard you took a bullet."

I nodded. "Bruised, but fine."

"Good. Go write your reports." He turned to go, then paused, looking back. "Did you speak to Dr. Glenn?"

"Yes, sir, everything's a go for tomorrow morning."

"Good, time's ticking."

32

TRIGGER PHRASE
MARCY

When I got home, I almost expected to see Agent White waiting for me in the parking lot. I had felt sure he would come after me again since we'd gone to see Dr. Glenn. I figured he'd have some objection to that, but I didn't see him. He didn't even call and disrupt my sleep. I wondered if he'd given up the fight. The thought made me smile.

It was a brief bit of joy that I knew wasn't going to last. My alarm had gone off at four thirty so I could be ready for when Angel picked me up. I stood staring in the mirror at the purplish-blue-green bruise blooming over my left breast and over my sternum. I pushed on it, seeing how painful it was. It darn near stole my breath. Putting on a bra hurt like crazy, and I almost went without, but didn't. Instead, I put on one of my more comfortable sports bras that wouldn't press too hard on the bruising.

I was dressed and ready to leave the apartment by five fifteen. Angel arrived just as I exited the building. He pulled up, and I climbed up into the Suburban.

"Mornin'," he mumbled, trying to hide a yawn.

I laughed. "Good morning, sunshine. Late night?"

"Couldn't sleep. You?"

"I did okay. Got about six hours."

We went to our coffee shop, which thankfully opened at four a.m. for all of the early-morning commuters in the area. Once we were caffeinated, we headed for Dr. Glenn's office in Melrose Hill. We arrived at five minutes till and saw that Flora, the boys and their lawyer, Jackson Declan, were there waiting.

"Good morning, thank you so much for bringing the boys."

"We want answers as much as you do, and if we can help prove that Matthew caused this, all the better." Flora had her arms crossed over her chest and looked mutinous but determined.

"Thank you all for showing up on time," Dr. Glenn said as he joined us, keys in hand. He opened the building and led us inside. He opened the next door and held it as we all passed through. "I'll set the four of you up in the observation room." He spoke to Flora, Jackson, me and Angel; then he looked at the boys. "Hello, boys, I'm sorry, I should have introduced myself. I'm Dr. Glenn. I hope you don't mind speaking to me this morning?"

The boys shook their heads, indicating they didn't mind. Gary even gave a small smile.

Within ten minutes, the four of us were standing at a two-way mirrored window like the ones we had down at the precinct in the interrogation rooms. I could see a video recorder set up facing the table where Dr. Glenn, Mike and Gary had taken seats. On the table was a stack of blank paper, colored pencils, crayons, and markers.

I watched Dr. Glenn pull his phone from his pocket and set it down. The moment he did, both boys' eyes widened, and they looked suddenly fearful, scooting back in their chairs away from the device.

"Does my phone make you uncomfortable?" Dr. Glenn asked.

Both Gary and Mike nodded, not taking their eyes from the phone.

"It's just an iPhone, there's nothing about it that can hurt you, but for now, would you like me to put it away?"

Again, they nodded.

"All right. I'll put it back in my pocket." He picked it up and then slid his hand down his side with it, into his jacket pocket. "Now, I can see that you both are able to answer yes and no questions with gestures such as nodding. However, I have this paper and all these different utensils for you to use to answer my questions. Is there anything here that you would like to use?"

Mike reached for some of the paper and the markers, while Gary chose the colored pencils and his own stack of white paper. They looked at Dr. Glenn expectantly.

He smiled at them and gestured toward the paper. "Can you draw me a picture of what your childhood was like? Perhaps of the times where you seemed to lose time? What was it you thought you were doing, and what were you actually doing?"

The boys nodded after a moment and got to work. Dr. Glenn used the drawings as well as some hand gestures and even got them to write a few things down for us. I was amazed. It turned out the boys often thought they were playing video games, only to find themselves somewhere else in the house or even outside, where they *woke up*, not having been playing games at all.

They'd even check their games, looking to see if the characters on the screen had advanced as they had in their memories, but they hadn't. They were exactly where they'd been the day before on the screen. Mike had, at one point, pointed at his head and circled his finger as he made a face, indicating that he thought he was going crazy.

"You're not crazy, Mike," Dr. Glenn assured him. He tapped on one of the pictures Gary had drawn. "I think the supplements your father was giving you were causing that feeling in your head."

Mike and Gary both nodded and then began drawing furiously again. This time of their mother's death. It was a series of pictures drawn out quickly, showing what they had thought they'd been doing and then what they'd seen.

"I see. You again thought you were playing video games?"

They nodded.

"And you heard a scream, and it 'woke' you up?" Dr. Glenn used finger quotes on the word woke.

Mike was hesitant, but then gave an unsure nod.

Dr. Glenn tapped the object in one of the stick figure's hands. "This is a phone. Is it yours?"

Mike started to look scared and worried again, but he indicated that yes, it was his phone.

"And your father called you?"

Mike's body started to shake as though he was terrified, but he did nod to indicate that yes, his father had called.

"Okay, it's okay, Mike. You are safe here. This is a safe space. There are no phones here to worry you."

His shivering began to subside, and he took a deep breath, then nodded again.

"Can you draw or write out what your father said to you?"

Gary reached for a new sheet of paper and, in black block letters, wrote out the word Legacy. Then around the black he traced in red, only he made it look like the red was dripping off the words. I wondered if he was trying to make the word look like it was bleeding. It was kind of creepy looking.

"Legacy?"

Mike's face went blank as though he was staring at nothing. He was still as a statue.

I looked at Dr. Glenn and then over to Gary and realized that he too was sitting still as a statue. A moment later, Dr. Glenn snapped his fingers in front of each boy, but that did nothing. It was as though they were stuck.

"What's wrong with them?" Flora's whisper in the quiet room startled me.

"I'm not sure," I murmured, trying to keep my voice down.

Dr. Glenn stood and moved over to Gary. "Gottlieb, can you hear me?" he asked.

Gary nodded.

"Good." He pulled something from his pocket that looked like a stress ball and placed it in Gary's hands. "Can you tell me what your hands feel?"

"Soft, squishy," he answered out loud.

"Good." He grabbed a marker and waved it under Gary's nose. "What do you smell?"

Gary's nose wrinkled. "Grape?"

Dr. Glenn smiled. "Yes. What do your eyes see?"

Gary blinked and seemed to come into focus more. He

tried to speak, but suddenly his voice was gone again. It was as though his voice box wasn't working anymore.

"Don't worry about your voice," Dr. Glenn told him. "It will come back with some more sessions. You've done very well today, Gary."

Gary gave him a small smile and looked around, then frowned when he noticed his brother sitting as still as a statue. He reached over and pushed him off the chair.

Mike got up and frowned at Gary.

Gary frowned back and tilted his head at him, and it once again looked as though they were having a conversation we weren't privy to.

"Mike, are you back with us?" Dr. Glenn asked, drawing his attention.

Mike nodded, then looked down at his hands and frowned again. He looked around, his expression one of confusion. He looked back at Dr. Glenn, lifted his hands, and mimicked holding a game controller.

"You thought you were playing a video game?" he asked, then added, "You were looking for the TV and gaming system just now?"

Mike nodded again.

"It's okay. As you can see, no gaming system." He tapped his head. "It was a dream."

Mike looked over at Gary and returned to his seat.

"I think we're going to end things here today. Thank you, boys. I'm going to speak with your guardian and the police officers for a moment, and I'll be back to get you. Okay?" Dr. Glenn gathered up the papers they'd drawn on, then turned to the video recorder. He hit a button and lifted it off its stand.

A moment later he walked through a door, joining us.

"I'm going to make a copy of the tape for you to take with you, but I think we made good progress today. I'd really like to set up some more sessions with them, if you are open to it, Ms. Dixon."

Flora nodded. "I was so surprised to hear Gary speak; how did you do that?"

"The boys entered a fugue state when I said the word Legacy. Something about that word triggers them. I didn't know the word to bring them out of it, so I used another method called the five senses. It didn't take all of them to draw Gary out, which means he probably doesn't go as deep into the fugue state as Mike. Gary actually used another method to draw Mike out, though I don't recommend doing that. The touch was jarring enough to break the state of his mind, but it can be damaging if done incorrectly."

"Why did he lose his voice again once he was back?"

"It's involuntary mutism. Something we'll need to work on, but definitely fixable." He looked around at each of us and said, "Any other questions?"

"Not that I can think of. Well, except, may we also have copies of the pictures?"

"Of course. Ms. Dixon, you're welcome to collect the boys. If you do want to continue to bring the boys to me, stop at the desk and speak to my secretary. She'll get you set up with appointments and billing. This session was free though."

"Thank you, Dr. Glenn. I will set those up. I really can't thank you enough," Flora said, moving toward the door to get the boys.

"My pleasure, ma'am. The exit is just through this door." He gestured to the door we were about to leave through. "Detectives, if you'll follow me?"

We did, and soon we had copies of everything to take back to the precinct.

As we were about to leave, he stopped us once more. "I wanted to mention." He paused for a moment, considering his words. "There might be another trigger word or phrase that specifically gets the boys to act in a violent way. It's possible that the word we know triggers them is part of that phrase, so you need to be careful bringing it up."

"Thanks, we'll be careful."

"I'm glad to hear that. I will work on trying to find their release word in our next session." With that, he turned to go back to his office.

33

TIPPED OFF
MARCY

Angel and I headed for Captain Robinson's office. I held the DVD of the session, and Angel was carrying copies of the images the boys had drawn. I paused at Jason's desk, but he simply nodded before I could even ask.

"He's waiting for you."

"Thanks." I continued to his office, knocked, then opened the door. "Sir?"

"Yeah, come in, Kendrick, Reyes."

We joined him, and I handed over the DVD with a grin. "I think we've got enough, sir. You'll want to probably fast-forward to the last fifteen minutes; that's when most of the important stuff came out."

He nodded, put the disk in his disk drive and skipped ahead to the point I mentioned. He watched silently and then hit stop and moved the cursor back to that same mark. Instead of hitting play to watch it again, he picked up his phone and said, "Jason, get the chief and the mayor on the line."

My eyes widened. "Sir?"

He held up a finger for me to wait. A moment later, he was connected in a three-way call with both the chief of police and the mayor. I wondered why they'd left the deputy mayor out of the loop, but that was really none of my business. I fidgeted in my seat and looked over at Angel, who smiled. I wondered, if like me, he thought this was a good sign.

"Sirs, I have something you're going to want to see." He paused and listened to them. "Yes, it's from the Dixon-Pfeiffer session with that renowned psychiatrist, Glenn." Another pause and then he added, "Yes, that's the one. I have it ready to go as soon as you arrive."

They were coming here? I sat up a little straighter and tugged on my blazer. I wondered if I even looked well enough to be seen with the mayor. I'd woken up and dressed so early I couldn't even remember if I'd put any makeup on.

Angel chuckled softly, and I looked over at him.

"You look fine," he murmured.

I smiled at him and brushed my hair behind my ear.

The captain hung up and said, "They'll be here in five minutes. What else do you have there?" He nodded at Angel.

Angel handed him the pages. "These are the images the boys drew. When you go back and watch the entire video, you'll see everything in context, but most of them are pretty much self-explanatory."

The captain was still looking at some of the more disturbing images the boys drew when there was a knock on the door. "Come in," he called.

"Sir, the police chief and mayor to see you." Jason held the door open for them.

"Sirs, I'm sorry for the cramped quarters, but I thought it was important for you to see this immediately."

"Go ahead, Robinson," Mayor Taylor replied, his eyes on the frozen computer screen.

"Yes, sir." The captain resumed play, and all of us watched as Dr. Glenn spoke of the phone call, and then Mike and Gary as they entered the fugue state from Dr. Glenn saying the word Legacy. "That's enough to issue an arrest and search warrants, I would imagine, isn't it?" Robinson glanced at them.

"Do it," the mayor said, his gaze hard on the screen.

"We'll hold off on arresting the boys," Police Chief Warren added.

I felt a spike of satisfaction at their words. I was finally going to get my warrants so I could nail that asshole for what he did to his boys and his ex-wife. "Thank you, sirs," I said.

"Talk to Judge Harper; he'll sign off on it; tell him to call my office if he has any hesitation about it." Mayor Taylor shook our hands and left.

Police Chief Warren followed him out as he said, "Keep me updated, Robinson."

"Yes, sir," Captain Robinson agreed. He looked at us with a determined look. "I'll have that warrant by lunch."

He wasn't wrong. The paperwork was delivered at eleven forty-five. "Kendrick, Reyes, contact patrol, get a team to go with you, call in CSI and get over to the Pfeiffer estate. You've also got search warrants for his office and any other buildings that you may discover he's connected to while conducting the search. And you can arrest the suspect as soon as you see him."

"Thank you, sir."

I was anxious to get going. I took the paperwork he

handed me and pulled my phone out to coordinate with Lindsey as we headed out to Angel's Suburban. Once we were in, he called in the request for a couple of patrol units to meet us at the Pfeiffer estate. We were going to search there first, and if Dr. Pfeiffer happened to be there, then all the better.

Of course, when we got there, the only person at home was a housekeeper, who was shocked to see us. She complained loudly as we trolled through the house looking for evidence. Any kind of bottle that looked like it held pills was confiscated. So were all the files in his office. Angel and I were in the bedroom, opening drawers and going through the closet.

I dug through the top drawer and found it was full of socks and underwear, but underneath those items, he'd stored a stack of letters. I pulled them out and looked at them. They were all addressed to him from various women. I pulled one from the envelope and started to read. The woman mentioned how much she loved him and how she couldn't live without him. Shaking my head, I put it back in the envelope and set the stack aside. We'd take them with us, just in case there was something in them.

I opened the next drawer, but it was full of T-shirts and polo-style shirts. Slipping my hand between the fabric of each shirt, I couldn't find anything hidden there. I moved on to the next, and it was full of shorts, but again nothing else. I sighed and squatted to open the bottommost drawer.

"Huh." Angel grunted.

"What's up?" I turned my head to look at him. He was staring into the closet.

"Take a look here."

I stood up and joined him, but all I saw was a bunch of

empty hangers. Then it hit me. The man had been tipped off. "Son of a bitch. Officer Mendoza!"

"Yes, ma'am?" Mendoza popped his head in the doorway.

"Where's the housekeeper?"

"Outside with Peters, ma'am."

"Thanks." I strode from the room and out the front door. "Mrs. Henderson, was it?" I asked as I approached her.

"Yes, but you can call me Margaret."

I gave her a tight smile. "Margaret, did Dr. Pfeiffer return home at any point today and pack a bag?"

"Well, he did come home, but I didn't see him with a bag." She frowned. "I'm not saying he didn't pack one, only that I didn't see one when he came into the kitchen to speak to me. He told me I wouldn't need to cook dinner and that I could have the rest of the afternoon off once I finished my cleaning."

"What time was that?"

She thought about it and then said, "About twenty minutes before you all arrived."

"Did he happen to say where he was going?"

"No, ma'am."

"Great." I sighed. I turned to get Angel, but then realized he was standing just off to my left. "Let's go."

"You think he was tipped off?"

"I know he was. I just want to know who he has in his pocket. Robinson is going to hit the roof. Not to mention the mayor."

"What about Pfeiffer's office?"

"We'll head over now with the arrest warrant, see if he's holed up there. It's going to take Lindsey's team a bit to finish here anyway, so we'll do the search there tomorrow." I remembered the letters and stopped to tell one of the CSI techs about them, then continued on with Angel to the SUV.

"We should get an officer to sit on the office overnight. Just in case we don't get him, and he shows up to destroy files."

"I'll talk to Robinson once we've checked the office."

When we arrived at Pfeiffer's office, his receptionist informed us that after receiving an urgent call, he'd left around ten forty-five with orders to cancel all his clients for the next few days. She had no idea when he planned to return, nor where he'd gone off to.

"Great," I muttered as I shook my head. Pulling out my phone, I dialed the line for Jason and asked him to put me through to Robinson. "Sir?"

"Tell me you have him in custody, Kendrick."

"I'm sorry, sir. He was tipped off. Just spoke to his secretary. He got an urgent call around ten forty-five and then left. Housekeeper confirmed he was there and gone about twenty minutes before we arrived. CSI team is still at the house. Thought we could save the office for tomorrow, but put an officer on the building just in case he shows up and tries to get rid of files."

"I'll talk to Patrol and arrange it. Stay there until an officer arrives; they'll have a plan in place to keep watch. Tell the receptionist to leave the keys."

"Yes, sir. What about Pfeiffer?"

"We'll issue an APB and get his image out to the news stations. I want this asshole found."

"You and me both, sir." I hung up and turned back to the secretary. "I need the keys to all of Pfeiffer's doors. Including the building." I held up the search warrant. "And I'm going to need you to leave."

"But—"

I shook my head. "No. You can't call any more clients. I know it's an inconvenience for them, but you can leave a note on the door."

She sighed and quickly made up a sign and stuck some tape on it. She grabbed her purse and handed me the office keys. She gave me a worried look. "Am I going to lose my job?"

I shrugged. "You're going to see it on the news, so I suppose you have a right to know. We have an arrest warrant for Dr. Pfeiffer. He's going to jail. I don't know for how long, but probably long enough that you might want to start looking for a new job."

Tears spilled down her cheeks, and she nodded. "Thank you."

"Hey," I said as she started to walk away. When she turned back, I added, "Leave your number in case we have any questions, please."

She moved back to the desk and wrote down her number on a pad of paper. She tore the page off the pad and handed it to me. "Can I go now?"

"Sure."

Angel and I checked all the rooms in the office to be sure Pfeiffer wasn't hiding in any of them, and then locked everything up and went downstairs to await the patrol officer. While we waited, we checked out the other psychiatrists' offices, speaking to each one to see how close they were with Pfeiffer. It turned out there was no love lost between them; they merely rented the space from him.

As we finished with the psychiatrists, a patrol vehicle pulled up, and two officers got out. Angel and I met them at the door.

"Banks, Jones, drew the short straw, did you?" Angel teased.

Officer Banks laughed. He was a nice-looking guy in his late twenties with dark brown hair and green eyes.

Jones just shook his head. He was also in his late twenties, and he had black hair and brown eyes. His build was much larger than Banks' though. He reminded me a bit of Mike Tyson in his younger days pre-face tattoo.

"I'll leave the keys with you. I want hourly checks on all of the offices that belong to Pfeiffer. We'll show you." I led the way. "You know what our perp looks like, right? Tell me Patrol has been given his pictures."

"Yes, ma'am. We were all sent them."

"Good. If you see this guy, call it in immediately."

"We will. We've got Braun and Garcia replacing us at two a.m., we'll give them your orders, ma'am."

"Hey, so maybe not the short straw, then." Angel chuckled.

Jones laughed heartily at that. "Yeah, man, I'd rather have first shift than that one."

Angel and I left them with the keys and headed back to the precinct to regroup.

Later that night, after I went by and fed Stephen's fish, I called him to check in. I smiled as he answered. I leaned back on the couch and said, "Hey, big brother, did you see the news?"

"You've put out an arrest warrant on that Dr. Pfeiffer? Yeah, I saw, but it looked like he's gone to ground?"

My smile slipped a little. "Yes and yes, unfortunately. Some jerkoff clerk at the courthouse warned him. Turns out he was paying for information. The clerk is in huge trouble. Might even find themselves liable for fines along with being fired. I think they're looking at racketeering charges."

"Wow, that's not good for them. I'm glad you're going after that doctor though. I've been thinking about those twins. I can't help but feel for them. I mean, having a parent do that to you... it's just not right."

I hadn't thought about Stephen identifying with the boys. Mom had abused him, and Pfeiffer had abused the boys... yeah, I could see the connection. "No, it's not," I said softly.

I still had a lot of regrets about not having recognized what was going on back then. Looking back now, I could see it, but at the time, I'd been just a kid. All I'd seen was that because Stephen was older, he got to do more things with Mom. It was almost like she was two different women, or maybe even three. One with me, one with Stephen, and then one with her clientele and pimp.

I shook my head, pushing away the memories that I no longer liked to recall. They'd been tainted by what I'd learned of her. Now, instead of thinking of her fondly, it made me almost nauseous. If I could, I would have all my memories of her wiped away. Packed up in boxes and incinerated, never to be seen again. Of course, life didn't work like that.

"Marce?"

"Hmmm?" I'd been lost in my thoughts and missed what he'd said. "Sorry, what were you saying?"

"What's going to happen to the boys now?"

"I'm not sure. We may still have to charge them with manslaughter or something, but hopefully there will be accommodations made for them. They aren't bad kids, just really messed up from their dad screwing with their brains. I think they're going to get help with Dr. Glenn. He is known for deprogramming cult victims, so I think he'll be good for them."

"That makes sense. I also saw you had to deal with active shooters at that hotel yesterday?"

"Oh, yeah. It's fine. And the captain said that while IA would have to look at the shooting, it was obvious it was a clean shoot. The hotel cameras caught the whole incident, so I don't anticipate any trouble."

"How's Jordan treating you? He hasn't jumped down your throat?"

I suddenly realized I hadn't told him about Jordan's suspension. "You'll never believe it."

"What?"

"The captain suspended him."

"No way!"

I laughed and told him all about how Jordan had been acting and what I'd said and how the captain had come in and put a stop to him. "So yeah. He's out for two weeks."

"I don't like that he even considered putting his hands on you, Marce."

"Well, Robinson did mention Jordan will have to attend anger-management classes, so hopefully I won't have to worry about that in the future."

"Good. I'm glad." He yawned. "Ugh. This medication is kicking my ass."

"You're fighting it. It's supposed to help you sleep."

"Yeah, but I'd have missed your call."

"I'll try to call a little earlier from now on. I'm sorry. It's just been kind of crazy lately."

He yawned again. "Ugh, sorry. I should probably go."

"Get some sleep. And if you wouldn't mind wishing me

luck in catching this guy, I'd appreciate it. I think I'm going to need all the luck I can get."

He laughed. "Good luck, Marce. You'll get him. You always do."

With that, we hung up, and my thoughts returned to Pfeiffer. I wished I had Agent White's number. I would call him up and ask him where he thought Pfeiffer might have gone.

Then a worrisome thought crossed my mind. What if Agent White picked him up? What if right now, Dr. Pfeiffer was sitting in some CIA interrogation unit, having his own brainwashing conducted upon him? They wouldn't dare, would they? Not in the middle of a murder case?

The thought was troublesome, and it kept me up for hours.

34

A NOT-SO-FORMER WORKPLACE
ANGEL

I picked Marcy up bright and early the next morning. Pfeiffer was still in the wind, and there had been no sightings of him by the time we checked in at the precinct. We made arrangements again with the CSI team and Patrol and then headed for Pfeiffer's psychiatric office.

Officer Braun met us at the door and opened it for us, then handed the keys to Marcy, who, after opening all the doors in Pfeiffer's office, turned them over to Lindsey. Braun stayed on the door, making sure no unauthorized personnel entered the building.

Marcy and I headed for the room where we'd spoken to Dr. Pfeiffer. We started with the bookcase, but there wasn't much but patient records, and they all seemed to be pretty standard. We'd leave those for Lindsey and her team to go through.

I turned to the desk and started going through drawers. I pulled one open and noticed there was a false bottom to it. Whipping out my pocketknife, I slid it through the side, lifting the edge up so I could remove it. Inside was a file folder. I opened it and started to read. It was about a particular drug, but the interesting thing was the company logo at the top and the date on the page.

"Hey, take a look at this." I held it out for Marcy.

She turned around and moved to my side, taking the paper. "No way. That bastard." She huffed. "If I get my hands on him, I'm going to wring his fucking neck."

"Who?"

"Agent White. He has to know Pfeiffer is still working for California Medico. All this time..." she trailed off, shaking her head as she pulled out her phone. "I'm calling Robinson. Making sure this search warrant is good for California Medico. He did say it was good for any place we found that Pfeiffer did business with or kept things at. But I want to be sure they aren't somehow exempt."

"Yeah, that would blow."

I went back to the file, looking through it. It seemed to be a recent study of test subjects who were only listed as Mr. A, Mr. B, and Mr. C. As I read on, I realized there were also three others, Mr. D, Mr. E, and Mr. F, who were in the control group. I didn't really understand what it was I was reading, but I was sure it was important.

I put the papers back in the folder and set it aside. Lindsey's team would want pictures of the drawer and where the file was found. Marcy got off the phone and confirmed that yes, California Medico was included in the scope of the warrant.

Ten minutes after she hung up, the captain called her back, and she sighed as she listened to him.

When she hung up, I asked, "What was that about?"

"The mayor wants us to call California Medico and let them know we're coming as a courtesy." She rolled her eyes.

"They are pretty connected. Doesn't the governor's brother do business with them?"

"Does he?" she asked, not really sounding all that interested.

I chuckled. "So, you going to call them?"

"After I talk to Lindsey. I might have to have a second team come with us while she handles this place."

She left the office only to return a few minutes later with Lindsey in tow. I showed her the drawer with the false bottom and the file.

"I'll make sure it gets photographed and documented. As to the other team, I'll see what I can arrange. Give me twenty."

Marcy nodded. "Might as well call them and tell them we'll be coming today at some point." She pulled her phone out and made the call. By the time she was done, Lindsey returned. "All good?" she asked.

"Yeah, you heading over now? They're just waiting for the go-ahead to leave."

"You ready, Reyes?"

"Sure. I haven't found anything else like this folder."

"Let's go, then. Thanks, Linds."

"Drinks later?"

"Can we play it by ear? Not sure how this is going to go."

"Sure, see ya."

Thirty minutes later we rolled into the parking lot of California Medico. It was a large square white cement building with black-framed windows spaced evenly across every side of the building. It was very sterile looking. I watched several men and women in white lab coats come and go from the building.

The CSI team followed us in through the glass doors,

and the alarms beeped as we passed through their metal detectors, drawing the attention of their security officials.

Marcy and I drew our badges out and held them up. "Detectives Kendrick and Reyes and our CSI team. We're looking for Dr. Pfeiffer's office here. And whoever happens to be in charge."

"If you'll wait here?" one of the guards asked as the other got the alarms shut down.

"Sorry about that. If we'd known when you were arriving, we'd have shut them down prior," the second guard said as the sounds stopped.

"It's not a problem. Do you have a lot of issues with armed people entering?"

"Oh, no. Most people who come are armed, but they know to check the weapon through there. This is mostly to discourage outsiders who don't know our systems, but also to deter theft. You'd be amazed at the amount of low-level espionage we have around here."

I arched a brow at the chatty guardsman. I thought Marcy was going to have a fit hearing him speaking so freely. I couldn't imagine what she'd do if she caught an officer giving out that kind of information to unverified people. He hadn't even examined our badges. For all he knew, they could be fake. I just shook my head.

The other guard returned with a well-dressed woman who smiled at us. "Detective Kendrick, I believe we spoke on the phone? I'm Diana Johnston, CEO of California Medico. Please, come with me, and I will show you to Dr. Pfeiffer's office."

"Thank you," Marcy replied as she shook the woman's hand.

As we walked, Diana said, "Just so you are aware, Dr.

Pfeiffer hasn't been here to his office or his lab in at least two weeks."

That was a little surprising, and I had to wonder why. "Was he supposed to be here?"

"Oh, yes. It's very strange. He's usually here at least three days a week." She opened a door and said, "This way. His suite of rooms is down this hall."

"What can you tell us of Dr. Pfeiffer's work here? What is it he's working on?" I asked.

Diana sighed and then hesitantly said, "There's a lot I'm not at liberty to tell you about what we're working on here, due to corporate espionage and the like, not to mention some of the things are patented, and we cannot share that information. What I can tell you is that Dr. Pfeiffer is currently working on strong psychotropic drugs that we hope can be used for deprogramming in severe cases."

She opened the door and let us into a room that had a large glass window on a wall that looked out into the hallway, a couple of windows on the opposite wall were set into the wall, and I could see out to the parking area. The room itself was very clinical, like you would see in a medical lab. In one corner sat a desk with an office chair and file cabinets behind it. The rest of the room had those counters like you'd see in a lab or a science setting along with computers and various scientific equipment.

At her description of what Pfeiffer was working on, Marcy said, "Ms. Johnston, are you aware that the reason we've got an arrest warrant out for Dr. Pfeiffer is because we suspect him of using drugs on his boys to make them susceptible to suggestions like murder?"

She looked appalled. "You think he used his work here to get his boys to murder their mother?"

"That is absolutely what we think." As I spoke, a person walking by the hallway window caught my eye.

It was a man wearing a white lab coat. He stared at Marcy, giving her a hard look. My eyes slid to Marcy, and she seemed to notice the man and tense up. "What is it?" I murmured. "Who is that?"

She gave me a brief shake of her head and said, "Later."

I turned back to Ms. Johnston, getting back to our questions. "Did you know his boys? Or his ex-wife? Did you ever meet them? How did he treat them?" I asked in rapid fire.

Diana shrugged. "We of course knew that he was married when he started working for us, but Dr. Pfeiffer always kept his home life just that. He never brought his family here. And they never came by to see him. I don't think he even has a picture of them on his desk."

"Is there anyone here, a co-worker or assistant, he is close to?" Marcy asked. "We're trying to discover where he might have gone."

"No, I'm sorry. I'm not aware of any interpersonal relationships he had with anyone here. He did have assistants, but they come from a pool of assistants who work in various aspects of our company. I don't think there's any that he used consistently during his time here. He would just grab whoever was available at the time."

"Can we get a copy of whatever notes there are on the drugs he was working on?" I asked.

"Of course, I'll download all the files I can for you. Would you like to wait, or would you like me to have them sent over to you?"

Marcy turned to the CSI team lead, Jeff Calhoun, and waved him in as she spoke. "We'll wait. We'd also like to take any of his personal effects he has here. If there is someone who is available to assist us in going through things?"

"I'll send someone over. Was there anything else I personally can do for you?"

I shook my head. "No, thank you for your time, Ms. Johnston, and for being so cooperative."

"Of course." She smiled and moved to the door. She stepped out, but continued to keep an eye on us through the window as she spoke to someone in the hallway.

"Jeff, you've got this. I think we'll leave you to it; we've got all were going to get out of Ms. Johnston," Marcy said.

"Yes, ma'am. We'll take care of it and get you the report ASAP."

"Thanks." Marcy gave him a nod; then we met Ms. Johnston in the hallway. "Thank you again, our team will go through everything here; if you'll have your person work with Mr. Calhoun, we'll be on our way."

"Of course, let me walk you out, Detectives."

Back in the SUV, I looked over at Marcy. "Lunch?"

"Definitely." She put the car in drive.

"So who was that man?"

"What man?" Marcy pulled onto the street.

"The one in the hallway in the lab coat. The one who stared at you."

"Oh. That was Agent White." Her gaze slid to mine, then back to the road.

35

THAT WHICH IS HIDDEN WILL BE REVEALED

MARCY

"We're missing something."

Angel looked up at me questioningly over his double cheeseburger. "What do you mean?"

I wiped my mouth on my napkin. "Okay, so we didn't see anything in Pfeiffer's office to indicate where he might be doing experiments on anyone let alone those boys. So where is he conducting these experiments? There has to be another lab somewhere."

"True. Especially if you take into account that one picture Mike drew."

"The creepy one of the stick figures in beds with computers next to them? Almost like a hospital room?"

"Yeah, that one."

"So, what are you thinking?"

"I don't think he would have any personal experiment stuff at California Medico. Ms. Johnston seemed to keep a pretty close eye on the goings-on there, and she or someone would definitely have seen him bringing those boys in there."

"She could be lying," Angel suggested, eating a French fry.

I thought about it, but shook my head. "She was definitely hiding shit, but I don't think she'd lie about that. She seemed genuinely shocked at the idea he was experimenting on the twins."

"True."

"I think we need to go back to the house. Maybe there is another false-bottom drawer with more files. But first I'm calling Lindsey; she might have discovered something and not gotten around to sharing it yet." I ate the last of my fries and pulled my phone from my purse. I dialed her direct number, knowing if she wasn't in the office yet, it would redirect me to her cell phone.

She answered, "Stone."

"Hey, it's Marcy. I wanted to ask if you found anything else hidden like that file Angel found. Or anything pertaining to the boys?"

"Nothing so far. We've got a lot of documentation to go through though. And the laptops at both his office and home."

"He's got another at California Medico. Jeff will be bringing it."

Lindsey sighed. "This is going to take a lot of man-hours."

"Yeah, sorry." I wasn't really; it was normal to have all this to go through in a case like this.

"Liar." She laughed.

I laughed too, then said, "Do you have the keys to his home?"

"No, but we left an officer there, just in case he shows up. Why?"

"I'm thinking we missed something. Maybe another false-bottom drawer with more files. They have to be somewhere."

"That's possible. I don't even know how Angel found that one in his office desk; it was pretty hidden. I put it back together, and even knowing it was there, I don't think I'd have realized it if it had been me."

I glanced over at Angel and grinned. "Well, you know Angel, he's got skills."

Lindsey laughed. "Anything else?"

"Not right now. I think we're gonna head back over to his place and see if we can find what we missed."

"Keep me updated; if I need to send another team over, I will."

"Sure thing. Catch you later." I hung up and looked up for our waitress. I caught her eye and asked her over.

"What can I get you? Another soda?"

"Not for me, no," I said, looking at Angel.

"I'm good," he answered. "I think we need the check."

"Give me just a minute, and I'll get it for you." She hurried away toward her computer station and was back with it a moment later.

We paid and went back out to Angel's SUV. "So, Pfeiffer's again?"

"Yeah."

When we arrived, we saw Officer Curtis posted outside. Angel parked in the driveway, and we got out, walking toward the door where Curtis was waiting.

"Shouldn't you be inside? We don't want Pfeiffer seeing you and taking off," I said.

"Yes, ma'am. I only just came out when I saw Detective Reyes coming up the street. I got a heads-up that you were on your way." He opened the door for us and let us in.

"Glad to know you're so vigilant." I smiled. "We're going to have another look around, see if we missed anything."

"Yes, ma'am." He nodded, moving to take up his post again at the living room window, peering out between the curtains.

Angel looked around. "Where do we start?"

"Might as well start here with those bookcases." I nodded toward the wall. "Maybe he's hidden stuff in books?"

"If not in here, then maybe in the bedroom? There's another bookcase there."

"Let's check here first. We'll go room by room."

An hour later, there was nothing in the living room or kitchen to indicate he was hiding stuff. We moved down the hall to the bedroom. Angel got started on the bookcase, and I returned to the dresser, but none of the drawers had a false bottom. I took out the drawers to see if there was anything hidden there, but found nothing. I moved on to the closet and flipped on the light. It was a walk-in closet, and the empty hangers hung on one side. There was a set of shelves on the back wall that had a few sweaters stacked on them, so I started pulling them off and shaking them out, seeing if there was anything there.

As I pulled the last one from the shelf, emptying them completely, I noticed something odd. "Hey, Angel, come here."

"Did you find something?"

"Maybe."

He joined me, and I poked at the wall where there seemed to be a seam where the panels of the wall with the shelves didn't quite meet exactly with the solid part of the wall.

Angel looked at me and raised a brow. "Hidden room?"

"That's what I was thinking."

He started pushing and pulling on each shelf, and on the third one, it pulled forward, and he grinned. It opened onto a staircase that led down into a darkened hallway. "I saw a flashlight when we were in the kitchen. It was in one of the drawers; let me go get it." He hurried from the room and was back a minute or two later. "I told Curtis we found something and to get another officer here, just in case."

"Good thinking."

Angel switched the light on and pointed it down the stairs. It was wide enough that we could go down together, but just barely. Still, we started down the ten steep steps and then stood at the bottom, gazing down a cement hallway. Something flashed on the wall as the beam of light hit it.

"What was that?"

"Looked like a mirror," I said, then added, "Point that thing around here; see if there's a light switch."

Angel did as I asked, and off to my right on the cement wall was exactly what we were looking for. He clicked it, and the hallway was illuminated; then he turned the flashlight off and shoved it in his jacket pocket. We moved forward and could now see what looked like windows that were mirrored glass and steel doors with locks on the outside. They reminded me of the kind you'd see in solitary confinement at the jail.

We moved closer and peered through the window of one room. Inside was a metal cot, a toilet in the corner of the room, a wooden table and one chair. It looked almost like a jail cell.

"Well, this is creepy as shit," Angel murmured. He tried the handle, and the door opened. "Yeah, can't see out from this side. It's like a prisoner's room."

I nodded. "Let's check each of these and move down the hall. It turns a corner up there."

There was nobody in any of the prisonlike rooms, thankfully. When we turned the corner, there were a couple more rooms, but these were slightly different. They had the same kind of mirrored window and door, but the insides were more decorated. They had regular twin beds, dressers, and an enclosed bathroom with a shower, sink and toilet. There was a TV and video game system too in each room. And on the small nightstand next to the bed was a picture of Audrina.

"These rooms belong to the twins," I said with surprise. "He kept them in here." I was furious seeing he'd treated them basically like prisoners.

"Look," Angel said angrily, his eyes up toward the high ceiling.

I followed his gaze and saw there were cameras in every corner of the room, even in the small bathroom. "Fucking bastard."

"He was watching them, like they were science experiments or something." His voice was full of disgust.

"Looks like it." I backed out of the room and stepped into the hall. The floor sloped downward up ahead, so I started following it. "There's another door down here," I said over my shoulder.

Angel came out of the room and followed me.

I pulled the door open, and it led to what looked like a huge hospital room. It was the room Mike had drawn. There were the metal cots, the computers, medical equipment, lab stations and microscopes. I moved over to the big metal refrigerator that stood against the wall, wondering if he kept food in here for the boys; maybe that was how he got them to take the pills; he put them in their food?

I was surprised to find the fridge wasn't full of food, but of oddly labeled drugs. "Look at this," I said as I pulled a bottle from the shelf. "Psilocybin," I read the label, then turned it so Angel could read it.

He pulled his phone from his pocket and typed the word in. "Looks like it's made from fungi, has effects like LSD, mescaline, and dimethyltryptamine."

"Scroll down; look, it lists the effects it has. Euphoria, hallucinations, a distorted sense of time... Maybe this is what he was giving them?" I pointed to his screen. "Look at the adverse reactions."

Angel read and then said, "Nausea and panic attacks, isn't that what happened to the boys? The panic attacks? Do you think they're still being given this stuff?"

"What does it say? Does it give a timeline?" I asked, then recalled that Flora had said he'd stopped.

He scrolled farther down and then said, "So, yeah, it typically lasts from two to six hours, so if they're still experiencing those effects, then maybe they are?"

"I doubt Flora would allow that. She's pretty attentive to those boys. And prior to that, I doubt their mom would have either, not after what came out in court. So if they're taking this, then they're doing it secretly or unknowingly."

I set the drug back in the fridge and closed the door. "Let's keep exploring; we'll get Lindsey down here once we've seen everything."

He nodded and moved past the fridge. "Hey, Marce, there's another hidden doorway." He pushed on the wall in a couple of places, and it popped open, revealing another lab with monitors.

I followed him in and saw they were the surveillance monitors. Each one was of the rooms we'd seen as we'd entered the hallway. On the wall was a shelf with DVD cases. I pulled one out, and it had a date on it. I opened it and moved to one of the stations with a monitor and put the DVD in the player. A moment later, Mike was on the screen.

"He recorded everything. It's all here," I said, looking back at the shelf.

"There's a vault-like door over here," Angel said from the far side of the room. "What is he stockpiling in there, do you think?"

I shook my head. "I don't know; let's find out." I had a weird feeling about it though, so as Angel opened the door, I drew my weapon.

The massive door opened slowly, and inside, seated on a comfortable-looking bed, was Dr. Pfeiffer. He stood up, and a bag of Cheetos went flying as he scrambled to grab something.

A moment later, he was pointing a weapon at us.

36

CONFESSIONS AND THREATS
MARCY

"Drop it, Pfeiffer," I ordered, sliding the safety off my weapon with my thumb.

"I'd do it if I were you. She's pretty notorious for killing murderers," Angel said, aiming his own gun at Pfeiffer. "What's the body count now, Marce? Six?"

"Seven, there was that one just a few days ago," I replied, not taking my eyes off Pfeiffer.

"Oh, right. At the hotel. Heard about that, didn't you, Pfeiffer? The gangbangers? They had M16s, nothing like that little twenty-two you've got that won't do shit."

Pfeiffer dropped his gun on the bed and sighed. "How the hell did you find me down here?"

"Skills," Angel replied, holstering his weapon as he pulled his cuffs from his jacket pocket. "Hands behind your back."

A few minutes later, we led him through the maze of hallways back up the stairs and out of the house to Officer Curtis' patrol car, where Curtis read him his rights and deposited him in the back seat.

Back at the precinct, Angel and I headed into the interrogation room, where Dr. Pfeiffer sat handcuffed to the table like every other criminal charged with murder. He looked angry and mutinous, and I wondered if he was going to be stubborn and refuse to answer questions.

Angel clicked on the tape and said, "Detectives Reyes and Kendrick have entered the room; the time is 5:46 p.m." He took his seat.

I sat down and stared at Pfeiffer across the table. "Officer Curtis said you don't want us to wait for your lawyer. It is your right to have one with you."

"I want to get this indignity over as quickly as possible. I don't need to wait for my lawyer to tell you that my experiments worked." He smirked at me, but there was fury in his gaze.

I arched a brow and gave him a confused look, I did know or at least suspected what he was getting at, but if he wanted to run his mouth, I wasn't going to stop him. "Experiments?"

"My experiments on programing Milgram and Gottlieb. My plan worked perfectly. I was able to program them to kill their mother at whatever time I chose. I waited and bided my time for the perfect moment. I wanted to be sure it was well after any conflict I'd had with her. I didn't want suspicion to fall on me, of course, and I do have an alibi for Audrina's death, so you can't pin that on me."

He was wrong. We actually could pin that murder on him. He'd loaded the gun. He'd ordered the murder. "So you wanted revenge against your wife?"

His eyes narrowed. "She was rebellious and stupid. And wouldn't do what I asked. She deserved what she got."

"But you used your children to get back at her. You turned them into weapons."

"They belong to me. I can do whatever I please with the things I own. We have that right here in America. Life, liberty, and the pursuit of happiness, right?"

"Pretty sure that right ends when it affects another person. You can't just murder people who interfere with you."

"They all belonged to me," he hissed as he leaned across the table. "I can do with them as I please."

"The courts will see it differently. You're going to go away for a very long time. You see, you might not have been there when Audrina died, but you ordered the murder. We know you did; we have proof. And I'd like to thank you for keeping such wonderful records of all your 'experiments.' It will go a long way to helping the twins."

The smirk fell from his face. I supposed he'd probably just figured out he was in a lot of trouble.

"You might as well tell us what you did to their brains; we're going to see it on those DVDs you made anyway."

His smirk returned. "Some of my best work to date. The work I've done will have lasting impacts for the right people."

I waited, knowing if I stayed silent, he'd continue. He just couldn't help himself. He wanted to brag. I could see it all over his smug face.

"I was able to reach their subconscious and manipulate it so that it no longer belonged to them," Pfeiffer continued. "They are completely mine. I have planted command words there, words that will turn them into killing machines. Not just toward their mother, though that was an excellent first human experiment for me to test them on. No, they will kill whoever I point them at."

The idea that he had turned his fourteen-year-old boys into killing machines was appalling. Still, I kept my mouth shut and stared at him, waiting for the rest of what he was clearly dying to boast about. I gave a sideways glance to Angel and noticed he was leaning back in his chair, his arms crossed, his stoic expression aimed at Pfeiffer.

Pfeiffer's expression grew even more smarmy as he grinned. "In fact, I'm only one phone call away from them taking out that meddling Flora. I just have to give the order, and it will be bye-bye auntie bitch."

He seemed to be finished and awaiting a verbal reaction now, so I said, "What are the command and release words?"

He just smirked and said, "That's classified."

37

ONE PHONE CALL CAN CHANGE EVERYTHING

MARCY

We had most of what we needed from Pfeiffer, all that was left were the command and release words, but he was stubbornly keeping them to himself. I gave Curtis the nod to take Pfeiffer down for processing. He'd be jailed pending a hearing on bail, but who knew how long that would be. I really hoped the DA would request no bail. The man was dangerous and a flight risk, in my opinion.

"We should call Flora and let her know we've got him," Angel said.

"Oh, yeah. Could you? I'll get started on the reports."

"Sure thing."

We returned to our desks in the detective pool. I got started filling out the reports and then picked up the phone to call Lindsey. She didn't answer, so I left her a message to listen for those command and release words on the DVDs Pfeiffer had made of his experiments on the twins. Surely they were on there somewhere.

"Hey, nobody is answering at the Dixon house," Angel

said a few minutes later. "I tried her cell phone too; nobody is picking up."

I frowned. "Let's take a drive over there. Make sure everything is good."

It was nearly eight p.m., and by the time we arrived, it would be close to nine. Still, I figured she'd want to know, and if she wasn't picking up the phone, then something could be wrong. Angel drove a little faster than normal, though we didn't put on the siren.

He pulled into the driveway and rolled his window down to push the intercom button.

Shelby answered, "We aren't receiving visitors at this time—"

"It's Detectives Reyes and Kendrick; this isn't a social call, Shelby."

"I see. Very well."

The iron gate swung open a minute later, and Angel pulled through.

Shelby was at the door waiting, his arms crossed and a look of disapproval on his face. "Why have you come so late, Detectives? Ms. Dixon has already gone to bed. Was this not something that could wait?"

"We did try to call, but we got no answer. We were concerned, and we have news."

"Yes, well, Ms. Dixon ordered the phones silenced by seven. She doesn't like to be disturbed in the evenings. However, if you will wait in the front parlor, I will let her know you're here."

"Thank you."

We went into the smaller room that reminded me of a living room.

It didn't take long for Flora to arrive, dressed in a silk

robe and looking very unhappy. "Detectives, I would have assumed if you had something to say, you would do so at a more reasonable hour."

"We did try to call you, Ms. Dixon; however, we were concerned something had happened when we received no answer. And we do have news. We have Dr. Pfeiffer in custody."

Flora brightened. "That is wonderful news. I am so relieved. Yes, that was worth being woken."

From behind us I heard a phone ringing. Of course, that didn't seem strange, not normally, but Shelby had said the ringers were turned off. I glanced at her, and she looked confused. "Ms. Dixon? I thought the phones were off?"

She shook her head. "That's not the ringtone on my cell, nor is it for the house phone, and Shelby always has his on vibrate. I don't know where it's coming from."

It hit me like a freight train. Pfeiffer had somehow managed to have a phone delivered to the boys. Not only that; the bastard must have used his one phone call to give the boys his order to kill Flora. "Angel, it's Pfeiffer!"

"What?" Flora panicked.

I moved in front of her and said, "Stay behind me."

I glanced at Angel as the boys entered the room. Mike held a gun, and Gary had a large butcher knife.

38

RECOVERY

MARCY

"Angel, I got Mike," I said. "You—"

He didn't even give me a chance to finish before he tackled Gary.

Mike wasn't paying any attention to his brother; instead he was moving forward, a blank look on his face. He had his sights set on Flora, but I was in the way, and I wasn't wearing a vest. I didn't want to pull my weapon. I didn't want to kill him. He kept coming forward, and I took a chance. Rushing toward him, I grabbed his arm, and he pulled the trigger, but I'd managed to force his arm downward as he did, and felt the bullet graze my calf.

Angel was suddenly there, grabbing Mike from behind as I took the gun from his hand. Flora was speaking, but I couldn't make out what she was saying. I was too focused on taking Mike down before he hurt me, Angel, or even Flora. We needed to get him to wake up. Angel was wrestling with him; the boy was much stronger than he appeared. I slapped him across the face, hoping that would do it, but he just stared ahead blankly. He was deep in whatever trance

Pfeiffer had put him in. I then remembered what Dr. Glenn had done with Gary.

"Milgram, what do you feel?" I said, knowing his hands had a hold of Angel's jacket.

"Soft. Fabric." His struggling paused.

"Milgram, what do you smell?"

He took a deep breath. "Woods, copper, flowers."

I tried to remember what other senses there were. "Milgram, what do you see?"

He blinked, and the blank expression fell from his face, and he looked confused. "Detective?"

"Yes, good, good job, Milgram." I blew out a relieved breath.

Mike looked around, the confusion still on his face. Then his gaze hit the floor, and his eyes widened. He pointed to a spot next to me.

I looked and noticed what had him worried. There was a pool of blood where my leg was bleeding. "It's okay, just a graze." Now that the adrenaline was wearing off though, it was feeling like maybe more than a graze. The bullet might have actually torn through my leg.

"I'm calling an ambulance," Angel said, pulling out his phone.

"I don't understand; how did this happen? How was he able to make them do this?" Flora asked as we waited for the ambulance.

I was getting a little light-headed, though Angel had made a tourniquet from Flora's robe belt and bandaged it with gauze Shelby had brought him. I sat down on the floor to wait. I could barely think. All I could focus on was my breathing.

Thankfully, Angel answered her. "Pfeiffer somehow had

a phone delivered. He was allowed one call, and he used it to call the phone."

"But how did the boys get it? I don't understand."

"I'm afraid that's my fault, ma'am," Shelby said from just inside the doorway. "I gave Mike the package when it arrived because it was addressed to Mike and Gary. I assumed it was something you ordered for them. You were at your hair appointment, so I didn't ask."

"It's okay, Shelby, you didn't know."

"We'll be adding additional attempted murder charges to Pfeiffer's charges," Angel said.

I nodded, feeling faint.

I was never so glad to hear the sirens of the ambulance approaching.

I ended up sitting in the ER waiting room for four hours this time before they finally brought me back to a room. I was exhausted, and all I wanted to do was sleep, but those plastic chairs weren't at all comfortable, and my leg hurt so much. I felt as though my body had been used as a punching bag for the past couple of weeks with all the crap I'd been through. The car accident, the shooting at the hotel and now this.

I didn't blame Mike at all though. All of that would be settled on Dr. Pfeiffer's head. I'd make sure of it.

I sighed as the nurse wheeled me back to a room with a curtain.

"I'm going to take your vitals, but first I need you to change into this gown, okay?" She set it on the bed. "Can you manage on your own?"

"Yeah," I muttered.

"Once you're done, you can have a seat on the bed." She stepped out of the small room and pulled the curtain.

I undressed, though I didn't take off my bra and underwear. I tossed my clothes on the guest chair and put on the gown, then sat on the hospital bed and waited.

It wasn't long before she knocked on the glass behind the curtain. "Ready?"

"Yeah, I'm covered."

She smiled as she entered and did all her tests. Taking my blood pressure—it was a little low—and my temperature—that was a little high—and my pulse, which was surprisingly average. "Dr. Sahu is on duty tonight, so he'll be in to see about your wound in just a few minutes."

"Great."

Her few minutes were more like an hour. It was nearly three a.m. before he came in to see me. I was leaned back against the bed, my eyes closed, when he entered. I heard the curtain move, opened my eyes and sat up.

He smiled and said, "Hello, Detective, I hear you were shot?"

I nodded. "I haven't looked at it, but when it happened, it felt like a graze. It's bleeding a lot though, so I'm thinking maybe it was more than that." I indicated my calf where the gauze had been soaked through with blood, and there were now stains on the white linens of the bed where my leg rested. The tourniquet had helped to slow the blood flow, but didn't stop it.

"Let's have a look." He undid the tourniquet and then removed the gauze.

I hissed as he did because it stung, but I didn't look.

The nurse came in and began to hand him things as he cleaned my wound and poked at it.

I waited patiently for the verdict, but all I wanted to do

was pull my leg away from his prodding and lay back down to go to sleep.

"A bit more than a graze; looks like it entered here, tore a gash all the way through. That's why there's so much blood. Good job on the tourniquet. It probably helped keep the blood flow to a minimum." He continued to dab at the wound. "I'm going to disinfect it, put on a localized anesthetic, and then I'll stitch you up."

"Thanks."

It took a hundred and thirty stitches and nearly an hour for him to finish. I was ready to pass out just from sheer exhaustion. I wanted to go home. The problem was I was still about forty minutes from my house, and I was without a car. Angel had gone back to the precinct after confiscating the boys' phone, and I had no idea when he'd be back to get me.

"All right, we're all done, Detective." He patted my leg. "You rest here, and I'll get you a prescription for some painkillers, and then we'll get you released."

"Thanks, Doctor." I leaned back on the bed.

He left, and then I heard Angel's voice just beyond the curtain; he was speaking to the doctor. A moment later, he knocked and poked his head past the curtain. "Hey, did you slaughter a pig in here or something?" He grinned.

I glanced at the bloody sheets that the nurse had pulled off after Dr. Sahu had finished with me. She'd put them in a basket, but the bloody mess was still noticeable. I laughed. "Funny man."

"Heard you've got a hundred and thirty stitches. I think that's a record for you, isn't it?"

I thought about it and smiled. "Yeah, highest one was only eighty-three." It wasn't from a gunshot though.

He patted his leg. "No iron like me though. Can't call you Robochick."

I burst out laughing. "There is only one Robocop, that's you, and even if I ever end up with that kind of metal in me, you will never refer to me as Robochick." I couldn't stop laughing.

He sank down in the guest chair as he laughed too.

A nurse popped her head in through the curtain and gave us a disapproving look. "Please, you need to keep it down; we have injured and sick people out here who need the quiet."

"Sorry," I gasped out between giggles. I took a few breaths to subdue the laughter.

Angel's expression turned more somber, and he said, "I've got some news. Not really great news, but news."

"Are Flora and the boys okay? They didn't have another episode, did they?"

"No, they're fine. Pfeiffer can't get a hold of them anymore. Though from the looks of it, he won't be doing much talking to anyone for a while. He's been admitted to the hospital."

"What? Why?"

"Two of the guards at the jail overheard what he was saying on the phone to Mike. And beat the crap out of him."

"Holy heckfire. That's not good; we could lose the case because they put their hands on him," I muttered.

"It's all on camera, and it started with a scuffle to get the phone away from him, but he started hitting, and well... they can claim self-defense. And the camera picked up the call as well. We've got the command phrase."

"What is it?"

"Remember my legacy. We still don't know the release word, but hopefully Lindsey's team will find it."

The curtain slid back a bit, and a nurse came in with paperwork. "You're all set, Detective. You can get dressed and head on out."

Angel followed her out, and I quickly dressed. I couldn't wait to get home. I wanted to sleep for a week. Not that I'd be able to. There was still too much work to be done. Angel drove me home with orders to stay in bed for the next twenty-four hours per the captain's orders. That made me smile. We'd filled my painkiller prescription before leaving the hospital, so I was set.

I put on my pjs and climbed into bed. I think I was asleep before my head even hit the pillow. I didn't dream, didn't have any nightmares, I simply slept.

I woke up feeling more refreshed than I'd felt in months. Glancing at the clock, I saw it was nearly three in the afternoon. I got up and took a quick shower, then put on a pair of sweatpants and a T-shirt, not bothering with a bra. I wasn't going anywhere.

After fixing myself a meal of scrambled eggs and bacon, I decided to call Stephen and let him know what was going on. "Hey, big brother, you doing okay?"

"I'm good. Heard you caught Pfeiffer?"

"We did." I went on to tell him all about how we found him and about the hidden underground rooms the man had created and how creepy it all was. "Horror-movie kind of stuff."

"Glad he's behind bars."

"Me too," I said as my phone beeped, alerting me I had another call. I glanced at it and saw it was Angel. "Hey,

Angel's calling, so I need to go, but I'll call you again tomorrow."

"Okay, sis. Bye."

I clicked over to Angel. "Hey, what's up?"

"Just checking on you; how are you feeling?"

"Pretty damn good, actually."

"Feel like getting beers with Lindsey and a few others?"

"Sure, where at and what time?"

Angel gave me the details, and I said I'd be there.

Things were finally looking up. I wasn't feeling so guilty about Henry anymore, and I'd put another dirtbag behind bars.

Life was good.

39

THE HANGED MAN

MARCY

The next morning, I woke still feeling pretty good. I'd gone out celebrating with Angel, Lindsey, Damien, and a few others. It had been a difficult case, and it was nice to have it end with the culprit being jailed pending trial. And despite Agent White's threat that the case would never make it to trial, that was exactly where it was heading.

Lindsey had all the proof of the so-called experiments Dr. Pfeiffer had been doing on his boys as well as random homeless people he'd conducted studies on. His notes showed that he'd just released them back to the streets once he was done digging around in their brains. The man was psychotic. He had no conscience, no empathy for his fellow man. It was disgusting.

Angel and I were driving separately today because he had an early physical therapy appointment. He said he'd just meet me at the station. I kind of missed him on the drive in to work. It felt weird swinging through the drive-thru at the coffee shop and only ordering one drink. Still, I needed it. I didn't know what the day would bring, but since we'd pretty much wrapped up the case, I'd probably have to go out on more of the everyday calls.

I started toward my desk when Hummel waved me over. "What's up, Hummel?"

"Did you see the news?"

"No, what's happened?"

He gave me a look of sympathy and patted my shoulder. "It's on nearly every channel."

Now I was really worried. I headed for the break room, where there was a TV. My eyes widened as I read the scrolling feed. *Death at the county jail...* "No!" I muttered and grabbed the remote, turning up the sound.

"—was found hanging in his cell early this morning. Dr. Pfeiffer had been charged in connection to his wife's murder. Yesterday there was an incident involving Dr. Pfeiffer, and he ended up being admitted to the hospital. He was returned to the jail just hours before he was found. Despite there being cameras in the cell block, there was a malfunction rendering all video evidence of the hanging nonexistent. Stay tuned to Channel—"

I hit the mute button. I didn't need to hear any more.

Camera malfunctions, my ass, I thought. I would bet a million dollars that somebody turned them off. And I had a good idea who that somebody might be. Feeling frustrated, I stormed out of the break room. I wanted this thoroughly investigated. I knew Agent White and the CIA were behind this. I wanted them brought up on charges.

I saw Angel and headed for him first. "He's dead."

Angel looked at me and frowned. "Who?"

"Pfeiffer. They found him hanging in his cell."

"Well, I guess it just saves the taxpayer money."

"Angel, the man was not suicidal. There is no way he did it to himself. Somebody un-alived him."

He gave me a sardonic look. "Aren't you being a bit paranoid? Come on, Marce, who would kill this guy?"

"Oh, I don't know. Agent White maybe? Another CIA spook who didn't want their precious mind-control secrets getting out?"

"You're being ridiculous. He probably just realized he was going away for a long time and took the easy way out. I'm sure the cameras will show him doing it."

"Oh yeah? Well, magically the cameras weren't working at the time he was hanged. Explain that one."

He faltered and looked unsure of himself. "Huh. That's odd, definitely."

"I'm going to talk to Robinson. I want to go investigate." I had my hands on my hips. I was seething and ready to make some heads roll over this gross negligence at minimum or government interference in the course of justice at worst.

"Okay, I'll back your play, but don't be surprised if Robinson shoots you down."

He walked with me to Jason's desk. "Is he in?" I asked, looking at Jason.

"Yes, one second, Detective, let me see if he'll see you." Jason picked up the phone. He spoke for a moment and then said, "He'll see you."

I gave him a nod, and we passed him as we headed toward Robinson's office door. I knocked and then opened it. "Sir?"

"Kendrick, Reyes, come in. Good work on closing this case. The DA is working up a deal with the boys and their lawyer; they won't have to spend any time in jail."

"That's good to hear, sir," I started.

"I'm sure you've heard about Pfeiffer. It's all over the news." He shook his head.

"Sir, that's what I wanted to talk to you about."

"What about it, Kendrick?" He looked concerned; his brow furrowed.

"I want permission to head over to the jail and investigate—"

"Sorry, that's not going to happen, Kendrick; you know they have their own system to deal with deaths of this manner. We can't overstep here. Once he's in their custody, it's out of our hands."

"But—"

"No, Kendrick. Let it go. There's nothing we can do. You did your job. You found the guilty party, and it looks as though he got his just reward. Not only that, but we don't have to put the city to the expense of a trial."

"But you know he was murdered, sir—" I protested.

"Be that as it may, it's not in our jurisdiction. Now, I'm sure there are other things that need your attention. Just know the chief and the mayor were impressed with everything you uncovered, as well as the capture of Pfeiffer in the first place. So again, good job. Now get back to work."

I sighed. He wasn't going to budge. I was beyond frustrated, but like he said, there was nothing I could do.

"For the record, I'm sorry." Angel bumped my shoulder.

"Yeah, it just kind of steals some of the satisfaction I felt at catching the bastard."

He nodded. "I gotta admit, his death is pretty suspicious, but you know, if it was the CIA guys who made it happen, maybe it's better that we don't dig into it."

I shook my head, disagreeing because to me, that wasn't justice. Still, it didn't look like I had a choice in the matter.

Just as we were about to take our seats, the captain ordered us out on a call.

The morning sped by with various calls; first a domestic violence call, then a stabbing and after that a shooting. By lunch I was ready for some peace and quiet.

"Want to hit a drive-thru or check out the food truck?" Angel asked.

"Food truck. I think I want to just go sit and eat in the park. Just kind of veg."

"I think it was the tropic one. I'll drop you off. I'm kind of wanting just a regular burger."

"Okay."

Angel dropped me at the corner by the precinct, and I headed for the food truck and ordered their Mahi-Mahi burrito. I took it and my drink across the street to the park and sat down on one of the benches. I was just about to take a bite of it when someone sat down next to me. I froze when I realized it was Agent White.

"I have to admit, Detective, you've got spirit. I've enjoyed watching you navigate this case and even get your man."

I glared at him. "Seriously? You had him killed before he could go to prison for the shit he did."

He shrugged. "Count it as a win. I could have hidden him away, and you'd never have gotten all the evidence you had to connect him to the murder."

"You only killed him to cover the CIA's ass. You were afraid that if it went to trial, Pfeiffer would reveal his connection to you. You don't give a shit about justice."

"Look, his work was important to us, yes, but don't think for one minute that we didn't want to see him pay for using that knowledge outside the scope of the organization. That's not allowed. So yes, I am glad you were able to get your hands on him, but make no mistake, Detective, national security comes first, and there are certain things that don't need to be made public." He stood.

"You know killing him isn't really justice for his victims."

He shrugged and walked away, leaving me without an appetite.

40

AN INTEREST IN LIFE
MARCY

Six weeks later

Case closed. I shook my head as I read over the documents I'd been able to get on Pfeiffer's death from the jail. They'd barely done an investigation. It turned out one of the new hires, who had been fired over the bribe they'd taken, had been the one to shut off the cameras. As to who had done the asking, it had been a guard, or someone dressed as one, as it turned out.

My guess was Agent White had gotten his hands on a uniform, paid the staff person a thousand dollars to shut down the cameras in the cell block, and then he'd gone down and murdered Pfeiffer. After that, he simply removed the uniform and disappeared, leaving no trace of himself anywhere at the scene. He'd as much as admitted it that day in the park, so it wasn't just a subjective guess.

I slammed the file folder down on my desk in frustration. "There's nothing here."

"Did you really expect there to be?"

I glanced over at Angel and sighed. "No. Doesn't mean I don't think something shady went down."

"We know it did, but there's nothing we can do, Marce. Come on, you gotta look at the silver lining."

I arched a brow at him. "And what's that?"

He smiled. "Pfeiffer can't brainwash anyone else, and the twins are recovering."

I smiled back. "That's true. Except for the part where the CIA has a record of all his research, and somebody in their organization is bound to use that knowledge on someone else."

"Yeah, well, we can hope that 'someone' they recruit is a volunteer for them and capable of allowing themselves to be turned into a weapon for the betterment of the country and that the people that someone is aimed at are the evildoers."

I rolled my eyes. He was incredibly optimistic if he thought they were going to use the knowledge in that way. Somehow, I didn't think that would be the case. Maybe I was just paranoid though. Actually, I knew I was paranoid. I had been looking over my shoulder, watching for Agent White ever since that day in the park.

I both expected to see him and not. It was a very strange feeling.

I shook my head at Angel and smiled. "I guess you're right. We can't control them; we can only hope they use it responsibly."

He smirked. "Like the force, young padawan. It can be used for good or evil," he joked.

"You're a dork." I laughed, as he'd meant me to. My desk phone rang, and I answered. "Kendrick."

"Hello, Detective, it's Flora Dixon."

"Yes, Ms. Dixon, what can I do for you?"

"Well, the boys have been asking about you, and I was hoping you and your partner might come around and see them?"

I glanced over at Angel, who was listening to my side of the conversation with curiosity. "Yes, of course, Ms. Dixon. Detective Reyes and I would be more than happy to come by. When would you like for us to come?"

"I could have a nice lunch prepared, if twelve thirty works for you?"

"We'll be there."

"I look forward to it, Detective." She hung up.

I set the phone receiver down and looked over at Angel. "We've been invited to lunch at the Dixon residence."

"Oh, well, la-dee-da, do we dress for the occasion, do you think?" he asked, his eyes sparking with humor.

I laughed. "I think we'll just go as we are." I rolled my eyes at him. "I'm going to let Jason know, so we don't get sent on a call."

"Hey, Jason, would you let the captain know Angel and I are headed up to Beverly Crest, please? We received a call from Flora Dixon; the boys are asking to speak to us."

"I can do that; he and the lieutenant are in meetings with the deputy mayor all afternoon. Captain gave me a roster of who to send on calls. I'll just skip you and Angel until you get back."

"Thanks," I said and then joined Angel at the door.

Two and a half hours later, we pulled up to the Dixon

house. Shelby already had the gate open, so we just drove through.

"Detectives, do come in. Everyone is already seated in the dining room."

"Are we late?" I glanced at my watch; it was twelve twenty-five.

"No, ma'am, not at all." He led us to the dining room.

"Detectives, come in, welcome." Flora stood from her seat to greet us, a brilliant smile on her lips. "Boys, what do you say?"

"Hello," Mike murmured.

"Hi," Gary said.

"You're talking," I said with surprise.

The boys both turned slightly pink.

"They are. Dr. Glenn has done tremendous work with them."

"I am thrilled to hear it."

"Please, have a seat, Detectives."

Angel and I sat opposite the boys while Flora sat at the head of the table. Once we were seated, staff started bringing plates out and setting them down in front of us.

"This looks delicious," I said, eyeing the lobster tail and steak.

"It does."

"The boys and I just wanted you to know how grateful we are for everything. And for speaking with the DA on the boys' behalf."

I smiled at them. "It was my pleasure. What was decided?"

"We have to continue with therapy," Mike said.

"But we get to stay with Aunt Flora," Gary added.

"That's wonderful. I'm so glad, and I'm very glad to hear you're speaking more."

"Yes, they have made great strides," Flora said, looking fondly at them. "I've hired a tutor, and they'll be starting classes next week. My hope is that they'll soon be caught up in their education within the next year."

"That sounds like a great plan, but I hope you aren't only focusing on therapy and education," Angel put in, looking at the boys. "I hope you've got some hobbies and interests you can pursue as well. Sports maybe?"

Gary nodded and picked up his phone, typed something out, then slid it across the table to Angel.

"You've taken up chess? That's a great game. What about you, Mike?" he asked.

Mike hesitated, then picked his phone up. As he typed his response, Angel slid Gary his phone back. After a second of typing, Mike passed his phone over.

"Fishing in the lake on the boat?" Angel looked over at Flora.

Flora smiled. "We have a lake on the estate. Mike likes to take the rowboat out and fish. He finds it relaxing."

"It's a great hobby. I don't get to go out very often, but when I do, I enjoy it as well."

Mike smiled and took a bite of his steak.

I was so glad to see them taking an interest in life. They were too young to have to deal with all the crap their dad had put on them.

We enjoyed the meal with the Dixon family, and Flora informed us that both boys had dropped the Pfeiffer ending from their names when she'd gotten guardianship, and she was having it legally changed for them. I was pretty happy about that. The man didn't deserve to have a legacy with them after what he'd done.

Flora had also shared that Dr. Glenn had finally figured out the release word trigger phrase for the boys. It was hot potato. It had come about in a session where he'd asked them about some games they'd played as kids. Turned out hot potato was one of them, and Mike had realized that was an important phrase.

Since Pfeiffer had ended up dead, the team had boxed up all the evidence and put it away without going through everything, as they would have done on a still active case. So Lindsey had never learned the release words for us. Thankfully, Dr. Glenn had continued to work with them and had.

After work, I headed home, taking an alternate route just in case Agent White got it in his head to start following me again. Was that paranoid of me? Yes, probably. I hadn't seen him since that day at the park, but I didn't want to take any chances. I went inside and locked my door, then kicked off my shoes.

I pulled out my phone and dialed Stephen. He'd been back home for a week, and he started work again today. I wanted to see how he was doing and invite him for dinner.

"Marce, what's up?"

"How about pizza and a movie tonight?" I said.

"Sounds good, your place or mine?"

"Your choice."

"I'll come to you, and I'll pick the pizza up on the way," he said with a chuckle.

He sounded good, and I was glad.

"Okay."

Forty-five minutes later, he was at my door, pizza in one hand and a two liter of Pepsi in the other. That was another positive thing. He'd stopped drinking altogether. I smiled and let him in.

He set the pizza on the coffee table and headed to the kitchen, returning a moment later with two glasses filled with soda. "What movie did you choose?"

"*Deadpool.*"

"Perfect."

It felt great to just sit and relax with my brother, enjoying pizza and a good movie. Even so, my mind wouldn't entirely let go of the Pfeiffer case. I still worried about the CIA and how they'd missed seeing that he'd been doing experiments on his kids using their techniques. I sighed.

"What's on your mind?" Stephen asked, pausing the movie.

"Just thinking about how shady our CIA is. I don't understand how they were so lax and didn't notice what Pfeiffer was doing to his own kids."

"You know, Marce, maybe it's better to let it go. Not think about it so much." He frowned and reached for my hand. "I mean, look at Watson. All he did was focus on them and how shady they were. I just don't want you to end up the same way."

His words hit me hard. He was right. I had to let it go. I leaned over and hugged him. "It's good to have you home."

"It's good to be home."

THANK YOU FOR READING

Did you enjoy reading *Blood Line*? Please consider leaving a review on Amazon. Your review will help other readers to discover the novel.

ABOUT THE AUTHOR

Theo Baxter has followed in the footsteps of his brother, best-selling suspense author Cole Baxter. He enjoys the twists and turns that readers encounter in his stories.

ALSO BY THEO BAXTER

Psychological Thrillers

The Widow's Secret

The Stepfather

Vanished

It's Your Turn Now

The Scorned Wife

Not My Mother

The Lake House

The Honey Trap

The Detective Marcy Kendrick Thriller Series

Skin Deep - Book #1

Blood Line - Book #2

Dark Duty - Book #3

Kill Count - Book #4

Made in United States
North Haven, CT
23 September 2024

57790592R00200